EVERY

BODY

HAS

A

SECRET

EVERY BODY HAS A SECRET

PAMELA CRANE

Rockin' C Reads
Raleigh, North Carolina

Thank you for supporting authors and literacy by purchasing this book. Want to add more gripping reads to your library? As the author of more than a dozen award-winning and bestselling books, you can find all of Pamela Crane's works on her website at www.pamelacrane.com.

For Tim.
There are not enough words to fill a book with how much I miss and love you. Thank you for sparking the confidence in me as a self-conscious ten-year-old girl to write.

Prologue

Opening the package only took thirty seconds, but covering up the murder it led to will cost me thirty to life. This realization comes too late, since the package is sitting at home, its contents hidden behind a locked bookshelf wall along with another secret that's even worse. Meanwhile I'm here wondering what to do with this body.

For the record, I didn't set out today to conceal a murder. It just sort of happened. Things like that seem to "happen" a lot to me lately. I came here to relax, and it takes a lot to ruin a brisk hike under an autumn-colored canopy, but hiding a body will do the trick.

The trek up to the waterfall isn't an easy one. Only the most determined of nature lovers survive the climb up the mountain, and due to yesterday's downpour, the mud keeps most hikers away. Sunlight slices through the burgundy and goldenrod remains of leaves clinging for dear life above me. The dirt footpath that winds along the shore of Doomwood Falls dips and curves around the massive roots of hibernating trees. I inhale the woodsy scent, but it's no use. The panic itching under my skin still persists.

I thought this might ease the growing tension between my shoulders, but after the week I've had, I'm not sure anything will help. The fistfight. The break-in. The police interrogation.

The hit-and-run… It's all too much for one person to handle, and the package I received has me constantly on edge. I have an ominous feeling my past has found its way back to me.

I'm almost on the other side of the river when something large floats toward me, giving the distinct feeling that it's about to complicate my day. As if it could get any more complicated. Most people see nature and think serenity. I see it and start planning my alibi.

The current nudges whatever it is toward me, while rocks disturb its path as it bumps against them. A branch snapping behind me yanks my attention away. The sound reminds me that I'm probably being watched, as I have been since my neighbor went missing a week ago. But her disappearance is the exact reason I'm here, because my gut tells me I'm close to finding her and this place holds the clue I'm searching for.

Another crack is followed by the rustle of leaves.

"Is someone there?" I call out, hoping to scare away a predatorial animal… or predatorial human. Nothing would surprise me these days.

Of course no one replies, and I can't see anything through the dense brush. So I return my attention to the water's murky surface, which shimmers innocently in the daylight. But it's just a facade masking a sinister truth about Doomwood Falls: This town is full of secrets. Even the name *Doomwood Falls* zaps an icy shiver down my spine.

The lump floats closer, then snags on a branch jutting out from the shore. At first I think it's a log, but it's not quite the right shape or color. It dislodges itself and the river spits it out, depositing it onto the pebbled bank downstream. Mud suctions my boots as I squelch near it. Only when I'm a few steps away do I comprehend what I'm seeing.

A ragged gasp catches in my throat as the definitely-not-a-log spins slowly around, a gruesome dance in the current's lazy embrace. It's a body. Facing downward, a head lolls on the waves with long, dark hair matted in river sludge. Both arms are outstretched in a gesture of surrender. The clothes are nearly translucent, and the skin peeking out between folds of fabric is an unnatural, sickening shade of gray.

I don't move, not at first. Then I inch closer with a morbid curiosity like a leash pulling me forward. Is this… no, it can't possibly be my missing friend. I stoop down, but the face is pressed into the muck, showing only the back of a head and curve of a neck. But her waves of ink-black hair are the right color—or terribly wrong color, if this is who I fear it is…

Closing my eyes, I can't allow the worst-case scenario to surface in my brain. Instead, an awful silence replaces it, and all my usual ADD thoughts are now replaced by the *lub-dub, lub-dub, lub-dub* of my racing heart. I crouch with a foolish flicker of hope that the woman might still be alive, so I flip the body over with a grunt.

Nope. Definitely dead.

Debris masks her face, so I kneel to wipe it aside, revealing features that are unrecognizable. The flesh has been picked apart by fish, or the Loch Ness monster, or whatever lives in these waters. Whoever this woman is, she has been dead in the water too long.

A glint catches my attention, and it's not her face that my eyes are drawn to anymore, rather something else on the body. A gut-wrenching realization steals the air from my lungs as my gaze travels downward and lands on something so shocking it sends me butt-first onto the ground.

What I'm looking at is impossible, but it's right there in front of me. I jump to my feet and remove the object with shaky fingers. I pocket it with a dreadful awareness that this is more than just a random drowning I've stumbled on. This is intended for me, just like the hit-and-run and the note left in my home. And if anyone finds this body, any hope of a future for me will unravel. This woman's death was planned to put me behind bars… or six feet under, whichever comes first.

Panic spurs me to action. I have no choice but to disappear with this evidence, because although I could plead my innocence in this person's murder—and yes, I am now one hundred percent sure it was murder—I'll definitely be convicted for it. Especially because I have a prior record. One scrutinous look into how my husband died and I'll be sharing a cell with Blanche Taylor Moore, the Black Widow of North Carolina.

I recall the snap of wood behind me moments ago and scan the brush. Has anyone witnessed me here tampering with this body? I listen for human sounds: breathing, footsteps, a Snapchat alert, anything that might reveal someone else is here. Nothing but silence. An eerie, suffocating silence. It's just me and this dead woman. Hopefully.

Now what?

I should run. I could turn around, get back in my car, and flee for another town. Or another state. Heck, to be safe I should probably pick another country. I hear Indonesia is nice this time of year, and it has a no extradition policy with the United States. And yes, I double-checked. But my feet are rooted to the spot, two heavy anchors in the soft earth, because I'm tired of running.

I consider an unthinkable option and take a step toward the body, then another as the wet ground sucks at my soles. Then I do something very stupid.

I touch the body.

Just the sleeve at first. Then the arm. It's cold, stiff, and heavier than I expect. The flesh is waterlogged, and I have a horrifying image of skin sliding off the muscles and bone as I grab both arms and start dragging her back into deeper water. By now something primal has taken over, and I don't know what I'm doing until I'm already doing it.

I scramble up the embankment and grab a large rock. Then another and another. My limbs move on autopilot, like I've done this before—burying the evidence. In a way, I suppose I'm a pro at this now.

With my palms blue and bleeding and my nails caked in mud, I keep collecting handfuls of rocks until I figure it's enough. Then I pull the corpse deeper into the river at my waist level, while my heart punches at my ribs. The cold seeps through my sleeves, against my skin, into my bones. But I keep pulling her deeper while my boots slip and slide further in.

When I reach as far as I can safely go, the body groans, a soft, gassy sound of protest that bubbles up to the water's surface. I yelp and let go, imagining her eyes popping open as she comes to life, but that's not what happens. The bubbles eventually stop, and she's still dead.

Now submerged up to my chin, I drop the largest stone onto her chest cavity. It lands with a sickening splash, and the body sinks about an inch. Not even close to where I need it. Taking the handfuls I've got tucked into the folds of my shirt and pockets, I jam more rocks under the waistband of her pants, into her pockets, down her sleeves… shoving them anywhere they'll fit while watching the body sink below the surface, slowly, like it's thinking about it.

I return to shore for more armfuls, loading her with rocks again and again until finally she disappears. And then she's swallowed whole.

I heave myself back to land and collapse onto the dirt, breath gone, muscles shaking. I'm not relieved, because I know what's coming. Someone's going to find the body eventually. And when they do, they'll come looking for me. And what will I do then? I'll do what I've been doing since I first arrived in Doomwood Falls. I'll disappear, just like that body. Well, let's hope it's not *exactly* like that body, because I'd prefer to make it out of this alive.

Placing my hand into my pocket, I touch the object—still there. It's evidence that ties me to this crime, but it's also a clue. I don't know who killed this woman or why, but if I do know anything, it's this:

I never should have opened the package.

Chapter 1

One Week Earlier

Nothing wrecks a girl's wedding day like the spray of brain matter all over her white dress.

A glare off the portrait's glass hides the bloodstain, until I shift just enough to reveal the splatter of burgundy caught in a swish of white chiffon. Tucked behind a gilded picture frame, I'm smiling in my wedding photo, unknowingly wearing a dress that looks like someone took a paintbrush to my fairytale dream and smeared it in red. Tragically, it's not paint staining my dress.

"Very beautiful wedding photograph," a man's voice behind me says with a slight Farsi accent he's worked hard to cover up since 9/11. Ali Azad clearly hasn't spotted the bloodstain on my dress yet.

I wait for him to notice and correct himself, but when he doesn't, I say, "Thanks. That is what today's photography lesson will be about—wedding portraits."

"Very good. Maybe someday I will wed…" he replies, glancing over his shoulder at the cluster of women gathered near the entrance to my studio where I offer photography classes.

Several ladies join us, and my heart squeezes with an anxiety that never lets up. I don't fit in here on Hemlock Drive, where the grass is emerald green all year long and the women wear two-hundred-dollar workout outfits instead of the sports bra and swishy shorts I'm used to. I inhale a reassuring breath, then turn around to face my students, who mostly consist of busybody neighbors and bored housewives with a knack for underdeveloped ISO knowledge and overdeveloped gossip.

The group trickles into my 411 Hemlock Drive studio that has my business name printed across the glass door: *Shoot to Thrill*. The studio is attached to my house, which I'm not exactly happy about, but it was the only way I could open up a business without hurdling the red tape of a background check and year-long lease.

Always early is Ali Azad, an Iranian refugee who has the biggest crush on Zala, whose last name I can never seem to remember and lives two houses down. Giving herself an extra three inches of height, she's wearing shoes with so much arch support they could only have been designed by a structural engineer. In her mid-fifties, Zala tends to take too many pictures of birds and is convinced that every blurry shot is *avant-garde*.

My best friend and across-the-street neighbor, Ivory Cobb, hangs at the edge of the small gathering. In front of Ivory, a girl wearing red leather head to toe stomps in with the subtlety of a drumline. She's painfully Gen Z and wearing an expression like the whole world just said something offensive.

Grimacing at my bridal photo hanging on the wall, Ivory lifts one hand to shield her eyes from the golden glare streaming in through the floor-to-ceiling window of the studio where I host classes to aspiring photographers. Most of them are neighbors who pity me—and Ali, who only comes to orbit Zala because he's too nervous to ask her out. In fact, the whole class has been trying to help him `muster the courage for months.

Truth be told, most assume Zala would be out of Ali's league if she had better style, especially with footwear. Ali is short and pudgy, while she towers over him with her high cheekbones, almond-shaped eyes, and hair so platinum it's debated—behind her back, of course—if she dyes it. I tend to think they'd be a great match, that the heart yearns for what completes it. That's what made me first fall in love with my husband, then more recently pick Ivory as a best friend: We are absolutely nothing alike.

To the residents of Hemlock Drive, paying for my lessons is akin to charity and gives them bonus points of good karma to balance out all the Amazon packages—and much worse secrets—they're hiding from their husbands. Or what their husbands are hiding from them. Secrets are why mine is dead. They don't realize that I know about the skeletons in their closets, mainly because I'm also an expert skeleton hoarder, so I'm familiar with the tells.

"Shari, honey, I swear I've seen this photo a hundred times and never noticed this." Ivory's pointy fingernail scratches against the glass, as if she's trying to scrape off the bloodstain from the image beneath it. Her voice is laced with a curious bewilderment. "Please tell me that's not *blood* on your wedding dress."

I gently set my vintage 1953 Polaroid land camera down like it might explode. It took me months scouring the internet to find this exact model, of which less than a hundred still exist. I don't want to tell Ivory the truth about what happened on my wedding day, because secrets are like cockroaches. Where there is one, there are a hundred more ready to scatter from the corners.

"Why would you assume it's blood and not red wine?" I answer her question with one of my own. "You know how clumsy I am."

Ivory tilts her head, her ponytailed braids brushing her collarbone. "That's not merlot, Shari. That's arterial."

If anyone would recognize blood spatter, it's Ivory. Although her field was in cybersecurity, the Doomwood Falls Police Department outsourced her on numerous occasions to handle overflow work on unsolved cases. You wouldn't believe the graphic images she had been *exposed to*—ha! I can't resist a good photography pun even if I tried.

"Fine, you got me," I concede. "Yes, it's blood, and no, I'm not telling you how it got on my wedding dress."

"Seriously?" Her frown is so natural I can't tell if she's upset or just resting her face. "You're not going to tell me the story behind that?"

"I like having a little mystery."

If Ivory knew just how much of a mystery my life actually is, I doubt she'd still be my friend. She's always been an open book to me, from the moment she sauntered—and I do mean *sauntered* at five-foot-eleven—across the street to introduce herself to me the day after I moved in. The first thing she did was hand me a plate of burnt homemade brownies along with a bottle of Kahlua, then proceeded to introduce herself as Ivory Cobb, my new best friend.

Half an hour later she was in my living room unpacking moving boxes with me, while refilling our glasses and retelling an abbreviated version of her life. By the end of the day, I knew pretty much everything about her. Including that she had dozens of uses for Kahlua, including in coffee, over ice cream, and on yogurt. She had the lightest skin tone of five siblings, hence the name *Ivory*, and she gave up a thriving full-time cybersecurity career to be a part-time headhunter and stay-at-home mom to her ungrateful teenage daughter.

"Best friends aren't supposed to keep secrets from each other," Ivory says, jabbing me with her elbow. "Especially ones involving a wedding that looks like a crime scene."

Oh, if only she knew the half of it.

"My wedding day was very traumatizing."

"I can tell," Ivory says, then graciously drops the subject and glances at the girl whose outfit looks nearly identical to Eddie Murphy's in his *Delirious* stand-up comedy special. "So who's the new girl?"

The red-leather girl's expression remains sour. "Uh, you can ask me directly. I do know how to speak."

"This is Wren." Zala steps in, swishing her hair behind her shoulder as she introduces her. "She just moved to our neighborhood. I invited her so she could get to know everyone."

I hold out my hand, but Wren hits it with her knuckles in an awkward one-sided fist-bump. "Welcome to Shoot to Thrill. I'm Shari Catalano, resident photographer and studio owner."

I get an unimpressed look in exchange. "You call this a studio? It looks more like a clearance rack for ugly backdrops."

Admittedly, I didn't have much in the way of décor, but being bad at decorating didn't make me bad at photography, did it?

"Well, this space is only used for lessons, not actually taking portraits," I explain.

Wren idles by my photography wall. "These look amateur to me. How can I trust you to teach me proper photography technique when it looks like a kid shot these?"

"Look, *kid*." Ivory floats up to us like she's the queen of suburbia and merely letting me borrow the castle. According to most of Hemlock Drive, that's pretty accurate. "If you want to do paint by numbers, there's a craft store in town. The rest of us actually appreciate Shari's expertise."

Ivory fiddles with her necklace that matches mine—a delicate gold chain holding two handcrafted lilies, a symbol of beauty and our special friendship talisman that Ivory had custom made on our first girls' trip to the beach shortly after I moved to Doomwood Falls.

"So either show some respect, or leave." Ivory points to the door.

"Down, girl," Wren mumbles before slinking into the corner. "No need to get volatile. I don't have money for the class anyway."

Seriously? Zala brought a broke girl who is going to give me trouble. Not my ideal customer.

"I'm covering the cost of her session today," Zala explains.

Some days the money just isn't worth dealing with people like Wren. But I paste on a smile and begin class with the usual pep in my step because I need to eat. I take coats, pass out lidded coffee cups, and direct everyone to the table of cameras to use at their *disposal*. Did I mention I can't resist a good photography joke?

"So you're teaching us how to take wedding portraits." Ivory examines my photo wall—also known as my *Wall of Exile*—that gives examples of all types of photography I teach my class, from portrait to landscape to wildlife. I don't include photojournalism, which is my professional background, for good reason. It nearly got me killed.

"So exciting, yes?" Ali glances longingly at Zala as he says this.

Ivory shrugs. "There's no reason for me to learn this because I have no intention of getting married again."

"Third time's a charm, right?" I glance at her.

"Third time is till death do *him* part."

Ivory's been divorced twice—to the same man—so when her now-husband Fred proposed marriage, she proposed a pre-nup with a clause that stated she could take everything from him if he left her, including his life, if need be. They laugh about it like it's funny, but I can't even force a grin because it reminds me of my dead husband.

I walk toward the front of the studio where Wren is perched on a chair sipping over-sweetened coffee from a lidded mug that I keep stocked out of necessity, not hospitality. After one too many coffee spills near my priceless cameras, I insisted all cups were required to wear lids.

"I find it hard to believe *you* were married, Shari." Wren clearly has never met a boundary she couldn't trespass with her bold statement shoes.

"Why is that so shocking?" I ask, wondering if my biggest insecurity is true—that my past is so dark that no decent man on earth could possibly want me.

"I don't know. Maybe it's because you strike me as..." Wren assesses me carefully and scrunches her nose, "a homebody. Just not the type to put yourself out there, you know?"

"You're saying I look frumpy," I clarify for her.

"Well, I could always help with that and give you a

makeover on my podcast. It's my specialty." Wren fluffs her dark waves with tips dyed fading pink. "Where's your husband now—did he get tired of vanilla?"

I assume she's referring to my cream-colored wardrobe and house. Certainly she can't know my sex life was as boring as my wardrobe apparently is.

"He's dead," I say flatly. "I'm widowed."

"Oh. That sucks."

I don't judge her inappropriate response too harshly, since she's barely legal drinking age and probably doesn't know any better. "Yeah, it does suck."

"What happened to him?" Wren leans in with morbid interest. "Like, how'd he die?"

I stiffen, and Ivory must notice my discomfort because she comes to my rescue. Again.

"Wren, we don't talk about—" Ivory pauses, because she doesn't know my husband's name. It's been four years since I've uttered it aloud. "—Shari's dead husband, okay? Let's focus on aperture and shutter speed, not ancient history."

"I'm guessing it was bad?" Wren persists.

"Well, his death sure wasn't *good*."

I should have known when the accident happened at my wedding that my marriage was doomed. All the red flags waved even before I said *yes* to Stewart Dobson's proposal, but I chose to ignore them. When I told my future mother-in-law that I would be keeping my own last name, she warned me we wouldn't last. Which was why I shouldn't have been shocked on the day of our nuptials when we released doves at the ceremony, and someone mistook it for a dove hunt and proceeded to shoot each bird, spraying my dress with guts.

Ironically, it was the very same gun my husband would later die by.

Wren's gaze sweeps over the photo gallery of my former lives, my *Wall of Exile*: a blood-sprayed wedding portrait; a sun-drenched California beach; a rural Pennsylvania Amish market; snow-capped Colorado peaks; and my post-prison-release seedy apartment with the buzzing AC unit and peeling wallpaper. Most recently added is the cabin near the waterfall at Doomwood Falls, framed in the last gift my husband ever gave me before his untimely death. The collage serves as a visual autobiography of a woman on the run, frozen in perfect symmetry across my drywall.

"Did you take all of these pictures?" Wren taps her fingernail on the picture of the cabin. I grab her finger to stop her.

"Don't touch that. It's sentimental." The edge to my voice makes Wren quirk an eyebrow at me. "The frame is from my husband before he died."

Her mouth puckers as she returns her attention to the photos with more interest than makes me comfortable. "Why'd you move around so much?"

"I just needed a change," I answer.

"A change… or an escape?" Her question hangs in the air like fog.

My cheeks flush and heat creeps up my neck in an unspoken confession. I've always had a terrible poker face. "I happen to have an adventurous spirit, Wren. I like to see the world."

Wren grins like she's won a debate. "*Adventurous spirit,* huh? Is that why you're a widow—your husband couldn't keep up with the mysterious Shari Catalano?" She laughs like she hasn't just thrown a grenade into the middle of the room.

"Nothing is as adventurous or as mysterious as your outfit choice, Wren," Ivory chimes in.

I chuckle along with them, even though it sounds wrong in my throat—too high, too hollow—while Ivory shoots Wren a look sharp enough to puncture tires. My past is a monstrous shadow I've tried to outrun until my feet bled, until the memories blurred, until I found this quiet corner of the world, hoping to finally outwit its relentless pursuit. But every time I think I've left it behind, I feel it breathing down my neck.

Yes, it is my fault my husband is dead. And yes, I buried him while wearing an orange jumpsuit and handcuffs. And when I finally walked out of that prison three years later—I got lucky with the sentencing due to a technicality—the air didn't feel like freedom. It felt like punishment, because freedom meant living with everything I'd lost. Everything *he'd* taken. But I don't need some ignorant girl to remind me of this.

"Can we get back to today's lesson?" Apparently Ivory senses my distress and steers the conversation into safer terrain with a practiced ease that only best friends and therapists possess.

The scent of developer and acetic acid from my dark room hangs in the air. We're about an hour into the basics of wedding photography when Ivory's phone buzzes. She answers it with the same enthusiasm she has for tequila shots.

"Hey, baby!" she says, grinning at her husband's face on the screen. She glances at me, cups a hand over her mouth, and whispers, "It's Fred. He's pretending to clean out the garage but I know he's only just moving stuff around." Fred continues talking, then Ivory says, "One sec—" and holds the phone out to me. "He actually wants to speak to you."

I blink. "Why does he want to talk to *me*?"

"No clue. Here. Find out." She pushes the phone into my hand like it's a ticking device.

I hold an empty screen in front of me. "Uh, Fred, you there?"

The image jostles as if the phone is being passed along, making me slightly nauseous from the jarring movement.

"Is this Sharon?" The screen is still black, but the voice isn't Fred's. Not unless Fred started smoking ten packs a day and has a cold.

"Uh, it's Shari," I answer.

Then a bleach-white smile fills the screen, and it's not Fred's either. "Nice to finally meet you, Sharon. I'm—"

That's it. That's all I hear, and it's more than enough. Before he finishes his sentence, before I can throw the phone at Ivory and pretend I don't know this man, it slips from my hand onto the floor and makes a dangerous *crack*. Because I know that face intimately. But it's someone who's supposed to be dead.

Chapter 2

"Nice to finally meet you, Sharon. I'm Marshall," his introduction echoes from the floor, eventually catching up with my brain.

Marshall? Correction: The man on the phone is not the dead man I thought he was, though the resemblance is uncanny. Ivory picks up her phone and hands it back to me with a warning glare to be more careful. The image is angled awkwardly, showing part of his face and the shoulder of his orange collared shirt. An industrial fan spins behind him, which looks like the one in Fred's garage. Somehow, even half of his face makes me feel like I need a locked door between us.

"Sorry about that," I apologize.

"Ivory warned me you were clumsy," he says. "I'll be sure not to give you any sharp objects."

At this point I realize the resemblance isn't as strong as I thought. It's the eyes that bother me most, the pale gray of a foggy day, eerily similar to the ones that linger on the edge of my nightmares. But this guy has an extra chin or two, with red hair in a mess of shiny curls like he just got back from surfing or falling into a vat of oil. He grins a little too confidently. Definitely not my type.

My ideal man is nerdy and introverted, and if he'll dress up for a Renaissance Festival or watch Monty Python with me, even better. I had married my ideal man and he's now dead. But this guy looks like he'd bully my ideal man.

"Ivory told me a lot about you, but she never mentioned how beautiful you are." He's oozing with charm. And I do mean *oozing*, because it feels gross coming from the mouth of a total stranger.

"Well, we all know how Ivory loves to exaggerate." I desperately want to end this awkward video chat.

"No, I mean it. Ivory didn't do you justice, Sharon. You are," he pauses, "gorgeous. Spitting image of the hot chick in that *Barbie* movie. Do you get that a lot?"

"My name is *Shari*, not Sharon," I repeat, "and I can't say I've heard that comparison before."

I'm an olive-skinned, brown-haired, thick Italian woman, the exact opposite of Margot Robbie's fair skin, blond hair, and size zero waist. Three Margots could probably fit into one pair of my jeans.

"So…" he smiles and his unnaturally white teeth twinkle like he's auditioning to be the charming-but-dangerous prospect on a dating show, "I know we've just met, but how do you feel about dinner tonight? I've got a place on the beach, just over the border. Sweet sunsets. Sweeter wine."

I force a smile so hard my jaw twitches. "I can't. I have work."

"You call taking pictures work?" He laughs like I've told a joke. "I swear I'm worth it."

"No, what I mean is," I lower my voice and step a few paces away from Zala and Ivory and Wren, who are pretending not to listen but are absolutely eavesdropping, "I don't really date."

He tilts his head, amused. "Why? Afraid you'll like me too

much?"

Because my parole officer will never let me cross the state border without a ton of paperwork. And you creep me out.

"I'm not able to just drop everything and run to the beach." At least not for this guy. But for Ivory on another girl's trip, I'd be willing to beg my probation officer.

Something about this guy makes me fidgety, like my body can't decide whether to run or combust. Heat crawls up my chest, then my neck, beading tiny jewels of sweat on my forehead. My necklace feels too tight, and I tug at it, trying to loosen it to breathe. My finger snags on the chain and I feel a *pop*.

"Shari, honey," Ivory cuts in with a stage whisper, "I think you two would hit it off great. Fred knows him from work and can vouch for him being a nice guy. Plus he loves to travel!"

Ivory points to my *Wall of Exile*, indisputable proof of my love for sightseeing.

"I appreciate the offer," I manage a stiff grin in a silent plea for her to stop playing matchmaker, "but I'm not looking for a relationship right now."

"I bet I can change your mind on that." He sounds like someone who gambles big money on golf games and says things like *you should see my Lambo* after two bourbons.

"I don't think so." I touch my neck to fiddle with my necklace, but there's only bare skin. "Sorry to cut this short, but I'm in the middle of teaching a class and have to go. But it was nice meeting you."

"You're not even willing to let me buy you a drink?"

"No, I'm *really* not interested…" I can't remember his name for the life of me. Was it Michael? Or was it—

"Maxwell."

"It's Marshall," he corrects me, then grins. A slow smirk that slips a little at the edges. "Are you sure you don't want to give me a chance? Because if not, I can promise you that you'll regret it."

At first I think he's trying to be playful, but something about the way he says it lands like a threat. An inside joke where I don't know the punchline, but I do know I'm the target. No one else in the room seems to notice. They're all chatting again, holding their cameras, adjusting settings. Wren is demonstrating some filter app that makes her look like an anime and calling it art.

"My loss, right?" I try to match his playfulness, but I'm not feeling it. "It was fun chatting, but I've got to go."

His eyes now start to resemble an approaching storm. "You're being rude, by the way."

I scoff. "Rude how? Because I won't date you?"

"Because I'm offering to buy you a drink and you're being a bitch about it."

"Wow, I think this conversation is over." I'm about to hang up when his next statement stops me.

"No, *I'll* say when the conversation is over. And by the way, I was lying. You're not as hot as Margot Robbie. Be prepared for a short, lonely life with your dozen cats to keep you company. I can guarantee you'll be sorry for this."

There's no playfulness in his tone this time. Was he actually threatening me?

"Then it's a good thing I'm a dog person," I retort to a blank screen, because the call has already ended.

I hand the phone back to Ivory. "That went well."

"I don't get you, Shar." After tucking the phone in her purse, she raises an eyebrow at me. "What is your deal? He has a huge house and is single!"

"So is the Pope," I mutter. "It doesn't mean I want to date him."

Ivory sighs. "Girl, you've got to start living again. The past—everything you went through with your husband—shouldn't control your future. We've all done stuff we regret. Believe me, I know all about how the past can wage a war your present has to finish. But there's a point when you have to surrender and end it."

In a way, Ivory is the only person who understands me. We share a secret grief, a self-imposed blame for losing our first loves. While her husband wasn't murdered like mine was, she, too, has navigated the treacherous waters of a broken heart, of rebuilding a life from wreckage.

Cupping my cheek, she forces me to look at her, and there's something quiet in her demeanor, the woman who is a walking party with a never-ending arsenal of conversation. It's not pity I find in her expression, but something else. Something haunted.

Her first and second divorce weren't just messy, they were apocalyptic. She's never given the specifics and I never asked, but right now I want to. But this isn't about her, it's about me. And she's the type of person to remind me of that.

"I don't think I can move on after what happened to—" I almost say my husband's name but can't force it out. I stare at our wedding portrait and my blood-spattered dress.

"I know, I know. Hurt doesn't disappear. It relocates. But you need to at least try."

I press my hand to my chest, where it always aches the

worst. Where my wedding band used to rest against my collarbone on a necklace I have since replaced with the new one symbolic of hope and friendship. Except my lily necklace isn't there.

I gasp. "Where is it?"

"Where's what?" Wren asks, naturally gravitating toward the drama.

"My necklace. It's gone. It looks just like Ivory's…"

Ivory places her hand on the exact same spot at her collarbone where her twin necklace rests. Searching the floor, I eventually find it knotted in a tiny heap from when I yanked too hard and broke the clasp during the phone call with Maxwell… Michael… Marshall, whatever his name is. I bend down slowly, my knees crunching, and scoop it up.

"How cute!" Wren squeals. "Are those, like, friendship necklaces? That is so retro. I used to have one with my college roommate. Well, before I slept with her fiancé." She says it like it's an accomplishment.

Ivory laughs too hard, the way she does when she wants to stab someone with her nail file. "Yeah, Shari and I got them as a symbol of friendship and strength. We're committed to keeping each other strong. Right, Shar?"

I give her a nod that's more conceding than agreeable. "Yep, girl power!"

My gaze drifts back to the wedding portrait—white dress, red blood. A flash of orange moving outside the studio window invades my peripheral. Someone is standing in my yard, mostly hidden by a tree except for a shoulder jutting out. I know that shoulder.

Marshall. It's the same shirt he was wearing during our

conversation, and now he's outside my house watching me. But there's something he doesn't know about me, so he better keep his distance. Not everyone has a murdered husband and a prison record, but I do. And I could easily make it happen again.

Chapter 3

The pull of the string is followed immediately by the electric hum of a single sixty-watt bulb dangling from a wire. It flickers once, then twice, before settling into a yellow glow too faint to reach the corners of the room.

I step over the threshold and grab the white five-gallon pail, heavy in my right hand. The wire handle digs into my flesh, cutting off the circulation to my fingers, turning them a mottled purple. It's the kind of bucket you buy at a hardware store to mix grout, rigid and industrial, but the weight shifting inside isn't grout. It sloshes with a thick, viscous movement. Like slop.

My sneakers squeak against the concrete floor. I hold my breath, counting the steps to the far corner where the shadows are thickest, huddled together like frightened children.

Thud. Thud. Thud.

The muted sound hammers from the front door. Someone's here. My heart hammers back, and for a single precarious moment, the bucket tilts. In that second, time stretches as I watch the rim of the bucket dip. The liquid inside surges toward the edge, cresting like a miniature tidal wave. My free hand shoots out to grab the rim.

The liquid laps at the edge of the plastic lip, a single droplet trembling there, held back only by surface tension.

Do not drop it!

The knocking ends but the doorbell chimes. My visitor's impatience is going to cost me my life, if I'm not careful. Because if this bucket tips over, it's not just a mess. It's the end for me. It's police tape and handcuffs and a Breaking News banner across the bottom of every TV screen in America. It's my face on the cover of the *Doomwood Falls Daily*. It is the total and complete annihilation of the life I have carefully constructed over the last year.

The droplet rolls back into the depths of the bucket and I slowly exhale. For now I leave the bucket in the corner. It looks innocent enough in the shadows, just a bucket. I back away and yank the string again. *Click*.

Darkness swallows the room instantly, eager to hide what I've done.

Chapter 4

The doorbell rings just as I'm crawling out of the wall. And no, that's not a metaphor about escaping the confines of my mind-numbing life. I mean it literally. I'm exiting the secret room hidden behind a bookcase door that I built using a YouTube do-it-yourself video. No one but me—and maybe the Home Depot employee who helped me pick everything out for the project—knows about that room, and I'll do pretty much anything to keep it that way.

As the doorbell chimes again, my American bully, Zoomie, does what he does best. He barks his gigantic head off while zooming around. Although he slobbers all over my walls and is missing half his teeth, it was love at first ugly sight.

Years ago, my husband and I found him wandering along a rural highway rooting through garbage, and I instantly recognized that this skin-and-bones dog had been a bait dog in a fighting ring. Emaciated with roughly chopped-off ears and a tail broken in several places that give it a zigzag lightning bolt shape, he and his overactive salivary glands found a home in our bed instantly, despite my husband's objection. As a photographer, I couldn't resist the name Zoomie when I realized he had a midnight adrenaline habit.

The bookshelf door swings shut behind me with a *click*, sealing the entrance. After double-checking to ensure my secrets are safely locked away, I smooth my hair in the hallway mirror, plaster on my *I'm perfectly normal with nothing to hide* semi-smile, and open the door. On the other side is Ivory, dressed like she's ready to go clubbing while I'm wearing sweatpants and a coffee-stained sweatshirt I bought at a thrift store.

"Ready to go?" Ivory gives me a once-over with a hint of disproval.

"All set."

"You're going out in public wearing *that*?" Ivory physically turns me around and gawps. "Your butt says *Juicy*, Shar. How old are you again?"

I assumed the bejeweled word across the pants' rear was fashionable again since other Y2K trends had made a comeback, but apparently not for a woman in her thirties. "What's wrong with what I'm wearing?"

"Where do I begin?" She blinks her obviously fake eyelashes. "First of all, your pants predate Britney Spears. Second, every time you make a public appearance, you could potentially meet your future husband. But looking homeless… well, that's not going to attract the right clientele, if you know what I mean."

"Did you just say *public appearance* and *clientele*? You make me sound like a prostitute. We're going to the jewelry repair store, not the disco."

"And third," she adds, "no one goes to the disco anymore because they've been extinct since the 1970s. Look, hon, you never know where love might find you. But with that outfit, you're more likely to attract loose change than a man."

"I could use the money, so I'll consider that a win."

"Ug, what am I going to do with you?" she groans. "Let's go."

While Ivory descends the porch steps, I glance back at the bookshelf and think of what's behind it, the room full of things I've hidden so well I sometimes forget they exist. But not today. All because of Marshall. I can't shake the feeling that I know him, or maybe he knows me. Either way, he's too familiar not to ignore. And the way he said *"you'll regret it"* like he meant it creeps me out. I deadbolt the front door behind me, forcing my secrets to remain hidden for another day.

Half an hour later, I'm still wonderfully comfortable in my *Juicy* sweatpants as I drop off my necklace to get fixed. Then we head over to our favorite coffee shop, The Alibi Café.

The sky is a wet gray-blue, so we sit inside. It smells like espresso and permeates with hope for a better future as book nerds fill nearly every table with their overachieving book club picks. I luck out and find a table next to the window near the door, the one spot no one wants due to the draft every time someone enters.

Sitting across from me, Ivory is draped in an expensive sweater probably spun from the coats of endangered cashmere goats. She stirs her oat milk latte, the spoon a tiny, silver baton conducting a symphony of flavors.

"I think Freida is dating an ex-con," Ivory opens the conversation with an explosion.

Her daughter Freida, named after Fred, is still in high school. If I had an eighteen-year-old daughter dating an ex-con, and a husband who wasn't dead, I'm pretty sure she would be sent off to a convent, if they still exist. Though it's pretty judgmental of me to think this since I, too, am an ex-con.

"What does Fred think of the guy?" I ask.

"He doesn't know about him yet. I haven't for sure verified it either, but when I do… well, her ex-con will be made extinct."

I laugh, because imagining Ivory doing anything as messy as murder is hilarious. "Let's keep homicide off the table for now. I'm sure he's not as bad as you think."

"Speaking of bad, what do you think of your newest student?" she asks me, and without a name I already know she's referring to Wren.

"She's… opinionated, I'll give her that."

"You know, if she ends up enjoying your class, that could really boost business."

"How so?"

"She's an influencer, Shar. Didn't you hear her mention it only a thousand times in class?"

"No, I must have missed that during Macho Marshall's weird FaceTime call."

"*Macho Marshall*?" Ivory chuckles. "Anyway, so I checked Wren out, and sure enough, she's got hundreds of thousands of followers on pretty much every social media platform. Plus she has a popular podcast." Ivory taps the screen of her phone and shows me the podcast: *Zen with Wren*.

I'm not as impressed as Ivory seems to be. "Doesn't everyone have a podcast these days?"

"Don't mock it," she warns me. "A little word-of-mouth praise from her could go a long way in building your business. Wren has a lot of influence, so it's in your best interest to keep her happy."

With Wren's ability to destroy me just as easily as it would be to help me, I definitely plan to at least try. Though after spending an hour listening to her complain about how none of my photography techniques involved slimming filters or portrait mode, it might be an unreachable goal.

I'm sipping my hazelnut macchiato when my phone blinks with a notification that Shoot to Thrill has been tagged in a Facebook post. I've spent the past year scrubbing any internet presence of personal pictures that could lead someone to finding me here in Doomwood Falls. The only person I had worried about finding me is presumed dead, so I'm not regimented about it but I still try to be careful. It gets harder as more people have phones glued to their palms, constantly filming and TikTok-ing every minute of their lives.

When I check the post, my chest tightens. "Someone just wrote a negative review about my photography class."

The public bashing is left by a woman named Sue on the Doomwood Falls Community Page. Worst of all, it's not just a bad review. The more I read, the more I sense that it's a personal attack:

I signed up for a photography class at Shoot to Thrill, run by the infamous Shari Catalano, a woman whose résumé feels less "creative professional" and more "unsolved questions." The class itself was a masterclass in overexposure, specifically of talent and technique. The instruction felt like an endurance test—blink twice if you need help.

By the end, I wasn't inspired; I was terrified. Shoot

to Thrill isn't a studio name. It's a warning label. I suspect the fee doesn't pay for instruction so much as it aids whatever past she's outrunning. If you're thinking about booking, do yourself a favor and look into Shari's past. Not deeply—just enough to decide photography might be safer as a hobby you never pursue.

It makes no sense. I can name every person I've taught in my classes, and I've never taught a Sue. No one has ever complained. I can't imagine anyone hating me this much. But there is someone who strikes me as publicly opinionated, fluent in social media, and impossible to please: Wren.

"Did you hear me, Ivory? I got a bad review," I repeat.

"Okay, so what?" But she seems lost in whatever she's staring at out the window.

"Hello? This could shut my studio down!" I emphasize, because while it may not be a big deal to Ivory, who has job security and a well-off husband, this could bankrupt my fledgling business that I rely on to survive.

She glances at me and rolls her eyes. "One bad review isn't going to ruin you."

"It sure isn't going to help. You know how word-of-mouth spreads in this town." Especially the bad kind. Gossip is like catnip to these folks.

I wait for her to agree with me, to demand accountability, to seek justice on my behalf, but she doesn't. Instead, she's mutters, "You're overreacting," and returns her attention to the window behind me. She's miles away, in the labyrinth of her own mind, leaving me alone in this purgatory of social media cancellation.

"Forget it," I say, too stressed to sit here doing nothing. "You clearly are occupied. I'm heading home to deal with this."

Though I have no idea what dealing with this should involve. Running a sale price on all lessons? Calling my regular clients to make sure they're happy?

When I rise to my feet, the chair screeches across the floor. Ivory's head snaps back, a marionette yanked by an invisible string.

"Where are you going?"

"If you paid any attention, you wouldn't need to ask!" I grab my purse, hoping she'll beg me to stay since she is my ride home, after all.

"Sit down and stop acting like a child!" she demands loud enough to draw the attention of several customers around us.

"What's the point of spending time together if you're just going to ignore me?" I yell back.

"Boo hoo. Get over yourself, Shar. The world doesn't revolve around you."

I stand there dumbfounded, seeing a cruel side of my best friend she's never shown me before. "Ouch."

"I didn't mean to say that." Her tone is softer now. "But it's just a stupid review."

"A review that could lose the few clients I have." I sit back down, deflated. "You don't understand because you have Fred to support you. I have no one but myself."

"Hey, that's your fault. I tried to hook you up."

"With Macho Marshall? I'd rather be single and broke, thanks. Besides, I'm not looking for you to solve my financial problems. I'm just asking you to listen right now."

"I'm sorry I was distracted. I thought I saw someone." For the first time ever, Ivory does the impossible: She wrinkles her un-wrinkleable, Botoxed brow.

I twist in my seat, scanning the nearly empty sidewalk. A bearded man commits a crime against humanity by power-walking in Crocs, and the backs of two people cross the street with their Bernese mountain dog, who bounces all too happily in the brisk weather.

"Is everything okay?" I ask.

There's a slight tremor of her hand that I almost miss except that it bumps her mug and sprinkles droplets of latte on the table.

"Yeah, it's fine. Can we please talk about your situation instead?"

"I thought the world didn't revolve around me…" I mock her in my best Ivory impersonation.

"Oh, shut up. You know my world revolves around you," and we both laugh because it's true. My drama is way more interesting than hers. I pick up my phone and click my way back to the review, then slide it toward her. Her eyes narrow as she reads what's on the screen. "Wow, harsh. Any idea who wrote this?"

Navigating to the name on the Facebook account, I read it aloud: "Her name is *Sue Nimm*. But I don't remember having a Sue in any of my classes."

"Honey," Ivory states. "That's a fake profile. Sue D. Nimm—*pseudonym*. Get it? It's probably just a troll."

I feel infinitesimally dumb right now, but that doesn't negate that the threat feels very real. This person seems to know about my past. "Troll or not, whoever this is, they're out to get me."

"Who have you pissed off recently?"

The only person I can think of is… "Macho Marshall was pretty mad that I wouldn't go on a date with him. He told me I'd regret it, and now I do."

"Well, you don't have any proof it's him, but I can ask Fred if he thinks Marshall would do something like this." Ivory leans forward and makes direct eye contact, which I've never felt comfortable with. "But if it turns out to be Marshall, you need to report it to the police."

"The police?" I shake my head. "No way. They don't care about a stupid online review."

"They will if he makes a threat, which he did—twice! And this qualifies as communications harassment. Go to the police. Because this is creepy and stalkerish."

But the mention of police—even hypothetically—gives me a full-body flight response. There is no way I'm going to a police station willingly.

"No, it's fine. I think you're right. It's just one negative review. It's better not to engage."

"You're going to let guys like him get away with bullying? No, Shar! Stand up for yourself! Go to the cops with this."

But Ivory doesn't get my reason for wanting to let it go. Of course she doesn't understand that confronting someone who may or may not know about my past could backfire. She's never spent nights sleeping on a cement bench, with a toilet three feet from her pillow, the stench of stale urine a constant companion. She's never heard the clank of prison bars locking behind her, a sound of finality that echoes in the hollow chambers of her soul.

But I have. And I will never set foot in a police station again. Not after knowing the cold snap of cuffs around my wrists, the bite of metal against my skin, the familiar taste of fear. Even if Marshall torpedoes every client, costs me every dollar, shreds all the credibility I've painstakingly built, I'd rather start over with nothing than risk talking to the cops.

My phone rings with a jarring intrusion. The name on my screen says *Zala*. I already know what she's going to say before I pick up because the universe has a cruel sense of humor.

"Hey, Shari," she starts with a saccharine sweetness that precedes a punch to the gut. "I'm going to have to cancel our session this week. Something came up."

"You saw the review online, didn't you?"

"Well… um," she stutters, "it's kind of hard not to when I was tagged in it."

She was? I pull the phone away from my ear and scroll back to the post. Sure enough, half of Doomwood Falls was tagged on that review. Pretty much all of my clients. Or past clients, it's beginning to look like. Whoever did this lives in town and knows more of my business than they should. I'm not so sure Marshall fits the bill, but I'm sure as hell going to find out.

"Anyway, it's nothing personal," Zala continues. "I just don't have the time right now to take classes."

Her words are a practiced euphemism for *I don't want any association with the town villain*. I thank her anyway and hang up, then stare at the table and its landscape of crumbs and coffee stains.

"Zala cancelled on me!" I explode. "How much worse is this going to get?"

Ivory reaches for my hand, her touch tentative, but I pull back, wrapping my fingers around my coffee cup instead. It's lukewarm now, but I gulp it down anyway. Since I'm going to be broke soon, I can't risk wasting a single drop.

"You have to do something," Ivory scolds me. "Don't let him get away with this."

"I'll figure it out." I'm angry and not bothering to hide it.

"You'll figure what out?" Speak of the devil… Of all the coffee shops in all of Doomwood Falls, Wren shows up at ours. She pulls out the chair next to mine and sits down. "Aw, are you two having a lover's quarrel? Maybe I could help mediate."

"We're not fighting. We were just talking about…" Then I catch myself, because I don't know Wren at all. What if she was the troll who posted the review? So I quickly blurt, "…Norse folklore."

"Norse folklore—as in elves and trolls?"

I nod, watching her carefully. Whoever posted that review couldn't hide that level of disdain for me. "Yeah, it's fascinating stuff. I'm learning about it for Dungeons & Dragons."

"Okaaaay," she shrugs without even a hint of malice, "you're cooler than I thought."

I look to Ivory, who is shoving her chair back, then jumping up from her seat, completely ignoring me again. Whatever she's focused on outside the window is far more interesting than trolls. In fact, based on her expression it looks critical, like a Free People super-sale or someone dying.

"Mind getting a ride home with Wren?" Ivory isn't really asking because she's already halfway to the door. "I have to go."

She doesn't wait for either of us to answer, and as I watch her rush down the sidewalk and turn the corner, I have a horrible feeling I'm about to lose my grip on everything. This means only one thing: It's time to start packing. Not boxes… yet. But mentally and emotionally I'm planning my escape from

Doomwood Falls, one backward step at a time, a hasty retreat from a life that was never truly mine.

Chapter 5

I couldn't sleep last night. So this morning I decide to clear my head of Macho Marshall, of the anonymous review, of Zala cancelling her session, and go to the one place that brings me peace: Doomwood Falls waterfall. Though, even here dread tags along on my hike.

Something about nature brings comfort when nothing else does. Maybe it's because the pine trees never change, even when everything else surrenders to winter. Like wizened old men who have seen the rise and fall of civilizations, their pointed tops reach up toward a sky that's a vast, indifferent blue. There's tranquility here, and I need it to rub off on me and push all worry out of mind.

I press my back against a hibernating oak and shiver, the rough bark scraping a polite *hello* through my ill-equipped sweatshirt. Or maybe it's less polite and more like, *You really should have worn something thicker, you idiot.*

Raising my camera to my eye, the familiar weight is a comforting anchor in a world that's decided to go off-kilter. I manually adjust the zoom lens and capture my shot.

Click.

The waterfall is less of a gentle cascade and more of a full-blown tantrum, loud enough to drown out thought. To be honest, that is my current goal, to put that hateful review out of mind, along with whoever is dead set on ruining me. *Cough—Marshall—Cough*. After advancing the film, I catch the way the afternoon light filters through the spray like tiny diamonds suspended in air. I'm focusing the lens when something strange lingers along the edge of the frame.

The color is out of place here in nature: neon pink. Lowering the camera, I search for it again and easily spot it, clothing strewn along the mossy bank. A neon pink shirt sits on top of a crumpled heap of clothes, as if their owners were in a hurry to get out of them.

Teenagers, probably, swimming in the frigid pool beneath the falls, testing boundaries, trying to feel alive. Or maybe they're just trying to catch hypothermia. I don't see anyone in the water, which leads me to think they're hiding in the hollow behind the curtain of falling water. It's a popular place for clandestine hook-ups and adventurous indiscretions.

I smirk with fleeting amusement at the naïve joys of adolescence that I wish I could go back to, and I lift the camera. Maybe I'll catch their silhouettes in a frozen moment of rebellion against parental curfews and questionable life choices. Peering through the viewfinder, I readjust the focus and—

Click.

The tinny sound is followed by voices. I lower the camera and listen. A girl speaking joins the rush of water, but her words are drowned out. She's talking rapidly, growing louder as I approach the waterfall. This time a single word is clear:

"Stop!"

It doesn't sound like the playful shriek of a girl in cold water who's just lost her bikini top. No, this is distinctly sharp and terrified. Trekking along the path that winds behind the falls, I scan the rocky ledge beyond the cascading water, looking for signs of where she could be.

"Hello? Is anyone out here?" But I doubt they'd hear my voice over the roar.

The birds, who were in the middle of a cheerful singalong, go silent. Even the wind seems to hold its breath. Where did the voice come from? It's impossible to tell. The falls mask everything, a natural sound curtain.

"Do you need help?" I call out again, attempting to inject authority into my voice.

Once again nothing. No splashing. No giggling teens trying to get arrested for public nudity. Just the relentless crash of water.

I move closer, stepping over a tangle of roots that resemble grasping fingers, and I duck beneath a low-hanging branch. My boots sink into the damp earth, squelching in the mud. I scan the opposite bank through the blinding glare of the sun. The clothes are still there, but no people are in view. Ripples skim over the water's brown depths. I wait, but no one surfaces.

The plea *Stop!* plays on a loop in my head, but now I'm starting to doubt what I heard. It probably is nothing. They saw me coming and don't want to get caught. But the danger felt so real… *Stop!*

I advance the film and bring the camera to my eye again, my hands shaking so much the viewfinder wobbles. It could be hunger blurring my vision, but I snap a picture of the bank anyway, along with the clothes and the empty space near the waterfall where the clothes' owners should be.

Click.

I don't know why I feel compelled to take these pictures,

but something warns me that I need to prove I was here, that this happened. That I didn't just imagine a woman screaming. Or maybe it's just my traumatized subconscious begging for a therapist.

The wind picks up, sending a flurry of crispy red leaves swirling around me like a morbidly beautiful ballet. I step back, and the heel of my boot slips on the wet rocks. My breath catches as I almost fall into the water. I need to leave. My feet are already eager to put as much distance as possible between me and whatever is happening here. I've got enough of my own problems that I don't need to go chasing other people's.

I turn to leave, but something stops me. A nagging in the back of my mind, probably the same one that tells me to check if I closed my hidden bookshelf door all the way. When I glance back I see it, a disturbance behind the spray. Movement. And a streak of something pale.

Naked skin.

My finger, now numb with cold, hovers over the shutter release button on the 1954 Leica that my dad gifted me on my wedding day, now worth over $10,000 and irreplaceable. Not just because of its sentimental value, but it's literally impossible to find.

The zoom feels like an extension of myself, over the years capturing so many secrets and memories of my husband before… well, I try not to think about that. I watch two figures, shrouded by the ceaseless deluge. Anyone else would have walked right by, oblivious to them, but the camera, with its almost malevolent ability, sees what the human eye can't.

I twist the zoom ring, each slow rotation deliberate. The lens tightens, sucking them into focus. The shutter snaps, and they're ripped from their hazy world and dropped clearly into mine. I brace myself, expecting the usual suspects—two teens. But it's not. It's so much worse.

My stomach lurches with a threat of dragging last night's dinner up my throat. A man's face is caught in a shard of light that pierces the waterfall's veil. He turns just enough for me to identify his face. Then he looks directly at me.

Our gazes lock, only for a moment. But I know those eyes.

I duck, terrified of getting caught. Scared of what he'll say to cover up what he's done. Somehow he'll turn it around to make me the villain, even though I have the truth locked inside the heart of my camera. Something horrible just happened here, and I am the only witness.

Chapter 6

I'm crouching in the brush when my photojournalist brain starts piecing the facts together. The cheating bastard is Fred, the man who promised forever and till death do us part to my best friend. Even through the waterfall's haze, I know it's him the instant we make eye contact. He's not alone, and the woman he's with is a stark contrast to Ivory. First of all, the woman behind the waterfall is as white as a paper plate in a snowstorm. And Ivory wouldn't be caught dead wearing the neon pink shirt I'd seen tossed on the ground.

What the hell is Fred thinking? Cheating on Ivory is a death sentence. The questions claw at the inside of my skull while I'm hunched over, trying to shuffle my way out of here without him seeing me again.

A horrible stench and familiar squish under foot stops me mid-step. A massive pile of fresh dog poop covers my shoes. The size of it puts Zoomie's to shame, which means this dog must be massive… and is probably somewhere close by, based on the poop's soft texture. I'm not eager to stick around to find out, though.

After wiping my soles off with a few leaves, I scoot behind a bush and peek over the branches, expecting to spot the couple. But they're gone. The clothes are gone from the shore too. It's now or never.

I jump up and run. Branches scratch against my cheeks while I suck in gasps of air that burn my lungs. I push through the undergrowth, blind to the path, until I break through the woods into the clearing where I parked my car. Only once I'm in my car's silent interior do my thoughts unravel.

Fred is cheating on Ivory. Ivory is going to kill Fred. Why did I have to witness this?

What do I do? If I tell Ivory, I shatter her world and will be forced to testify in her inevitable trial for murdering Fred. But if I stay silent, I'm complicit in Fred's crime against my friend. A silent lie, a festering wound. Do I confront him? Offer him a chance to spin his web of excuses before I unleash the storm?

When I pull up my driveway, the sun is dipping below the horizon, painting the sky in bruised purples and angry oranges. My home looms before me, ominous in the fading light. The covered porch is hidden in darkness, but there's something unsettling about it. Something is moving.

A figure steps out of the shadows on to my walkway and into the dying evening light. All the air along with my frantic thoughts whoosh out of me in a single gasp. Oh, it's only—

"Wren? What are you doing here?"

"Ew, Shari, what happened to you?" Even as she sounds grossed out by my appearance, Wren's voice maintains a carefully modulated pitch of concern as her gaze rakes over me.

"What do you mean?" I touch my hair and feel the point of a jagger prick my fingertip, and my cheek burns.

"I mean you look like you just escaped an alien abduction." Her eyes are already dissecting me. Then she sniffs. "Do you smell that?"

Oh, crap—literally. I hadn't gotten it all off, apparently.

That means it's probably on the floor mat in my car.

I force a dry laugh. "Oh, that. I was hiking and went a little off the trail."

She's drafting her social media caption, I can feel it: *Neighborhood hot mess, unfiltered! #realtalk #suburbanlife #hotmessexpress*

"By yourself?" She glances at the lowering sun. "At this hour?" Wren's interrogation has begun.

I lift up my camera. "It's called the *golden hour* for a reason."

"Well, if you're having some kind of mental health crisis right now," she continues, her voice dripping with faux sympathy, "I totally support that. But maybe we should cancel today's class?"

My stomach clenches in a knot of pure panic. I had completely forgotten about it. "Cancel? No, the timing is perfect. I didn't realize you could afford classes. Last time you said—"

"No, it's cool now. I came into some money. I should warn you, though. People talk, you know?" She delivers the line with a practiced innocence, as if she isn't the primary architect of the gossip. "I don't want the neighbors thinking I'm, like, aligning myself with the town psycho."

She flashes her teeth in a smile that's less warmth, more weapon. This girl has lived on Hemlock Drive for barely a minute and already holds the social fate of our entire cul-de-sac in her hands. Everyone, from the empty-nesters to the harried young mothers, is desperate to remain in her gilded circle. Even me.

Why? Because she possesses a ring light and half a million

followers who hang on her every word about the transformative power of kale smoothies and *being your authentic self*—a self that conveniently aligns with her flawlessly curated aesthetic. And now she's threatening to dismantle my struggling photography business with a single, perfectly aimed social media reel.

"Wren," I say, forcing a calm worthy of an Oscar, "I'm totally fine." I recall Ivory showing me Wren's latest video promising tips on how to transform your selfies from *uggo* to *wowza* with the right angle. "I was going to teach you how to find your best angle and utilize it in photography. You don't want to let your fans down, do you?"

The bait is taken. "True. I did post a teaser story this morning."

"Great," I say, already ushering her inside. "How about I make one of your delicious kale smoothie recipes while you head into the studio?"

She glides past me in an entitled whirlwind of couture clothes and painstakingly tousled hair, her oversized tote bag thumping against the doorframe. I close the door behind her. My pulse still hasn't settled. I need to pull myself together. Now.

But then—

Thump.

We both freeze. The sound is muffled, indistinct, yet undeniably there. It echoes from behind the bookshelf, a heavy impact that seems to vibrate through the very foundations of the house. Someone found my hiding spot.

Wren tilts her head with sudden curiosity. "Is someone else here?"

"No," I blurt out, the word too quick that it practically

screams guilt. "It's probably Zoomie getting into something he shouldn't be."

Which reminds me… where is Zoomie? He's usually quick to greet all visitors with a slobbery unwanted kiss. I wonder if I hadn't fully closed the bookshelf and he managed to bulldoze his way inside.

Luckily Wren doesn't seem to notice that the thumping is coming from behind the bookshelf directly in front of her. But she does notice a picture sitting on that same bookshelf—the last place I want to draw her attention to.

"So what brought you here to Doomwood Falls?" Wren appears to be attempting small talk, which I've never been good at and have no desire to start practicing now. But I can't be rude, so I tell her what I've told everyone since I arrived here a year ago.

"Ivory Cobb, actually."

Her eyebrows lift. "Really? How so?"

"I was looking for a job, and Ivory's a headhunter. I don't know how she found me, but she offered me a temporary position taking photos for the *Doomwood Falls Daily*. She even found me this house on Hemlock Drive when I told her of my plans to open up my own studio. Ivory saved my life and gave me a second chance."

Ivory really did save my life, because having no support system along with a felony record makes it virtually impossible to get a job… a legal one, that is. No one else would touch me or my impressive professional resume once they completed the background check. Ivory was the first and only person who believed in me after my prison release. She's the reason I survived.

"And this is your dead husband, right?" she asks, and the careless way she phrases it makes me lose hope in our future generations.

"Yeah, that's him."

"What's his name?" she presses.

I can't speak his name; it feels wrong coming out of my mouth when I'm the reason he's dead. But it feels even worse trying to explain to this girl why I haven't spoken it in four years. A huge part of me, the part that wants desperately to move forward, wants to at least try.

"His name…" I suck a breath in through an invisible straw, "is Stew."

Something akin to relief, or freedom, or a feeling I can't put words to fills me up and pours over as I say it out loud.

"Stew? As in something you eat?"

"Yes, Stew, as in Stewart." It comes out so much easier the second and third times, and it's almost melodic. Definitely therapeutic.

"I thought he was Italian. Your last name is Catalano, isn't it?"

"Oh, I didn't take his last name after we got married." I don't want to explain why, that my father had forbid it because we were the last Catalanos in America and he didn't want his daughter's name being overwritten by some accountant unoriginally named Stewart Dobson.

"How feminist of you," she says. "And who is this yummy piece of man meat in this other picture?"

She points to a family portrait of me, Stewart, my mother, father, and my brother back before I knew how to fire a gun or make toilet prison wine.

"Oh, that's my brother Luca," I tell her.

"Why haven't you introduced me yet? He's hot and totally date-able. And I'm newly single."

"For exactly that reason—I would never want you dating my brother."

"And why is that? I'm a catch, Shari. He would be lucky to have me."

Wren would *not* be lucky to have him, because it's not Luca's welfare I'm concerned about. I know my brother, whose past is worse than mine.

"Trust me, you're better off never meeting him."

I head into the kitchen and rummage through the cabinet looking for the blender for our smoothies. Anything to hide that thumping. I find it and plop it on the counter and plug it in, hoping I have something edible I can mix together that won't end up tasting like sewage. Sure enough, I find yogurt and blueberries in the fridge. This will have to do.

"Besides, I haven't seen Luca for years, so I have no idea where he is or what he's doing." Probably in jail carving shivs out of bars of soap, if I were to guess.

She squints at me, her eyes narrowing into suspicious slits, then she slowly walks away from the bookshelf. I have to distract her before Zoomie draws more attention to the—

Thump.

This time she pivots toward the bookshelf. "It almost sounds like the noise is coming from behind this—"

I hit the blend button just as the perfect excuse hits me. "Oh, the laundry room is on the other side. Zoomie likes to sleep in there," I yell over the blender.

"It sounded like something fell. Aren't you going to check

on your dog?"

"Nah. He's fine. He does this all the time. I'll deal with whatever mess he made later."

Once the smoothies are done, I nudge her toward the studio entrance, as far away from the bookshelf as possible. "Ready to start?"

"Sure." But she doesn't sound sure, and she's moving slower than dirt. "I'm gonna run to the bathroom before we start. Cool?"

I point her back to the studio. "It's in there, like always."

But she doesn't head towards the studio, which is accessible through my living room. Instead, she pivots with her gaze fixed on the staircase.

"Upset stomach. I think I'll use the upstairs one… for privacy," she says breezily.

Who on earth spoiled this girl so much that she feels entitled to letting herself upstairs?

"You have makeup, right? I'll grab stuff to fix up your face while I'm at it."

I move to intercept her, trying to keep my voice casual, as if her demands aren't sending cold dread pooling in my gut. "Actually, the plumbing's been a bit weird up there. The studio bathroom's much better."

She stops and locks her gaze onto mine. Right now her expression is unreadable.

"Hmm," she says finally, the single sound loaded with unspoken meaning I can't decipher. I'm worried this interaction will lead to another disastrous review. "Okay. But you really do need to take care of that scratch on your face before you end up with a hideous scar."

She descends the stairs, but I can feel her suspicion in the air, a thick, palpable shroud. And I know two things with troubling certainty: One, that Wren does not believe my excuse about the thump. And two, she is absolutely not going to let it go.

We're in the hallway, me leading the way through the living room into the studio, when Wren suddenly stops behind me. Resting one hand against the bookshelf, she casually leans against it to adjust the strap of her shoe, and I hold a terrified breath that the latch will release and open the door under her weight.

Something tells me Wren is going to be my downfall.

Chapter 7

My hidden room is still hidden, despite the close call of Wren nearly stumbling on it. So my secrets are still safe… for now. But once she disappears down Hemlock Drive after a torturous hour-long session of her insisting that high-angle selfies make better portraits—ignoring my well-supported point that too-close angles can exaggerate features like noses and foreheads—I slam the front door shut.

Pressing my forehead against the wood, I try to staunch the thrumming behind my eyes and in my temples. Two pain pills later, Zoomie barks at the bookshelf, reminding me to slip inside and investigate.

A small table is knocked over, but that's the worst of the damage. A metal chest has been pushed aside but otherwise looks untouched. I pop it open just to make sure everything is still there, and a quick peek reaffirms me. I don't know how I managed to keep Wren from uncovering this, but I'll be more careful from now on. The last thing I need is someone discovering what's back here.

My nerves are shot, but I need to do something about the Fred and Ivory situation. It'll haunt me until I do. There's only one person I want to talk to right now.

It's twilight with the temperature hovering just above freezing, so I slip on my coat and cross the street with no preliminary phone call, like I have a hundred times before. One car is missing from the driveway—the one I had hoped wouldn't be here. I stand on the doorstep and jab the doorbell. The shrill chime pierces the quiet suburban air while I pace the porch like a caged animal until the door finally opens.

"Hey, Shar," Ivory says, her expression unruffled.

She's a vision of domestic tranquility in a soft gray sweater and leggings, her braids now undone in ringlets that skim halfway down her back.

"You busy?" I can't believe what I'm about to do to my closest friend.

"I just finished cleaning up after dinner," she says, then steps aside for me to enter. "Everything okay?"

"No," I blurt unedited, then I slip past her into the pristine sanctuary of her home. "I need to talk to you."

She doesn't ask questions. Not a single, probing query. She's patient that way. Instead, she silently leads me into her kitchen, pops a coffee pod into the coffeemaker, and pushes the brew button. When it's done, she places the mug in front of me with the gravity of a cop presenting evidence and makes a tea for herself.

"So, what's going on?" she asks as she sits down across from me at the island.

And then I burst, because I can't hold it in any longer. "I saw Fred with another woman."

The ugly statement hangs in the air between us. Ivory doesn't flinch, doesn't cry, doesn't even widen her eyes or mouth in shock. She simply takes a slow, deliberate sip of her tea. Earl Grey, I think, or perhaps chamomile—something soothing and incongruous with the bombshell I've just dropped.

"You're sure it was him?" she asks in a flat, even tone.

"Yes." My voice breaks. At least I'm pretty sure. Ninety-nine percent sure it was Fred. Or maybe more like eighty percent. Suddenly I regret being here, telling her this horrible thing that I might have gotten wrong. What if it wasn't Fred?

"When?" Her questions barges through my uncertainty.

"Earlier today, at the waterfall."

She sets her mug down gently, the faint click of ceramic against granite the only sound. "Did you see the other woman's face?"

"No," I admit.

"So I'll never know who she is unless Fred tells me, which let's face it, he'll deny until his last breath."

The calm way she says *his last breath* feels ominous. Ivory vowed never to let another man destroy her like her first husband, not without destroying him back. This betrayal… this could warrant nuclear-level destruction.

"Maybe it's best not to know who she is," I say.

"Why? So she can go around homewrecking without guilt? No, she should be held accountable, and I want the truth. I deserve the truth, Shar."

I wish I could help Ivory, but the truth is I can't be certain about anything I saw. I can't even with one hundred percent certainty guarantee it was Fred. Unless…

"I was taking pictures and have the roll of film. Once I develop it I'll see if I can find out."

Ivory nods slowly, a measured, almost dispassionate gesture. This doesn't feel like a heart-to-heart with a best friend, rather a business transaction. Ivory is way too clinical and detached considering what she just found out.

I stare at her, bewildered. "How can you be so calm right now?"

She glances towards the hallway, where the mint-green walls of her daughter Freida's room peek through her open door. A portrait I took of Freida and framed as a gift for her eighteenth birthday adorns the wall.

"Because we have a child together," she says, "and I don't want to ruin all of our lives over this."

Though Freida is not really a child anymore. She's technically an adult and college-bound after this year, her senior year of high school. Part of me wants to remind her that Freida's old enough to know what's going on, but the other part of me knows that I don't have kids and therefore I know nothing about parenting and should keep my mouth shut.

"I don't want to blow up her life without concrete proof," she adds. "I need to be sure. See what you can find in your pictures, and then I'll figure out what to do."

"What about Fred?" They're supposed to be coming over for dinner next week. I can't stomach the thought of pretending all is well when it isn't.

"We act like everything's normal," she answers, and rises from her seat with her empty tea mug.

She places it in the sink and flips on the light switch that swathes her backyard in a bright floodlight. I follow her with my own mug, rinse it, and place it in the dishwasher along with hers. She stands by the sliding glass door that leads onto the patio where trays of chrysanthemums, asters, and other fall flowers are lined up in a long row. Fallen autumn leaves dot the grass in colorful patches. At the edge of the floodlight I spot a fresh mound of turned-up dirt prepped for a new garden bed, roughly eight feet long by three feet wide. Interestingly, it's the size of a standard grave plot.

"I'm not sure I can act like all is fine," I admit.

"Shar." Her eyes firmly fix on mine. There's a flicker of frostiness I've never seen in her before. "You absolutely cannot let him know what you saw. Not yet. Not until I know exactly who the mistress is."

"Okay, if that's what you want." I nod like a bobblehead toy. "Are you sure you're okay?"

"I'm fine."

But something is profoundly wrong.

She walks me out to the porch and offers a slight almost perfunctory hug, then pulls back. "Let me know what you find on the film," she reminds me.

By now the sky is black. My skin feels too tight, stretched taut over my buzzing nervous system. I walk back to my house more concerned than ever. I don't know what I expected—screaming, tears, a smashed cup or two in a fit of rage. But this eerie acceptance? This chilling, almost pre-ordained calm? It feels more disturbing than any death threat Ivory could have thrown at Fred.

I thought I was doing the right thing by telling her the truth. I thought I was being a good friend. But now a heavy, gnawing dread has taken root in the pit of my stomach. I can't shake the sensation that I made a terrible mistake.

I'm halfway across my front yard when I stop short. For a full five seconds, I stand there in the grass unable to make sense of the slit of yellow light pouring out from my open front door. It's been forced open. I know this because I always lock every opening to the house—windows, doors, even my fireplace flue.

Ever since I was released from prison, locking all potential entrances comes as natural as breathing. The lock—my expensive, triple-deadbolt lock—appears busted clean through.

My biggest fear surfaces: *It's him.* I imagine him roaming the streets, one of my kitchen knives in hand, plotting his revenge. But that's not possible… is it?

I tiptoe to the house, every sound amplified—the crunch of dead leaves under my feet, the soft creak of the porch step, the long groan of the door being pushed open. Only three people know how to find me here in Doomwood Falls: One of them is presumed dead. The other hasn't spoken to me in years. And the third is in jail. It's anyone's guess which one might be inside.

When I realize Zoomie isn't barking, I know exactly who it is, which leaves me with only one other question: Can I make it to my lockbox in time to get my gun?

Chapter 8

Prison taught me many life lessons, one of which is that every second counts when you're faced with a threat. It will take me approximately six seconds to reach my gun in my bedroom safe, then another two to three seconds to unlock the lockbox and retrieve my gun. I don't account for the time it will take to find and engage the intruder, but I do know only one second is needed to shoot and kill. I plan all of this before I even step foot over the threshold into my home.

A kitchen light illuminates the hallway, but not much else. The first floor is loaded with a concerning silence, and I wonder if Zoomie is okay. My shoe scuffs the floor in an audible squeak. I stop and observe, my muscles tightly coiled. After a moment, I don't think anyone heard.

The staircase is only a couple more feet away. I'm about to rush upstairs when I realize my mistake. I can't *shoot* my intruder, even if I wanted to. As a convicted felon, I'm not allowed to have my unregistered gun. Any blood on my hands would mean another prison sentence. Most likely for life this time. Judges aren't as gracious the second time around.

Instead I head to the kitchen, drawn by an invisible thread. The knife block sits on the counter. I won't use it unless in self-defense—the kind of indisputable self-defense that even the worst public defender could prove wasn't my fault. My palm hovers over the largest butcher knife with an ethereal memory of my husband's death. First the gunshot that threw his body backward, then his chest splitting open as his blood soaked the leaves in crimson.

But there's no time for a trip down Memory Lane. Can I do whatever I need to this time? I guess we'll find out.

My fingers close around the smooth handle holding eight inches of gleaming stainless steel. The familiar weight of it settles in my palm. I aim the blade out in front of me and step back into the hallway. No one knows about the room behind the meticulously arranged book spines… but Wren heard the thump. Had she returned to investigate while I was at Ivory's house? And if so, what now? I couldn't kill her for uncovering my secret, and I don't have the kind of cash to keep a podcasting blabbermouth like her quiet.

I inch towards the bookshelf and reach for the second shelf. The dusty, leather-bound copy of *Nancy Drew: The Secret of the Old Clock* juts out barely enough for anyone but me to notice. I tug the book. A soft *click* vibrates through the wall. The heavy bookshelf groans as it begins to shift, revealing a dark seam of empty space behind it.

Then—

Movement. Behind me.

I spin around, knife raised, the polished metal glinting faintly in the dim light. I'm pretty sure I'm on the verge of a heart attack when I see a large dark lump bulging up from the sofa. It's not Fred here to confront me about what I saw. Nor is it Wren, with her calculating eyes and weaponized smile. And unfortunately it's not some random burglar here to rob me of my meager possessions.

It's someone I never in a million years would have expected to break into my house uninvited when I thought he was supposed to be in jail. Sitting on my couch like he owns the place is my brother Luca. And on his lap is Zoomie, his long tongue hanging sideways from his grinning snout and tummy turned up getting belly rubs.

Luca flashes a half-cocked grin that used to melt teachers and parole officers alike. It doesn't work on me because I know better. "Hey, sis."

"Hey, *bro*." My voice is almost as sharp as the knife I'm holding. "What the heck did you do to my guard dog?" Zoomie is supposed to scare intruders away, not welcome them in for a massage. "And my front door!"

Luca shrugs, like it's no big deal. "I didn't have a key."

"So you broke down the damn door?"

"I figured it was better than a window. I'll fix it, I promise." Zoomie has better handyman skills than my brother and dogs don't even have opposable thumbs.

I lift up the butcher knife. "I almost killed you!" My pulse is thudding, and my chest feels tight. The bookshelf is still slightly ajar, and I wonder if my brother noticed me opening it. I pretend to lean back to rest, clicking the door in place while masking it with a cough.

"Catching a cold, *Gianna*?"

"I go by Shari now, and it's more of an incurable virus." I glare at him and attempt to close the front door, but it won't latch now. The frame's split where he kicked it in. "Don't ever do that to me again. I thought you were—"

"I know who you thought I was," he cuts me off, guilt flashing across his face for half a second before he looks away.

"Sorry about that. I didn't have a choice, okay? I'm desperate and need a place to stay. Just for a few days."

It's at this point when I notice the massive duffel bag at his feet. I'm guessing there's a month's worth of clothes in there. This isn't going to be a weekend visit. I cross my arms, waiting for a better explanation.

Luca doesn't meet my eyes. Nudging Zoomie off his lap, he rises from the sofa and paces now, his hands shoved deep into his pockets. There's something off about him—his movements too jerky, his breathing uneven. He smells faintly of smoke and sweat and probably pot, though I'm such a goody-goody I wouldn't know. Well, I used to be one until my prison sentence.

"What's *actually* going on?" I ask.

He stops pacing and hesitates before speaking. "Do you want the condensed version or extended cut?"

"Spare me the details. Give me the main bullet points."

"I got kicked out of my apartment today."

I don't bother to ask why. Knowing my brother's history, I could name any number of potential reasons. Not paying his bills. Drug use. Kidnapping. Theft. Assault. You name it, Luca's done it. "I didn't even know you were released from jail."

"Yeah, I was only in for a month. No big deal. Free room and board, right?"

"And you didn't think to call me to let me know you were out?"

"I lost your contact info after the last time we saw each other, so I had no way to find you."

The last time I saw my brother was right after I got out of jail when he brought me a gift I would never forgive him for.

It's hard to believe it isn't as burned into his memory as it is mine. But at least the good news is that I'm not as easy to find as I thought.

"So then how'd you find me?"

"Mamma," he answers vaguely.

I haven't spoken to my mother since my trial four years ago. She didn't once visit, call, or write back. After I was released, I made sure to write her with my latest address and phone number, but she never put them to use. It was hard enough losing Stewart and my freedom, but to then lose my mamma on top of it all… It's the reason I depend so much on Ivory's friendship. I literally have no one but her. And Luca, if I'm crazy enough to count him as dependable.

"So you've been out of jail? Keeping clean?"

"Actually, yeah. I've been doing really good. I moved here to Doomwood Falls after Mamma told me where you were, so I've been here for about a month. Got a job bartending down at Dirty Dan's, and I even have a new girlfriend."

The information overload slowly starts to process, and I'm left with a few concerns. My brother has been living and working nearby for over a month without me knowing it. With his drug habit I'm not sure bartending is the best choice of job, but at least he's working instead of begging me for money. I want to ask who the unlucky lady is, but it's probably best I not know.

"Her name's Freida Cobb," he says as if reading my mind. "You might know her. She lives right across the street."

The name hits me like a slap. "You mean my best friend Ivory's daughter Freida?"

"Oh, so you *do* know her."

Zoomie paces the back door whining like he needs to go out.

"You are absolutely not allowed to date Ivory's daughter." I toss the words over my shoulder as I walk into the kitchen and let Zoomie out back. "She's still in high school."

"She's eighteen and legally an adult. And so am I. Which means we can do whatever we want."

"You're almost twice her age, Luca! And it's not always about you—it's about her. Do you really think you're good for her? Because we both know you'll end up ruining her life."

He rakes a hand through his thick black waves that he's grown out almost as long as mine. His olive complexion from our mamma's side is a striking contrast against the green eyes that he inherited from our father.

"You think I don't worry about that? It wasn't supposed to happen. But it did. And I—" his voice catches, "I think I love her."

What. The. Heck. I stare at him, trying to decide if he's kidding. He's not. The jade in his eyes brightens with a desperate wildness.

"Look, I won't hurt her. But promise me this stays between us," he says, almost a plea. "Her parents can't find out. And definitely not Mamma. Nobody can."

I close my eyes and exhale slowly. He's my brother. The only one who stood up for me when I couldn't. Like when our childhood neighbor would yell at me and steal my toys any time they landed in his yard. One day Luca paid him a visit—in his typical calm, friendly way—and pointed to the guy's bedroom window. *"I noticed you've been hoarding my sister's stuff in your bedroom closet. Don't worry—I let myself in to get it last night.*" That day the yelling stopped. Years later, I understood that it wasn't confidence, but it was practice… probably for the mafia.

"You swear on Dad's grave you're not going to do anything to ruin her life?" Even as I ask it I know it's an impossible request.

"I'll do you better. I swear on my own impending grave."

"How about… Stew's grave?"

His jaw drops at the sound of Stew's name slipping from my mouth so easily. He knows I haven't spoken it since the murder four years ago. I could never manage explain why speaking my husband's name shredded me for all these years, but it did. Finally, though, the curse seems to be broken.

Luca hugs me warmly. "Does this mean you're okay?"

I don't know if he means okay with moving on after Stew's death, or okay with him dating an adolescent, but I assume the latter.

"Yes, fine," I agree. "I'll keep your secret. And you can crash here, but only for a few days. And you're fixing that door frame first thing tomorrow." I know it's silly of me to assume my version of tomorrow matches my brother's.

Outside Zoomie runs the length of the fence, freaking out at something on the other side along the wood line. The spotlight doesn't reach the woods, but whatever it is has Zoomie in an aggressive state I've never seen.

"Yeah, yeah," Luca mutters, scooping up his duffel bag and heading for the stairwell.

"I mean it, Luca." My voice softens. "You know why I can't have a door that doesn't lock."

He pauses on the stairs. For a heartbeat, something like

shame crosses his face. "I know, Gianna—I mean *Shari*. I'll fix it."

He starts up the steps, his boots thudding against the wood. When he hefts the duffel bag strap up to his shoulder, that's when I see his knuckle, split and purple. Raw flesh stretches across the bones like he's been in a boxing match. A queasiness fills my stomach.

"Luca?" I say quietly.

He doesn't look back. "Yeah?"

"What happened to your hand?"

He hesitates at the top of the stairs. Then he says, "You don't wanna know," and disappears down the hall. The door to the guest room bangs shut behind him.

I stand in front of my wrecked doorjamb, the cold night air spilling into my house, and tell myself that letting Luca stay is the right thing to do. Outside Zoomie is still barking. Inside Luca's boots stomp across the ceiling above me.

Staring at the splintered frame, I catch a faint smear of blood on the knob. Luca's, I assume. Unless it's not, in which case now I have something new to worry about: his boxing opponent coming back for round two.

And here I thought things couldn't get any worse.

Chapter 9

"Special delivery!" I say aloud, but no one is listening.

The cardboard edge of the box of diapers saws into the meat of my fingers, right where the calluses from the garden shears used to be. I stop at the bookshelf door to hike the box up against my hip. My lower back gives a little *pop*—a dry, brittle sound, like stepping on a beetle—and a hot wire of pain zips down my sciatic nerve.

The bookshelf is dark-stained oak, filled with books I've already read. They're just camouflage, a wall of paper and glue and words.

I place the weight of the box on my left knee, balancing it there precariously so I can free up a hand. My fingers drift to the third shelf and land on Nancy Drew's spine. A *thunk* resonates deep inside the wall, the sound of a heavy bolt sliding back in a well-oiled track. I grip the side of the shelving unit and pull. The hinges don't squeak since I WD-40'd the heck out of them after Luca went to bed, but the runner rug protests, a low *shhh* sound as the bottom of the shelf drags across the pile.

The opening is a black mouth. I shoulder my way inside, the box scraping against the doorframe.

It's cooler in here by ten degrees, easily. I don't turn on the light this time. I don't need to. The hum of the dehumidifier in the corner chugs away like a sick lung, and I set the diapers beside it. Keeping my eyes trained on the bricks of the wall, I count pockmarks in the mortar. I don't like to look at what I've let happen in here.

I turn around and leave, stepping from the concrete back onto the hallway rug. I grab the edge of the bookshelf and swing it shut. The seam vanishes and the shadows are gone, sealed away behind the oak and the old paperbacks. I stand there for a second, rubbing the red indentations the box left on my fingers, wondering when this will end.

Chapter 10

The sleeping pills worked a little too well. In fact, I was so dead asleep that I didn't hear the sirens. Not even the commotion outside my house woke me. My phone ringing on my bedside table next to my head didn't even reach through my slumber. But somehow the tiny little notification beep of my phone startled me wide awake: one new voicemail.

In a world full of texting, hardly anyone leaves voicemails anymore unless they're a retiree or have too much time on their hands. Or in this case, both. I tap the message while rubbing sleep out of my eyes.

"Gianna, it's Mamma. Please call me back as soon as you get this. It's important."

It's been four years since I've heard my mamma's voice, but she sounds exactly the same as always. High and breathless and tight, like she's either been crying or doing jazzercise. Knowing her, it could be either one.

I frown. Even before my prison sentence, Mamma never called unless something terrible happened—her version of terrible, anyway. The last time she left a message like this was before Stew was killed, when she was dog-sitting Zoomie so that Stew and I could enjoy a getaway.

He'd eaten a battery. A large D battery, of all things. I had raced home expecting to find him foaming at the mouth or glowing radioactive green. Instead, he'd looked thrilled, wagging his crooked tail like he'd solved cold fusion. It turned out he passed the battery a day later, along with a sanitary napkin that may or may not have saved his life by soaking up the battery acid. My mother had cried harder about nearly losing Zoomie than she did on the day I got convicted.

So if my mamma is calling, it's either a national crisis or a minor inconvenience blown wildly out of proportion. With her, it's a coin toss. I call her back right after I brush my teeth because as a retired dental hygienist, it's always the first thing she wants to know about—my dental care.

She answers on the first ring just as I'm spitting out toothpaste. "*Bambina*, is it really you?"

"Hi, Mamma, yes it's me." I don't know why I'm trembling. It's my mother, the woman who birthed me, but my heart is racing and I'm sweating like I just finished a marathon. I feel like I'm cold-calling a stranger. "It's been a while. I tried reaching out but you never called me back."

"Oh," she sighs, and I have a feeling I know where the excuses are heading, "well, I just couldn't, Gianna. Not after what you did. You have to understand—"

"It's fine, Mamma," I interrupt.

I already know what she's going to say, because I've known her all my life. She's embarrassed by me. Her parenting was publicly criticized when I first got brought in for questioning, and I completely destroyed our family reputation when the prison sentence was given. To her, the damage to our family name was unforgiveable.

"I don't want to talk about the past, okay?" I continue. "You called me, so I'm just returning your call. Oh, and I go by Shari now."

"Oh, right. I forgot you abandoned your Italian heritage in order to keep your secret identity."

"I didn't abandon my heritage, Mamma. Shari's my middle name. I'm still the same person."

"You are *not* the good girl I raised, but I'm not going to argue. So, well, how are the teeth? Any cavities?"

"Mamma, please. My cavity-free teeth are not why you called." I figure I could at least throw her a little good news.

"Oh good," she says, then continues, her voice trembling, "I just… I wanted to make sure you weren't involved in what's going on over there."

"What do you mean?" I pull the phone away and stare at it like maybe I dialed the wrong number. "Mamma, what are you talking about?"

There's a sharp inhale on the other end. I picture her clutching her floral nightgown, eyes wide like she's watching the Weather Channel's end-of-days special.

"You mean you don't know?"

"Know what?"

"Gianna." Her voice breaks. "Didn't you hear what happened? Certainly you should have heard the sirens from right across the street!"

Sirens? Across the street? My mother's pitchy voice hurts my ear through the phone speaker. Or maybe it's sudden-onset tinnitus ringing, because I almost miss the next thing she says.

"Turn on the news. Your neighbor Ivory Cobb is missing."

I freeze in the middle of my bathroom, one hand still resting on the faucet. Ivory is not just a *neighbor*. She's my best friend.

"Missing?" I repeat, because I must have heard her wrong.

"No, Mamma, that can't be right. I literally saw her yesterday evening."

Yesterday. When I sat across from Ivory in her kitchen, watching her face remain stoic as I told her I'd seen Fred with another woman. When she told me not to say anything and to keep this secret. Did Ivory confront Fred after all?

"Yesterday *evening*?" she asks. "As in you might have been the last person to see her alive?"

Since when did my mother start working for the police department? I don't like this line of questioning at all.

"No, her husband Fred or her daughter who live with her were probably the last ones to see her."

"Well, that's good, at least. Maybe you should keep your head down, just in case anyone saw you over there. I'd hate to see you head back to you-know-where."

She says it like prison is just a mysterious evil character in a *Harry Potter* book.

"Okay, I appreciate the call."

"Alrighty, Bambina. Stay safe," she says.

Before she hangs up, I ask the only question that's on my mind after this terribly awkward conversation. "Did you want to maybe come over for lunch sometime? We could make *focaccia di recco* together." It was one of my father's favorite homemade dishes, and an olive branch to my brokenhearted mamma. My voice sounds flat and mechanical because I don't want to sound needy, but right now all I want is my mommy.

A dial tone answers for her. It feels like my heart is breaking.

Instead of giving in to the desire to curl up in a ball and cry, I immediately dial Ivory, which goes straight to voicemail.

Maybe she's ignoring calls today, finally processing Fred's infidelity. So I redial. Voicemail again.

A prickle runs down my arms. I cross my bedroom to the window that overlooks Hemlock Drive and pull the curtain back. My breath catches at the view. Across the street, Ivory's house looks like the backdrop of a crime show. Two police cars are parked in front of her house—one at the curb, the other in her driveway, their lights silently flashing. A news van idles at the end of her driveway, the big satellite dish pointed at the sky like it's listening for CIA secrets. A cluster of neighbors hovers on the sidewalk, presumably starting up the rumor mill.

"What the heck…"

My heart thuds so hard I feel it in my throat. I fumble for my phone, nearly dropping it, and open a browser. My fingers feel wooden as I type in the search engine:

Ivory Cobb Doomwood Falls Missing

A *Doomwood Falls Daily* article pops up at the top of the first result:

DOOMWOOD FALLS — Authorities have launched an active investigation following the disappearance of a local woman, Ivory Cobb, who was reported missing late yesterday evening. Cobb was last seen at her residence on Hemlock Drive, a quiet neighborhood bordering the river that gives Doomwood Falls its name.

According to the DFPD, her husband Fred Cobb reported her missing when she didn't arrive home that night. Officers arriving at the residence found no signs of forced entry. Her car remained parked in the driveway.

"She didn't just vanish without reason," the police chief stated during a brief press statement the following morning. "We're treating this as a missing person case and following every lead. At this time, we're asking the public for patience and vigilance."

Residents described Cobb as outgoing and friendly, someone who kept to a routine. "She is the glue that holds Doomwood Falls together," said a neighbor who wished to remain anonymous. Another neighbor Ali Azad said, "When I not see her yesterday, I knew something wrong."

Search efforts began overnight, with officers canvassing nearby woods and questioning locals in the area. By mid-morning, additional resources had been brought in, including county investigators. Police declined to comment on whether any persons of interest have been identified.

Doomwood Falls, a town better known for its annual harvest festival than criminal activity, has been unsettled by the news. Rumors have already begun to circulate, fueled by the town's long memory and the dense forest that presses in on its edges.

Authorities urge anyone with information—no matter how small—to come forward. Residents wait for answers, hoping the silence surrounding Hemlock Drive will soon be broken.

My mouth goes dry. This isn't a coincidence that the day Ivory finds out about Fred's affair she suddenly disappears. It can't be. As I stare at the article, something bubbles up in my memory, something I brushed off. But now, looking back, it feels urgent.

I vaguely recall something I noticed at the waterfall. And if I'm right, it might explain what happened to Ivory… and if she is dead or alive.

Chapter 11

The red glow of the safelight paints everything in my darkroom the color of dried blood. It's hard to focus on developing yesterday's film with police swarming Ivory's house and my mother's voice still echoing in my head, but my hands move on autopilot as I've done this a thousand times before. Something about the chemical smell wraps around me like a warm hug.

When I shut off the light, my darkroom is sealed from the world. The black is thick enough to feel against my skin. It's absolute—no shadows, no edges—just my breathing and the soft sound of film unspooling in my hands. The strip is curled tight, like it wants to hide what it's holding.

I load the film by memory alone. Fingers tracing the edges, the curl of it fighting me as I place it into the developer tank. When the tank finally seals, I exhale.

The chemicals are already measured. They have to be, because color doesn't tolerate mistakes. I pour in the developer and start the timer. I don't look at it, though. I always count in my head, the rhythm tight. The temperature has to be exact. Too warm and the colors bloom wrong. Too cold and they never arrive at all. I keep my hand on the tank, feeling the faint heat, like a pulse.

This is the worst part—working blind. With black-and-white developing, you see the image form, watch it decide what it's going to be. But color developing gives you nothing. It keeps its secrets until the end.

At first, nothing happens. Soon the images will begin to surface. Not all at once—just hints. Shapes pushing through the gray. The watery wall of Doomwood Falls materializes first. Then hazy figures emerge from behind it. Although it's too pitch-black for me to watch it unfold, I imagine it.

Once the initial developer is done, I bleach, fix, and wash the negatives. I remind myself not to rush. Rushing makes mistakes permanent. When the process is finished, I take the tank to the sink and open it. The film slides free, slick and fragile. I hang it to dry, the strips swaying slightly in the air, a thin ribbon of truth I wish I never stumbled on.

Standing longer than I need to, my hand rests on the light switch, but I don't flip it yet. Because once the light comes on, there's no going back. No more uncertainty. Just the facts. I breathe, then turn on the light.

The negatives glow softly, orange-brown and translucent. I lift one strip and hold it up. At first it looks ordinary. Then my eyes adjust on a detail that turns my unease into certainty. The color separates itself from the rest.

Red. A precise, deliberate red where it shouldn't be. I choose that frame to enlarge.

The room goes dark again, then I prep the paper for exposure, when I burn the image onto it. After the print is ready, it disappears into the chemical bath, and once more I'm waiting, blind and breathless.

This time, when the light returns, there's no doubt. The red holds. By the time the print is dry enough to touch, my hands are shaking. Not because I don't understand what I'm seeing, but because I do.

Two figures are tucked behind a wall of rushing water, the woman's body angled so that her face is mostly turned away, blurred by spray and motion. If only I could get a better look at her. I skim over the colorful images—the green edge of shoreline, the gray curve of rocks, the silvery blur of the waterfall… and a ribbon of red blood in the water.

I hadn't noticed it at the falls yesterday, because I was too focused on the people. But now that it's frozen in time, it's as clear as day. There is definitely blood at the base of the waterfall where Fred and the other woman are standing. But whose blood?

"Stop!" Now I'm more certain than ever that's what I heard the woman say, because here I am staring at a picture that looks like a crime scene. If Fred was capable of hurting whoever this woman is, he could be capable of anything. Including Ivory's disappearance.

The sound of footsteps echoes outside the darkroom door. Luca's looking for me, but I don't want anyone to see this. Not until I know what to make of it. My hands act before my brain catches up. I yank off the gloves, grab the photograph, and bolt out the darkroom door, running into my brother.

"Whoa there. What's wrong?" he asks as I bounce off of him.

"I'll explain later," I say, snaking around him toward the front door that he has yet to fix. For the time being a planter sits on the floor blocking it from blowing open.

"Where are you going?" he presses.

"I'll be back shortly. I need to do something." I shove the planter aside with my foot, something an intruder could easily do. This is practically an invitation to break in. "And fix this door, Luca!"

The cool air whips me in the face, but it barely registers. I'm already crossing the street, immediately noticing that the cop cars are gone, the news van has vanished, and Fred's house looks like it does every other day. Way too normal for its lead resident to be missing.

I pound on the door until my fist aches. It swings open to reveal Fred, eyes rimmed in gray circles, shirt wrinkled like he grabbed it from the dirty clothes hamper. Freida appears behind him, arms crossed, her expression permanently carved into disdain. Good—at least I have a witness in case I go missing next.

"Where's Ivory?" I shove the damp photo toward Fred's face, but he reels back and squints at it. "And who is this woman I caught you with?"

He blanches, then grabs my arm and mutters, "Not out here," while dragging me inside. He shoots his daughter a tense look. "We're going out back to talk. You stay here."

"Oh please," I snap. "Freida's an adult and should be part of this conversation. Her mother is missing, Fred."

Freida unfolds her arms and flings them up in exasperation. "Dad, just let her talk. I already know Mom put you in an impossible situation."

I whirl toward her. "What are you talking about? And why are you blaming your mother?"

"Mom likes attention." She shrugs, bored. "She's probably holed up somewhere five-star getting room service and will come back when she feels Dad's been adequately punished."

"Your mother is *missing*, Freida."

"And?" She lifts one brow. "It's not the first time."

Fred shoots her a warning look, but Freida ignores him.

"She used to leave all the time when I was a kid," Freida says, twirling her hair. "Sometimes for days. She called it *me time*. I call it being irresponsible. Honestly? I figured she'd leave for good eventually to go back to her ex."

I had no idea Fred and Freida knew so much about Ivory's ex-husband. Certainly he couldn't have anything to do with this, could he? But she *had* been acting cagey two days ago when we were having coffee at The Alibi Café and she had seen someone outside the window. Maybe it was her ex. Even all these years— and two divorces—later, she still carries a torch for him.

Fred closes his eyes like he's in pain. "Freida, that's enough."

But it isn't enough, not for me. The way Freida says all of this—like Ivory's an annoyance instead of her mother—makes my jaw clench. Even I don't treat my mother this way and she may as well have disowned me. But Fred hustles me out the sliding back door before I say something I won't regret but probably should.

It's early evening, and the backyard is quiet. Immaculately neat. The only sign of disrepair is their neglected garden shed barely visible along the woods. There's no trace of yesterday's fallen leaves, and the trays of flowers have been planted in the grave-sized garden bed, which I find odd. I can't imagine gardening being on Ivory's to-do list immediately after finding out her husband is cheating on her. But Ivory tends to make sure nothing looks wrong on the outside to hide the chaos going on inside.

As soon as I step onto the patio I round on Fred. "I saw you yesterday at the waterfall with another woman." I hand the photo to him again, and this time he actually accepts it. "Notice anything interesting about this picture?"

He examines it for barely a moment. "Well, first of all, that's not me," he says instantly and hands the photo back.

I bark out a laugh that sounds nothing like laughter. "Right. Because you have an identical twin we don't know about."

"Prove it's me."

"I will," I threaten. "There's more film developing right now." Which isn't exactly true. "And I'll take all of it to the police if you don't start explaining."

His eyes glint—with fear, or something close enough to count—before he looks away. "I don't know what else to say."

"Start by explaining why there's blood in the water." I jab my finger at the blossom of red right below the waterfall. "What did you do to Ivory, Fred? Tell me!"

He rubs a hand over the dimple in his unshaven chin. "Shari, I swear... I don't know where she is. I came home from work last night and she was gone. I already told the police everything. If they thought I hurt her, do you think I'd be standing here talking to you?"

I stare at him so hard my eyes burn. Every part of me wishes he was telling the truth, because that would make this simple and Ivory ran off for some *me time* without telling anyone. But the wizened part of me knows the truth is never simple. Sick, twisting guilt coils through me that if I had kept my mouth shut, if I hadn't told Ivory what I saw, none of this would have happened.

"Did you tell the police who your mistress is?" I scoff.

Fred doesn't answer, and his silence sounds worse than a

confession. "I'm done talking, Shari." When he storms away, I chase him to the gate that leads out to the front yard. He opens it, turns to me, and waits for me to leave. "Go home."

"Not until I have answers."

"Well, I can't give you answers, because I don't have them either. If you want to help Ivory, find out who she's been meeting with during the day when she doesn't think I'm watching."

I don't like the sound of that—Ivory having mysterious meet-ups. Or Fred watching her. What did she get herself into? Maybe she's been meeting up with her ex. Maybe she confronted the mistress. Maybe she found out something she shouldn't have. Every second that ticks by feels like it's counting down to something terrible. I just hope I'm not already too late.

I'm halfway to the curb when Fred calls after me. "Shari—wait."

I stop only because the desperation in his voice doesn't match the cool, defensive act he was giving me seconds ago. I turn slowly. "What?"

He's walking across the front yard, hands dangling at his sides. "You… you really think I hurt her?"

"I think somebody did."

His Adam's apple bobs as he swallows. "I would never—"

"She's missing, Fred," I cut in. "Vanished. After finding out you were cheating."

"That wasn't me," he repeats, and I swear if he says it one more time, I might shove the photo down his throat.

"It. Was. You." I toss the photo on the grass at his feet, because I can develop more. Lots more. "And I'm not the only one who will see it."

He looks past me toward the darkening street, the row of matching cookie-cutter houses full of witnesses to this conversation. He lets out a shaky breath, rubbing the back of his neck. I can practically see him calculating, plotting his next move. "You didn't tell anyone else, did you?"

"Does it matter?"

His gaze snaps back to mine. "Yes."

There it is. Not concern. Not grief. *Fear*. But fear of what? Being exposed for the cheating, lying murderer that he is?

"No one else will know," I finally offer, "until I'm done checking the rest of my film. And then—"

"You're going to the police," he finishes bleakly.

"Yes."

He doesn't respond. The silence between us stretches, constricting like a rope around my neck. He looks past me toward the dark street again. "Just... be careful, Shari."

The hairs on the back of my neck perk up. "Why?"

He meets my eyes, and the misery I see nips me in a way I didn't expect. "Because you don't know what you're getting into."

A hollow pit opens in my stomach. "Is that a threat?"

But Fred only shakes his head and leaves me standing awkwardly at the edge of his front yard wondering what his warning was all about. Obviously I don't know what I'm getting into, which is kind of the whole point in a missing persons case.

The blood in the water, the mystery other woman, my missing best friend—all of it spirals into one truth I can't ignore: Fred is lying, and I have no idea how to pry the truth out of him. As I head home, my skin prickles with the sense that someone is watching me.

It wouldn't be the first time. And it's easy enough to do in this housing plan. Cramming as many houses onto tiny lots produced the most profit, despite the discomfort that no one wants the whole street to be able to watch them wash their dishes or do Pilates in their living room. But that's the price you pay when you want a brand-new home with an HOA and neighborhood watch. You get watchers.

From my own front yard I can easily observe half a dozen neighbors. My gaze passes over Zala's dark house made to look empty, then glides over Wren's windows brightly glowing with what looks like a selfie ring light used to film her podcast. Ali's blinds are open and dimly lit, and a figure blocks one of the first-story windows… until the blinds suddenly flip closed.

Someone on Hemlock Drive had to see *something*, so why are they all hiding what they know?

Chapter 12

My rusted-out beater of a car has been stolen. And in its place my Fairy Carmother left a new one, a sleek black fancy Mercedes way above my pay grade. I want to believe it's a miracle. Some wealthy benefactor felt the urge to bless me with this gorgeous right-off-the-showroom-floor set of wheels because he never wants me to have to deal with breaking down halfway to the grocery store in the dead of winter again.

But no, I'm a realist, so the more likely explanation is that the vehicle belongs to some drug-dealing mobster my brother owes money to and they've come to collect. And my front door still isn't fixed, which makes their job of breaking kneecaps even easier.

"Luca!" I yell up the stairs. "You have a visitor!"

I feel bad for throwing my brother to the wolves, but I sure as heck am not going to sacrifice myself for him. I've done enough of that in my life, and it never once paid off. When Luca doesn't answer, I jog upstairs to look for him.

His bed is meticulously neat, the folds and corners exactly like I had made it for him yesterday—and every day in prison, or else I got a warning from the guards. This means Luca didn't sleep in bed last night. This normally should be alarming, but I've gotten used to Luca slipping in and out of my life with no explanation. I check the first floor and find a note I don't know how to interpret:

Headed out to deal with something and borrowed the car.

It looks like Luca has left me to deal with this kneecap-breaker, collector, henchman—whatever he turns out to be—on my own with no way of escape. Pale smoke from the exhaust, not black like my car emits, means it's idling as the driver sits completely still, face hidden behind tinted windows.

I swing open my front door and step onto the porch, with Zoomie steamrolling between my legs out into the yard. To my surprise, the car lurches forward, with tires squealing, shooting down the road like the metal ball in a pinball machine while Zoomie pursues for a hot minute before losing interest. Do I really look that formidable without makeup on? Or maybe my *guard dog* finally got the memo.

Pushing through the anxiety, I return to the kitchen where several new pictures I developed last night sit on the counter, edges stiff now that they're dry. After spreading them out, I look over each one. That blot of neon pink yanks my attention once again, and when I take a closer look I notice a letter embroidered on it. Due to the way the fabric folds, I can't make it out, but lucky for me the reflection of the water shows the letter perfectly: Z.

Next to the shirt a pair of men's pants hide in the corner of the frame, crumpled on the ground. Those pants could prove it's Fred in the picture. Real evidence. Something the cops can't shrug off and Fred can't deny.

Fred's car isn't in the driveway, and presumably the school

bus picked Freida up hours ago. I've got a couple hours before school lets out, so it could be my only chance to snoop around with no one home. I don't hesitate to weight the pros and cons of getting caught. I grab the photo, give a quick check to make sure no neighbors happen to be looking out their windows at this exact moment, and sprint across the street. Then I walk straight into Fred's house.

Technically "walk straight into" is an exaggeration. Not wanting to risk being seen at the front door, I resort to jimmying the garage side door open with a credit card. The fact that I'm a parolee probably means I should be averse to breaking and entering, but I might as well put the skills I learned from the pokey to use.

It took a bit more skill to maneuver through the garage. That space is Fred's domain where he keeps every scrap of lumber, every piece of pipe, every random hunk of garbage that he insists he needs but that Ivory won't let him bring into the house.

When I step through the garage entrance into the kitchen, the air feels heavy, like the place is holding its breath. Luckily I know Ivory's floor plan almost as well as I know my own, since the house developer lacked creativity and made them all identical, with the exception of a few custom or renovated homes dotting the street here and there.

The laundry room is the first place I think of where Fred would dump his dirty clothes. And if he's the man in the photo—and I'm convinced he is—those pants should be here, because Fred doesn't throw anything, and I mean *anything*, away.

Sure enough, when I open the slatted bifold door to the laundry room, the hamper is overflowing with sweatshirts, flannels, and several pairs of pants that look similar to the ones puddled on the shore near the waterfall in my print. I hadn't considered that men don't usually have as much variety in their wardrobe as women do, making my job of locating the exact pair in my photo harder. There are at least four pair of gray cargo-style pants that look alike.

Lady Luck strikes again, because Fred is inexperienced with laundry care and a basic knowledge of stain treatment. I dig down to the bottom and instantly know when I've found them— wet pants with muddy spots on the knees, already starting to smell like mildew and river water. Blood soaks one of the pant legs, which confirms it even more. I compare them against the photo. They're the exact same ones. Using my phone, I snap a picture of the pants in the laundry basket. Ironclad proof.

I check the time, and my *investigating,* which sounds better than *snooping,* has taken me longer than I thought. Returning the clothes to the hamper, I double-check to make sure there's no evidence I was here. I'm turning the knob to the door that exits the kitchen into the garage when a rumble vibrates my feet. Peeking through the opening, I'm met with a half-open garage door grumping and groaning upward, and Fred's car pulling in. I freeze stupidly, then quickly shut the door.

Fred should be at work. Why is he back so soon? And had he seen me?

I dash back into the laundry room, the one place in the house I doubt he visits very often, and hide behind the washing machine. Heavy footsteps thud past me into the foyer. I press myself deeper into my hiding place, heart ricocheting in my chest like it's on the verge breaking out.

"Yeah," Fred says loudly. He's on the phone. "I've been at

the police station all morning. They don't have a suspect yet."

This is bad. If he finds me here—inside his house, going through his dirty clothes—the cops won't care that I'm trying to solve my best friend's potential murder. All they'll care about is that I violated parole by breaking and entering. Then it's straight back to jail for me.

Fred's voice grows louder, and closer, as he lingers in front of the laundry room of all places. Since when is the laundry the place to hang out? Through the gap under the closed bifold door I spot his polished black dress shoes, and I imagine him in his suit and tie. I hadn't considered that the first thing he'd do after coming home is change out of his clothes.

"No, this whole thing is ridiculous," he snaps at whoever is on the line. When he resumes talking, his voice is further away. Thank God for small mercies. "And Freida's a mess."

His footsteps retreat. A cupboard door slams. I attempt to predict his next move—maybe a cup of coffee while turning the television on, which would give me the opportunity to run out the front door. But no, that's not Fred's routine. Instead it's exactly what I feared.

It starts with the clap of shoes hitting the floor and rustle of fabric dropping. I risk a glimpse around the door and huff. Fred is stripping off his dress shirt, unbuttoning it like he's peeling away a layer of skin. I duck back inside and through the slats watch Fred pace, half-naked with his pants gone and his shirt off, with six-pack abs that Ivory never mentioned. All that's left on him are his socks and boxers, and I'm in the middle of praying he doesn't take those off too when I see it.

A deep, angry gash carved across his thigh. It's fresh and raw and swollen around the edges. The blood in the water was *his*, not the mistress's. This revelation doesn't answer any of my questions, though. The injury could have been made in self-defense if Fred was attacking her. Or he could have hurt himself climbing up the waterfall. There's no way to know.

By now I assume Fred has hung up the call until he speaks again, low and dare I say sinister. "I'm taking care of it."

Every muscle in my body locks. I can only assume it's Ivory he's referring to. But *taking care of it…* That's mafia speak for *killing* someone, cutting loose ends. Did he kill Ivory? Or is he referring to his mistress to keep her quiet about what he's done? After all, a cheating husband is always the prime suspect when his wife goes missing.

Suddenly, Fred stops talking and there's a too-long beat of silence. Eventually the television clicks on to something sports-related, judging by the announcer's enthusiasm, and the sofa squeaks. I recognize it from the countless times I've sat in it next to Ivory. This is my chance.

The front door is visible from the laundry room, either an invitation or a trap. If Fred catches me, I'm done. If he doesn't catch me, I live to uncover the truth another day. I hold my breath, then I move.

One step. Two. Three.

Every floorboard squeaks under my feet like it wants to out me. My palms sweat so badly my phone almost slips from my hands. The entire foyer looms between me and the front door when a commercial break interrupts my exit.

I bolt down the hallway, nearly falling on the polished wood because my legs won't cooperate with the rest of me. They're jittery and rubbery, and my heart hammers so violently I half-expect it to punch through my ribs and leave a hole in Fred's plaster. I'm almost to the door when I do the absolute worst thing I could do.

I bump into the table along the entry and the corner hits the wall, loudly. Oops.

"Someone there?" Fred calls out.

I freeze, then press my back against the wall and clamp a hand over my mouth.

"What was that?" His tone is alert.

At any moment he's going to walk in here and find me sneaking around like some unhinged stalker. Then what? What lie do I spin? There's no rational explanation for rifling through his house. Especially not after our latest confrontation. I shut my eyes, as if that will make me invisible.

Then the announcer yells, "Touchdown Steelers!"

Fred whoops, having lost all interest in the mysterious moving table. When the commotion of screaming fans drowns me out, I'm already at the front door. Turning the knob one millimeter at a time, the latch releases with a tiny *click*. I fling open the door and bolt out, my body slamming right into—

Chapter 13

"Ali!" I flush with embarrassment and hurriedly close the door before Fred hears us. "I didn't see you there."

"You are in rush to leave?" Ali asks.

Ali Azad holds a gas weed whacker, his shoulders slightly stooped by the weight of it. Deep inside the house the television is blaring loud enough that I overhear something about a two-point conversion, so it's safe to assume Fred hasn't heard us. I just need to keep it that way. So I greet Ali with an authority like I'm supposed to be here and plant on a forced, wide grin.

"No rush. Are you looking for Fred?"

"Yes. I am returning his whacker of weeds."

"Oh, Fred's resting," I whisper, playing the part well, "but you can put it on the porch and I'll let him know it's here."

"And you are here why?"

I hadn't expected Ali to be so nosey, but I come up with a decent excuse pretty quickly. "I was just being neighborly and bringing food over for him. Without Ivory here, he's bound to starve."

"Maybe I should check on him, yes?"

I really need Ali to move along and not draw attention to the fact that I was inside Fred's house *not* bringing him food. "Like I said, he's resting."

Undeterred, Ali shifts toward the window next to the door

to check for himself. Then an idea forms. "Oh, I meant to tell you I ran into Zala and she mentioned you."

I'm playing with fire knowing how much Ali likes her, but I have no other choice than to break some hearts in order to save myself.

"She mentioned *me*?"

"Yes, you! In fact, you should invite her to go with you to this month's book club. I bet you she'd say yes."

"You think so?"

That's all it takes to divert Ali's attention, and it shockingly works. "Absolutely! I see how she looks at you. Go ask her right now."

"Thank you, Shari! You good friend!" Ali praises me, and I hate myself for it.

Ali practically skips towards Zala's house while I slink the opposite way to mine. My thoughts knot themselves into something tight and suffocating. I don't want to believe the worst of Fred, but the way he said he's *taking care of it* makes the worst feel like the only possibility. And on top of that, I can't shake the feeling that no matter who "it" is, I might be next.

My phone beeps with a text as I'm pushing the planter back in place while searching online for a handyman. I blink at the screen, and when I see the name, my back hits the wall and I slide to the floor.

Ivory.

After calling her phone several times since her disappearance yesterday, with no answer, she's finally texting me back. Or someone else is texting me from her phone. My thumb hesitates before opening the message, as if the words might explode when I read them:

I know you're freaking out, but seriously, I'm okay. Just don't tell anyone I messaged you. I need space before I totally lose my mind. When I found out about Fred's affair, something in me cracked. I just want him to feel what I felt for once—pain. So please don't say anything yet. Not until Fred's cooked. Please keep my secret like I've always kept yours. If my heart's a secret, you're the keeper.

It *must* be Ivory, because she's the only one who knows the secret grief I've carried since Stew's death. And she's the only one who knows what's inscribed on our necklaces: *If my heart's a secret, you're the keeper.* She's alive and safe! Or at least she says she is. That's what I should focus on.

Relief floods me, but it doesn't last long. Instead of settling, it pools in my stomach like something sour. Because the Ivory I know doesn't run away, no matter what Freida says about her. Ivory sulks, she fumes, she rage-cleans her house. But she doesn't vanish without telling anyone, especially not me. And she definitely doesn't ask me to lie for her.

And since when does Ivory use the word *cooked*?

I read the message again, waiting for it to feel true. But it doesn't. Maybe I'm paranoid. With my history, I know I have a habit of catastrophizing. I can admit my mind jumps to danger like it's a trampoline. But I also know what I heard Fred say:

I'm taking care of it.

Ivory might think she's teaching him a lesson, but I'm not sure he's the kind of man who learns. Or forgives. A chilling invisible finger scrapes its way up my vertebrae. My thumbs move before I can talk myself out of it:

I overheard Fred tell someone he's "taking care of it." I think he meant you. Please be careful. I need proof that it's you and that you're okay.

My heart does a panicky flutter. What if it isn't her? What if she doesn't respond? What if she's already—

There's another beep, but it's a photo this time. I open the image of a closeup of Ivory's necklace, the one that matches mine. It's dangling in front of a beach with blue ocean in the background surrounded by pale sand and the familiar wooden boardwalk that we've spent several girl's getaways at.

I'm skeptical because the closest beach is half a day's drive away. She would have had to drive through the night, then pay cash for a hotel room upon arrival in order to keep the charge off of her credit card. I mean, it's possible… but unlikely. Something is wrong. I feel it in my bones. My body always knows before my brain catches up, like an animal sensing a storm on the horizon.

The rose-colored glasses part of me wants to call the police and show them the text, the photo, the timestamp so the investigation can be closed. But the darker, more damaged part of me doesn't want them to stop looking until I see Ivory in the flesh. Plus, it might be wiser for me to stay as far away from this case as possible. The memory is still too fresh from when the police locked me up in prison without an ounce of mercy. Their suspicions, the judgements, the words they didn't say but thought anyway: unstable, liar, criminal.

I chew the skin around my fingernail, wondering who I could safely show this to. Not Fred—I don't trust a word out of his mouth. Not the police—not until I have more concrete proof of life.

I'm still sitting on the floor next to the front door when a sharp knock above my head rockets my pulse. I belly crawl into my living room to the window and peel back the curtain a fraction of an inch.

Zala nervously paces across my porch, and parked behind her on the street is the same glossy black car from yesterday. I walk upright like a normal person back to the entryway. Her back stiffens and chin lifts when she sees me.

"Hey, Zala. I thought you didn't want to take lessons anymore."

She shakes her head. "I don't. I'm not here about that."

"Oh, what are you here for?"

"Can I come in?" She inspects the street and wrings her hands so fervently I worry her fingers might snap. "Just for a minute?"

I hesitate, but Zala looks like she's about to fall apart on my porch so I step aside. "Sure. Aren't you going to shut off your car?"

She wrinkles her forehead and looks over her shoulder. "What? No. That's not mine. I walked here."

The hair on the back of my neck prickles.

Zala enters quickly, like she's afraid of being seen. I push the planter in front of the door to keep it closed, but she blocks me with her foot and the door limply swings back open. "I'd prefer it stay open."

The conversation instantly turns awkward.

"I didn't know if I should come," she lets out a shaky breath, "but I figured you deserve to hear it from me."

"Hear what?"

Zala won't look at me, and her fingers keep twisting. "Everyone in Doomwood Falls is talking about you."

They can't possibly know what I did. That part of my life is dead and buried. Literally.

"What—what are they saying?"

Zala bites her lip. Her eyes dart to the street, then back to me. She looks like she wants to run. "It's bad," she says finally. "I can't believe it's true. I really can't. That's why I needed to ask you in person."

My skin feels hot. My mouth goes dry. They know. They figured it out. The past has finally found its way back to me. My mind spirals too fast.

"I just need you to tell me the truth." Zala meets my eyes with a mix of fear and sympathy.

There are so many truths I can't say, and one truth I can't afford for anyone to ever find out. Then she hands me a piece of paper with an image on it and I realize everything is about to come undone.

Chapter 14

"What is this?" I ask, but I already know exactly what's on the page fluttering in my hand as the breeze tears through the gap in the door. A better question would be *How did you find this?*

Zala hesitates so long I start to wonder if she'll say nothing at all. Maybe she'll spare me her interrogation. But then her face goes taut, and she inhales as if bracing herself for a crash.

"Shari," her voice trembles, "or should I call you *Gianna*?"

My birth name is a fist to the gut. Congratulations, Zala must have done a deep dive internet search and figured out my real name—*Gianna Shari Catalano*. The paper she placed in my hand is a printout of my rap sheet, including my mug shot and conviction details from the Offender Public Information D atabase. I figured someone would eventually dig it up, but I didn't expect it to happen so soon, or for it to be Zala who unearthed it. I pegged her for a sweet bird-watching lady. I should have given her more credit.

"People are saying—no, this *proves* you have a criminal record." Zala keeps going, her words tumbling out faster now, as if she wants to get it over with. "They're also saying that you… that you have a history of violence."

Violence. Such a small word for such a big accusation.

I stare at her, my throat closing. I try to speak, but everything jams together in my chest, leaving no room for air or sound.

"And because Ivory is missing," Zala's gaze brushes over my face, then shies away, "the neighbors are wondering if maybe you had something to do with it."

My heart seizes, or at least it feels that way. I hear nothing. Not Zala. Not the hum of the car still idling on my curb. Not the tapping of Zoomie's paws across the floor as he sleep-chases a rabbit. Just the inside of my skull ringing like a struck bell.

And she's still talking. "I don't believe you hurt Ivory, Shari. I can't. That's why I came. I needed to hear the truth from you."

But I can't answer. I can't speak. I physically cannot form a single word without incriminating myself. Instead my breath shudders out as everything hits me at once. Ivory is the only person in Doomwood Falls who treats me like a sister, not a stranger with a question mark for a past. She's the one person I would take a bullet for, and yet the town thinks I'm capable of *disappearing* her.

"Can we sit down in my living room so I can explain?"

"Um," she edges away from me, and her thick-soled shoes—with extra arch support—scuff against the floor, "I'm not sure how comfortable I am being so far away from the door."

Wow, I'm right up there with Ted Bundy. Apparently Doomwood Falls clings to gossip like a drowning man clings to driftwood. They love a scandal. They love a villain. And right now I'm the easiest most scandalous villain they've ever been handed.

"Does everyone think I'm a monster?" It physically hurts to push the question out over the rock in my throat. "Did you even read my charges and convictions?"

"I did," she admits. "But I'm assuming there's more to it than this."

In a way she's right. There is a lot more to the story than this single page could ever cover. But that would require a sit-down conversation and half a bottle of wine, and Zala doesn't even trust me enough to step foot over the threshold of my home.

"There is nothing violent about my crime, Zala. I was charged with embezzling money from my last employer. Which I was wrongfully convicted of, by the way."

"Doesn't every criminal say that?" She props her hand on her hip, stares at her feet, and shakes her head.

"My boss framed me, Zala. Luckily the evidence was flimsy, which was why I only served three years." I point to the sentencing and release dates on the paper to prove my point. "Do you really think I would have gotten out so fast if it was a violent crime?"

She shrugs. "Look, Shari, I want to come to your defense, but it doesn't look good for you. Ali just told me he saw you over at Ivory's the day she went missing. According to the timeline, you were the last person to see her alive."

Damn Ali, now conspiring with Zala all because I played matchmaker! Never again.

"Talk to Freida. In fact, she's the one who told me her mom used to leave constantly for *me time*. I promise you I had nothing to do with Ivory disappearing." Except for the part of setting her world on fire when I told her Fred was cheating. That's on me.

Maybe if I show Zala the messages from Ivory, this will stop. The rumors will crumble. People will no longer spy on me from their windows. All of this could go away. But if I tell Zala,

I betray Ivory. Her last words rebound in my mind: *Please keep my secret like I've always kept yours.*

"So you weren't seen fighting with Ivory at The Alibi Café?" Zala tilts her head. "Because someone overheard it."

"Is that someone Wren?"

"Maybe," Zala admits meekly.

"To clarify, Wren overhead me yelling *to* Ivory, not *at* her. I was frustrated about that horrible review online. You know, the one you were tagged in and cancelled your session over?"

There's a big *oops* on Zala's face, because she didn't expect me to piece together that Wren is the rat or have a reasonable explanation for the fight.

"According to Wr—I mean *my source*, what you said sounded threatening."

I laugh, but it comes out a short, strangled sound. "Threatening? You're going to believe a girl who podcasts about what your junk drawer says about your personality over *me,* who brought you homemade chicken noodle soup when you had the flu last month?"

"You know how gossip works," Zala says softly. "One person exaggerates, and then someone else twists it, and by the time it travels around town…" She trails off, giving me a look that says *I'm just following orders.*

"Exactly! All this crap being said about me is gossip. And Ivory will come home soon. I'm sure she just needed some space." I try to sound confident. Convincing. But even I don't believe myself.

Zala narrows her eyes. "How do you know that?"

"I just do," I say weakly.

Zala's expression shifts from confusion to suspicion. "Is

there something you're not telling me?" Her intonation hardens just a little. "Because people are scared. And when people are scared, they look for someone to blame. And right now that someone is you."

"Because I did time in prison for supposedly stealing money? That's ridiculous."

Zala hefts her massive purse off her shoulder and holds it in front of her, digging through it in search of something. When she finds it, she hands me another piece of paper, this one folded into fours. I unfold it piece by piece, until I'm staring at a photocopy of a major news headline and a single article, printed slightly off-kilter on the page. The date typed across the top of the image is from right before my conviction date.

"No, Shari, we're not scared of you because you stole some money. We're scared of you because of what happened to your husband."

Apparently I didn't bury my past deep enough.

Chapter 15

It's been three days since Ivory disappeared and my brain spends all night running through worst-case scenarios. When my eyes finally shutter for the night due to sheer exhaustion, it's barely a minute before I'm jolted awake to the sound of pounding. At least it feels like a minute. The pounding stops, and at first I think it's my heart. But upon reaching full consciousness, it resumes as a frantic, insistent *thump-thump-thump* coming from downstairs.

After flinging off the covers, I stumble out of bed, my legs shaky and mind fogged with confusion and fear—mostly fear. The clock on my nightstand glows 3:14 a.m. Nothing good happens at this hour.

Another slam rattles the front door and the planter falls over with a loud *crack*. Only now does Zoomie perk up, only casually interested in whoever is here in the middle of the night. How he manages to sleep through the knocking is a mystery.

"Luca?" I yell from my bedroom, hoping it's just my brother coming home from a late night out.

I grab my phone and hurry down the stairs, gripping the banister with a sweaty palm. Halfway down, I notice something off. The hallway doesn't look right, even in the dark. When I reach the first floor, I see what it is. My bookshelf door is cracked open. Just an inch, but it's enough to notice it jutting out from the wall.

My pulse spikes so hard it's painful. I'm pretty sure I closed it earlier. The latch clicks loudly when it catches, but I've been in and out of this room so much lately it's hard to know for certain it fully closed. As long as Luca didn't find it and decide to check it out… which would be the worst possible scenario short of the police discovering it.

I creep forward and nudge the bookshelf open with two fingers. It swings silently on its oiled hinges, just enough for me to poke my head in. I don't need my phone's flashlight to notice the absence of the dehumidifier's hum. I step inside and feel along the inside of the metal chest butted against the wall. My grazing fingers rush frantically from edge to edge, but it's empty. The most important thing I was supposed to keep safe is gone.

"Shit, shit, shit." I don't usually swear, but this is swear-worthy bad.

There is the remote possibility that it had fallen out of the metal chest and onto the floor at some point. I'm about to pull the lightbulb cord and search for it when another knock makes the front door tremor. Whoever is outside isn't going away. I wipe my palms on my pajama pants and force myself toward the foyer where the broken planter has spilled dirt all over the entry mat.

"Sharon!" a man shouts urgently.

I don't recognize the voice, but whoever it is doesn't quite know my name.

Then conversationally, like he's luring a small child, he says, "I know you're awake and I'm coming in if you don't answer the door."

When I flip on the porch light, a hazy circle illuminates a man on the other side. Glancing at the slightly open bookshelf, for the first time tonight I'm not sure which side of the door I should be more afraid of.

"Michael, to what do I owe the pleasure?" By now I know his name is Marshall, but if he's going to keep calling me Sharon, I figure a little tit-for-tat with a drunk guy is good entertainment.

"My name is Marshall, bitch!" He's swaying on his feet, one hand braced against the fissured doorframe, the sour smell of alcohol drifting off of him. In the unsteady glow of moonlight mixed with porch light I notice his eye. A puffy black ring around a pale gray eyeball. "At last the queen arrives after sending her minion to do her bidding," he slurs, pointing a finger at me like he's delivering some kind of prophecy. "People like you… you can't hide forever."

"My minion? What are you talking about?"

He laughs, and it's a wet, sloppy sound. "Your brother."

Nothing this drunk man is saying makes sense, and I doubt my questions will help clarify anything, but it's worth a try. "How do you know my brother?"

"A simple internet search of someone's name can dig up a lot these days." He sways closer, and I recoil. Every word carries the scent of stale lager and garlic fries—heavy on the garlic. "Oh, I know all about your criminal background. Husband's suspicious death. Prison time. And your brother's name! Funny how your whole life is all right there for the viewing."

Speaking of my brother, I have no idea where he is. A rush of nausea swirls in my stomach. "Why would you look my brother up? What did he do?" *This time*.

He jabs a thumb toward his bruised eye. "You sent him after me!"

"What? No I didn't."

"Don't play dumb." He presses a hand to the welt. "Some guy jumped me at Dirty Dan's and told me to stay away from *you* specifically. So I looked you up and found out you have a deadbeat brother. And guess what! He did time in jail just like you. Put two and two together…"

I stare at him, bewildered. "Why would my brother jump you, Marshall?"

"That's what I want to know!"

I recall when Luca showed up three days ago, right after I found that nasty review online. There were his split knuckles that I hadn't given much thought to until now… Oh. No. He. Didn't. Luca must have saw the review, then figured out it was Marshall behind it. In his typical hot-headed way, he believes defending his sister means using his fists.

My phone is already in hand, so I navigate to the review and click on "Sue D. Nimm's" profile. A scroll down to some earlier posts reveals countless half-naked pictures of Marshall at the gym, him in a red Porsche, him drinking shots… lots and lots of Macho Marshall earning that nickname.

I aim my phone at Marshall's face with the review filling up my screen. "This is why. He kicked your ass because of that cruel review you left about Shoot to Thrill. My brother can get protective."

"It was a joke!" Marshall rolls his eyes, and it's more of an *I'm about to pass out* eyeroll than an *I'm teasing* eyeroll. "And *protective* is an understatement. He almost killed me. I went to the cops, by the way, and I'll be pressing assault charges."

"You brought this on yourself. If you don't want me to get a restraining order against you, stop stalking me. Stop parking in front of my house. And stop showing up in the middle of the night."

"Parking out front?" He snorts. "Okay, for real that's not me. My car's right there."

He gestures toward the curb where a flashy orange sports car is crookedly parked in my grass. Tire marks gouge two long dirt trails where he's torn up my yard. It's not the black Mercedes I've been seeing.

"Tell your brother if he comes after me again, he'll end up like your husband!" Marshall stumbles toward his car. For a second I think he's going to fall face-first into a tree, but he catches himself, muttering curses under his breath.

"My Sharona," he sings over his shoulder, and it takes him three tries before his hand makes contact with his car door handle, "I warned you that you'd regret rejecting me. And it's only just beginning!"

Chapter 16

I slip inside my secret room and wait for my eyes to adjust to the bleak light. I navigate the clutter, stepping around the bucket and beside the box of diapers until my shin bumps against the cold iron of the footlocker. I drop to my knees. The latch gives way with a heavy *thunk*.

I throw the lid back and search inside, but just like earlier, the key I had kept in the trunk for safekeeping is gone. An image of Gollum with the ring from *The Hobbit* surfaces over my own missing *precious*. My hand sweeps the interior again, scraping against the bare metal bottom. It's definitely empty. The hollow sound of my knuckles hitting the sides of the chest rings in my ears.

Scanning the room, it feels suddenly smaller, the walls pressing in. The key has to be here somewhere. My search starts along the corner of the room, covering every inch until it snags on something along the far wall. There, the shiny metal key sits on the floor, tossed haphazardly on a dirty paper plate, mostly obscured by the heavy, inky darkness of the corner.

I start to walk toward it, then stop. The shadows in that corner are deep and thick. I'm being ridiculous, scared of a shadow. I'm a logical grown woman, but my body doesn't care about logic. My muscles lock up, triggered by a reflex I thought I'd left behind in my prison cell.

Stay away from the blind spots.

For a second, I'm not in this dusty room. I'm back in the block. I've returned to where a shadow isn't just an absence of light; it's a hiding spot for a shiv, a fist, or a guard looking to make a quota. In prison, you learn that the dark bites. You learn that if you can't see into a corner, there is someone standing in it, waiting for you.

"Stop being stupid," I hiss under my breath. "You're at home, not in prison. You're in control here."

"Are you sure about that?" a whisper returns.

I ignore the intrusive thoughts and clench my fists, digging my nails into my palms until the sting grounds me. But the hair on the back of my neck is still prickling with the certainty that I am being watched. So I count to three.

On three, I lunge. I dive into the darkness, then close my hand around the key. I expect someone to grab my wrist, icy fingers to wrap around my throat. But of course none of that happens. Then I scramble backward until I'm safe in the hallway where my mind doesn't play tricks on me.

I don't stay to check the rest of the room. The adrenaline is sour in my mouth now. I slam the bookshelf shut behind me, leaning against it for a second. I calculate other hiding places for my *precious* key—on my car keychain, wearing it on a necklace, tucked into my jewelry box—but I discard them one by one until I land on the only place that makes sense that no one could ever find.

The studio. I have the perfect spot to hide the key there: in plain sight.

Chapter 17

Main Street, the unoriginally named road that runs through the heart of Doomwood Falls, is dressed in grays and browns. Massive flower pots cup a variety of fall flora, and bare dogwood trees jut up through tiny square gardens along the wide sidewalk. Moss creeps up brickwork, fog clings to ankles, storefront windows blink awake. The bell above the jewelry store exit dings as I step onto the stone walkway clutching my repaired necklace in a cream-colored bag. Of course it makes me think of Ivory.

I dial her number. It rings until it doesn't.

"Where are you?" I mutter, staring at my reflection in the storefront glass. My face looks thinner, stretched by the warped window. "Why won't you pick up?"

I don't leave a voicemail because I can't. Her inbox is full from all of the other countless messages I've left since she disappeared. Or ran off on her own accord. At this point it feels like the same difference.

A call comes in before I have a chance to return my phone to my purse. It's about time. I answer on the first ring, "Ivory?"

A bored female voice says, "This is Doomwood Falls Correctional Facility. We have an inmate requesting to speak with—"

"You've got to be kidding me." I already know who it is.

Only one man in my life turns the phrase *correctional facility* into something routine. "Put him through."

There's a click and then—

"Shari?" Luca sounds breathless, like he's escaping a burning building that he set fire to. Honestly, with Luca, nothing would shock me.

"Did your little tryst with an eighteen-year-old girl finally catch up with you?" My joke doesn't land well.

"Shut up. And no, it's not about Freida. She's not talking to me, so it's probably over." He lowers his voice. "If I tell you, can you swear you won't freak out?"

"I'm already freaking out. I have no money for your bail, Luca. Why don't you ask Mamma to cover it?"

"Yeah, right. Over both of our dead bodies. I cannot stress this enough, but please do not tell Mamma."

"What did you do this time? Is this about Marshall?" A stiff silence hangs between us on the line. "Because he showed up at my house in the middle of the night, Luca. My *home*!"

There's a long, guilty silence. I can practically hear him rubbing the back of his neck.

"Please don't leave me here. I can explain everything."

"Luca—"

He groans dramatically. "Can you just come bail me out first? You can yell at me as much as you want, and threaten to disown me, and that's fine, but can we please do it after I'm not wearing county orange?"

Of course I'm going to bail him out. What else am I supposed to do—let him rot? I may be irritated, under-caffeinated, and on the verge of a nervous breakdown, but I'm not heartless.

"I'm on my way."

I close my eyes, wishing for another life where I had a normal family, a live husband, maybe a kid or two, and a clean record. But instead I'm estranged from my mother, a childless widow, and Ivory is missing, or maybe not missing, or maybe screaming for help from the trunk of a car. Now my brother, the human tornado disguised as a man, has landed himself in jail again.

I lower the phone and slip it into my purse, then search for my car keys. Doomwood Falls exhales around me as wind whips through the narrow alleys between tall brick buildings. A delivery truck rattles by, radio crackling with a song from another decade. Somewhere a church bell marks the hour.

"Shari Catalano?" The voice is gravelly and holds authority.

I glance up. "Yes?"

The man speaking to me towers over me wearing a black leather jacket with jeans. His grizzled brown beard that skims his collar looks familiar, but I can't place where I've seen his face.

"I'm Detective Erazem Yankovic. I'm working on the missing persons case for Ivory Cobb. I understand you two were friends."

"*Are* friends," I correct him. I refuse to let anyone refer to Ivory in the past tense.

I eye him, suddenly remembering him from the news. He stands a few feet away, thumbs hanging onto his belt loops, coat too heavy for the mild weather today. He looks like he was born tired, with dark-rimmed eyes sweeping me the way people scan a menu they don't like.

"Detective Yankovic," I repeat. "Are you stalking jewelry

stores now, or am I special?"

His mouth twitches. I almost detect a smile underneath all that facial hair. "I've been looking for you."

"That makes one of us."

"I need you to come down to the station. We have some questions about Ivory that we need to ask you."

"What about her?"

The look he gives me is one I recognize from my past interrogations, like he's counting my lies before I tell them. "As you know, she's been reported missing. And according to our intel, you were the last person to see her alive."

It's not true, but apparently Freida doesn't count as a witness.

I swallow. "I can drive to the station and meet you there in," I check my phone, as if I have somewhere to be, "an hour."

"No," he says gently, which somehow makes it worse. "I'd prefer to take you. Your car will be fine here." He points out the street sign posted to the old-fashioned streetlamp that states free parking from 8:00 to 5:00. "I'll bring you back when we're done."

It's not worth the risk to argue with an officer of the law, so I unlock my car and drop the jewelry bag onto the passenger seat, tucking it into the growing accumulation of clothes, props, makeup, and other random photography-related stuff I might need at a moment's notice. I hesitate, fingers lingering on the jewelry bag like I'm saying goodbye to something alive. It's my only connection to Ivory right now, and I hate to leave it behind.

Detective Yankovic walks me to his cruiser and opens the back door for me. "You okay?"

"Yeah," I say, because lying is easier than explaining the

flashbacks of last time I was in the back of a cop car. "Just thinking."

He nods, like thinking is dangerous business.

The door slams shut on me, and the town slides past the window as we pull away. We pass The Alibi Café and the bank, but it's near the courthouse's neoclassical pillars when I feel a tingling between my shoulder blades. I glance down the alley between two red brick buildings. A man stands against a flagstone wall, half-hidden by a lamppost. Although his face is swallowed by distance and mist, the shape of him rotates as I pass. He's watching me.

Is it Marshall, with his lingering threat to destroy my business? Or maybe Ali, with his disarming smile and too-perfect timing. But the obvious choice is Fred, with an easy view of my house and who most likely told Detective Yankovic where to find me.

I blink and he's gone, along with everything else on Main Street as our vehicle turns the corner. One thought pulses louder than the rest: *Please, please let this day not get any worse.* This naturally means it absolutely will.

Chapter 18

If you've never been interrogated by the police, I don't recommend trying it. The cross-examination room is the color of a 1970s crime drama—puke green walls and faded yellow linoleum. Despair is palpable in a place like this, which I'm pretty sure is standard-issue. They probably pump it through the vents to make everyone behave.

Detective Yankovic sits across from me, jacket off now, sleeves rolled up to his elbows. He's got a legal pad he hasn't written on yet. A power move. Make the suspect fill the silence. But I don't.

"How long was it since you last saw Ivory Cobb?" he begins our interview with.

"Three days ago," I answer with ease. "At her house."

His pen moves with a light scratching. "Why were you there?"

I watch the clock on the wall tick like it's counting down to my doom. "I stopped by to tell her something she deserved to hear."

"And that was what?"

My brain grabs on to an image of Fred—sweaty, guilty, stammering—and the woman at the waterfall. "That I saw her husband cheating on her."

Yankovic's eyebrows lift, just a fraction. I caught his

interest. "You just drop by a friend's house to tell her that kind of news?"

"I do when the alternative is letting her live a lie," I say. "Ivory hates liars." And cheaters.

"Did she believe you?"

I shrug. "I think so."

"How did she react?"

The room hums as the heat kicks on. I have to think before I answer. "Calmer than I expected, which scared me a little."

"Did she say anything about leaving? About being afraid of Fred or his alleged mistress?" He taps the pen on his bearded chin, filing that away.

"No." Then his question strikes me as odd. "Why did you say *alleged mistress*? Did you ask Fred about it? Because when a spouse goes missing, a lot of times someone hasn't been faithful in the relationship."

The detective grins. "Yes, MacGyver, we asked Fred if he or his wife had been unfaithful in the marriage. He claimed he hasn't been, and his cell phone records and friends that we interviewed all seem corroborate that. No unknown calls or texts, and his time is all accounted for. From what his friends and daughter tell me, Fred was a strict nine-to-five employee who spent every other minute with his wife and kid."

"You don't think Fred could have had a burner phone and might be lying to cover it up? I mean, why would anyone with something to hide be honest with the cops?"

He leans forward and peers at me with a curiosity that makes me feel like I'm the one who cheated. "That's a very good question, Ms. Catalano. Do *you* have something to hide?"

"No." Except I do—Ivory's texts. If I want to prove he can

trust me, I need to show him my hand. "Can you look at something?" I take out my phone and open the messages from Ivory, the first text and the follow-up beach photo. "Ivory texted me from her phone. But I don't know if it was her."

He studies my screen. "Yeah, we traced these messages already. They pinged off a tower near a beach resort, the same place her phone was last active. The photo even matches the resort, right down to the umbrellas. We checked. But we haven't yet been able to confirm if it was her staying there. They don't have cameras, and the woman working the check-in desk that night has been unreachable so far."

I swallow hard. My stomach doesn't believe it's Ivory, even if the evidence does.

Detective Yankovic steeples his fingers. "When you told her about Fred, did you argue? Sometimes people get defensive when they don't want to believe something."

I lean back in the metal chair. It groans like it's uncomfortable being associated with me. "Detective, I think I'd like to speak with my lawyer before we go any further."

"You seem pretty well-versed in this whole interrogation process."

The unspoken conclusion hangs between us like my mugshot. I feel my shoulders tense up, a reflex I thought I'd unlearned. Prison teaches you posture. And how to convert fear into anger.

"I watch a lot of crime shows," I say lightly.

"Hm." He folds his arms and leans back, broadcasting a nonchalance better than I do. "Most people don't ask for a lawyer this early unless they've done this before."

I need to give him a convincing enough answer to deter him

from looking into me further. "I have a brother who's proficient in petty crime. Shoplifting, unpaid parking tickets, that kind of stuff."

That earns me a double-take. "And?"

"So I've had personal experience with this before." From the way he chuckles, I think I've succeeded. "Speaking of my brother, he's currently enjoying the hospitality of your fine facilities. Can you direct me to where I can bail him out once we're done here?"

Yankovic exhales, something between a laugh and a sigh. "You really don't miss a beat, do you?"

"I try not to. Silence has a way of filling itself in."

He closes the legal pad. "You're free to go, but we're not done, Ms. Catalano."

"I didn't say we were," I reply. "I only said I want my lawyer."

Yankovic stands and I follow suit. "I'll see what I can do about your brother." He pauses at the door. "For what it's worth, I don't think you hurt Mrs. Cobb."

"Good, because I didn't."

Afterwards I'm led to the front desk where a stack of paperwork waits for me. The officer taps the top document like he's proud of it.

"Your brother's charge sheet," he declares.

I scan it and read over the legal jargon, along with the bail bond agreement and receipt. Suspect information, arrest details, and charges. Under the additional notes the victim's name stops me cold.

Victim: *Marshall Szabo*

Yesterday's bruise-eyed, pride-trampled Marshall is not

only trying to threaten my business by writing bad reviews about my company, but also showing up at my house drunk and uninvited in the middle of the night. And now he's pressing charges against my brother for assault. This guy is the ultimate thorn in my side. But at least I now have his full name.

I look at the officer. "Did Marshall Szabo accuse my brother of hitting him?"

The officer taps the top page. "That's what the report says. Your brother punched him in the face during a confrontation at Dirty Dan's, but everyone's fine. One black eye, one busted knuckle. Happens more often than you'd think."

Oh, I believe it. Especially with Luca. By the time he emerges from the back—shoelaces returned, ego intact—his grin is so wide it must physically hurt.

"Shari!" he says, like he's greeting me at an airport and not a holding cell.

"Why can't you keep your hands to yourself? You got thrown in jail for punching a rich asshole with too much time on his hands and enough money to hire a lawyer."

"Whatever." He winces, flexing his bandaged hand. "I barely touched him."

"Define *barely*."

"I only hit him once! The rest was… gravity."

"Unbelievable." I pinch the bridge of my nose. "You know I can't afford this."

"I did it for you. You're welcome," he says sweetly. "Also, we should really get a jailtime punch card. You know, like one of those buy ten sandwiches get one free things? Except it's for getting processed. 'Welcome back, Luca and Shari! You've earned a free coffee for serving time in the slammer!'"

I stare.

He shrugs. "Hey, Mamma would be so proud."

"Oh, she'd be thrilled," I mutter. "And Dad would be rolling in his grave."

"At least we kept the family tradition alive." He pats my shoulder. "Some families pass down heirlooms, but we pass down arrest records. Let's just hope Dad's not watching from heaven aware of what you're hiding in that room behind your bookshelf."

I swivel toward him so fast my neck cracks. "What did you just say?"

"I found your secret, sis. But don't worry, I'm not judging. Sorry if I knocked things over. It was dark and uh, well, I didn't know what I was looking at until I ran into it."

I'm about to tell him to shut up because he's discussing this in a police station of all places. Then Detective Yankovic walks by and I remember why I was brought here for something other than my brother's latest disaster. It's not about me or Luca, but about finding Ivory. That needs to be my focus right now.

"Can we get food on the way home?" Luca asks as he hops down the steps toward the parking lot. "I fight better with carbs."

"No." Because my car is still sitting in front of the jewelry store probably getting towed. This means we can either hitch a ride with Detective Yankovic—no thanks—or pay money I don't have for an Uber.

The Uber is five minutes away from home and Luca is regaling the driver with a story about last night's bunkmate who got arrested for setting his mother's curtains on fire while attempting to flame-throw a kitchen torch with his fart. The idiotic story keeps getting drowned out by something tugging at the back of my mind. A detail I shrugged off. Something that could maybe help the investigation. Then the thought clicks into place.

Oh no.

I need to show Detective Yankovic immediately.

Chapter 19

I flick on the red bulb, and the darkroom awakens. My sanctuary. Or it used to be.

The counter to my left should have the waterfall photograph I need to show Detective Yankovic, particularly the one with the neon shirt and its embroidered *Z*. There is only one person I know of in Doomwood Falls with the letter *Z* in her name, and that's Zala. She also happens to be the one digging up dirt on me. Coincidence? I think not.

But the counter is empty. No, it's worse than empty. The Leica camera my father gifted me is sitting there, out of place, and something about it doesn't look right. I pick it up, and the lens falls off. The viewfinder is cracked, and the back to the film compartment hangs sideways. My priceless camera has been destroyed.

Under it a slip of paper sits where my developed photos should be. A single white square against the dark, like a baby's first tooth. I read the note without touching it, hoping maybe they can recover a fingerprint from the paper. The handwriting is jagged and hurried, like someone wrote it before fleeing the scene of a crime... such as a break-in.

Stop talking to the cops or you're next.

My throat dries instantly, turning into a desert canyon. A death threat left for me in my own darkroom. Fabulous. Exactly what every single woman wants to find before bedtime.

Whoever wrote this has been watching me and knows Detective Yankovic brought me in for questioning. Is it Z for Zala? Or the man I spotted near the jewelry store? It could be Zala and Ali working together. But my top pick is volatile, angry, unpredictable Marshall. The same Marshall who showed up drunk, pounding on my door at three o'clock in the morning, yelling my name—well, a version of my name—like a deranged psychopath.

Marshall knows where I live, even saw my broken front door, and he probably knows I talked to the cops. Plus he has motive and already threatened me twice. And once my brother got involved and beat him to a pulp, vengeance could very well be on the menu. I can't shake the feeling that he'd want payback.

There's a faint creak somewhere in the house. Probably the pipes. Or a serial killer. Hard to tell in this economy. I try to steady my breathing, but my heart's doing its best impression of a malfunctioning washing machine—*thump-thump-thump*.

Suddenly the darkroom terrifies me. I back toward the door without looking away from the empty spot where those photos should be. The threat is so real I can almost feel its presence.

Someone was here. Someone stole my photos. Someone has been watching me. Tomorrow my front door must get fixed, even if I have to seal it shut myself.

"Great," I mutter. "I always wanted to star in my own true-crime documentary."

I kill the red light and slip out of the darkroom. Whether it was Marshall or someone worse who destroyed my priceless camera and stole my photo evidence, one thing is suddenly very clear:

I'm not safe here.

Chapter 20

Detective Yankovic lied to me. My car was *not* fine by the time I got dropped off at the jewelry store. It took nearly an hour to figure out who towed my car and where they took it. I'll be sure to forward my impound bill to the Doomwood Falls Police Department, Attention: Detective Yankovic.

Last Stop Impound and Towing squats at the edge of town next to a junkyard, surrounded by a chain-link fence crowned with barbed wire and floodlights buzzing even in daylight. Cars sit nose to tail, their windshields filmed with dust, each one waiting to be claimed but probably forgotten about.

I push through the gate and it shrieks, the metal on metal needling my eardrums. Near the front of the lot is the office, dingy and empty. On the counter an old tube television plays a rerun of the soap opera *Shahrzad,* the actors all speaking in Persian. I'm beginning to get engrossed in the romantic drama between Shahrzad and Farhad when the screen goes black.

"I do not know how *that* got on there." Flustered at getting caught with his guilty pleasure, Ali Azad fumbles with the television knob before pivoting to me. "How can I help you, Shari?"

He stands behind the counter inside the cinderblock office, his short-sleeved uniform revealing a blanket of dark arm hair. A clipboard is tucked against his chest like a shield.

"You have my car." I keep my voice level, though my hands are fists inside my pockets because I'm ticked off at whoever did this. With Luca's bail costs and now an impound bill, my credit card is going to end up maxed out. On the plus side, I've been meaning to lose weight and a starvation diet is probably effective.

He nods, sets the clipboard down, and turns a computer monitor toward himself. The screen glow paints his brown skin a pale blue. "Catalano. Silver sedan."

"That's right."

One finger jabs at the keyboard a letter at a time, and it takes forever. I watch his knuckles and the faint scar across the back of his right hand. I've seen that hand wave from across the street, hold a Delster Iranian malt beverage at block parties, fiddle with the settings on one of my cameras during photography classes… which he also quit, by the way. It's one more hit against my business, but who's counting?

He prints the receipt and slides it across the counter at me. The paper curls at the edges.

I stare at the total in shock. "This has to be a mistake."

He doesn't look up. "It is standard fee."

"My car was legally parked," I insist, but the words feel brittle and useless. "Someone called you to tow my car just to be cruel. I want to know who."

Ali's jaw strains, but he doesn't answer.

"Who called the tow truck on my car?" I repeat.

He leans forward and props his elbows on the counter. "Does it matter?"

"Yes, it matters, because I was wrongfully towed." Someone else should be paying for this. Every dollar.

Ali's gaze drifts past me, out beyond the grime-crusted window that overlooks the lot. "You want your automobile or no?"

I plant my palms on the counter. The laminate is sticky, worn smooth by other desperate hands. Hoping to appeal to Ali's humanity and our months of friendship, I resort to begging.

"Please, Ali. We've been neighbors for a year. You know me! I think someone has been targeting me ever since Ivory went missing. I think whoever it is did this to me."

He exhales through his nose as his eyes slide back to mine. There's something new there—pity, maybe. "I was outside of jewelry store. On street."

A memory surfaces unbidden: the squad car door closing, the passing storefronts, the man watching me from the alley's shadows.

"So you decided to tow my car? What do you have against me?"

He studies me like he's weighing the cost of honesty. "I do not want murderer living on my street. I worry for Zala's safety having you here."

"I didn't kill anyone."

"No more lies. The whole neighborhood talks. We all know about your past, Shari."

I think of the blinds across the street twitching closed, the way conversations die when I approach a neighbor out in public. "You towed my car because you think I'm guilty."

"Yes."

"And you didn't bother to ask me about my past before you made a judgement about me?"

His eyes harden. "Why would I help you?"

Because I've invited him into my home. Because I've played matchmaker for him and Zala. Because last summer he borrowed my ladder and still has yet to return it. I don't say any of this as the words rot on my tongue.

"Whole neighborhood wants you gone," he adds, softer now. "This is just… encouragement."

Forfeit settles in my bones. I'm too tired to keep fighting back. I pull out my credit card and slide it across the counter. "Fine."

He takes it, swipes, and hands it back. Our fingers brush and he flinches. "Lot B. Row three."

I turn toward the door, then stop. "You know," I say without looking at him, "false accusations have a way of coming back around."

He has nothing left to say.

Outside, I walk past the rows of cars until I see mine, dust-streaked and dinged. Cupping my hands around my eyes, I press my face to the passenger-side window. All the usual junk is where I left it on the seat, except something is missing.

The jewelry bag with my repaired necklace. It's gone. I lift the door handle and it's unlocked, but I can't remember if I had locked it before heading to the police station with Detective Yankovic. This could be a random petty theft, or something more targeted.

I glance back at the office. Ali stands in the doorway, unwaveringly watching me. I meet his stare and smile.

Despite what all of Hemlock Drive seems to want, I'm not going anywhere.

Chapter 21

The Alibi Café's windows are fogged with coffee steam and moist breath. Bradley Reese, Attorney at Law, is already waiting for me. The back of his chair touches a brick wall decorated with old photos of late-1800s Doomwood Falls and random kitschy knickknacks that look like someone raided a yard sale. A briefcase sits at Bradley's dull gray loafers, and I swear he's wearing the same blue suit and yellow tie he wore the day I was sentenced. He's lost more of his already meager white hair since I last saw him four years ago, and he's only in his fifties. Some men age poorly, but Bradley fossilizes.

I slide into the booth across from him. Vinyl squeaks under me like it knows my weight has increased in all the wrong places since this whole ordeal started, thanks to stress eating junk food. Now that I'm broke it won't be an issue anymore.

"You look well," he says, which is lawyer for *you look alive*.

"You look expensive," I reply. "Still billing by the minute?"

He doesn't smile. Instead, he reaches into his briefcase and slides a small padded package across the table. Brown paper with my name typed across the front, not written.

"What's this?" I ask, already hating whatever answer he comes up with because anything from a lawyer is usually bad news and costly.

"Not here. Wait until you get home to open it. Don't share

with anyone the contents of this package unless you have to, and only with someone you trust." He watches my hands, not my face. "Certain people would kill over what's inside."

"What the heck is in here? Plutonium?"

"No, but before I explain that, Shari, I'm requesting that they reopen the investigation into Stewart's death."

The café noise dips. Or maybe that's just the blood leaving my ears.

"I filed a formal petition with the district attorney's office and the coroner. They found my evidentiary basis for the request compelling enough to take another look at the facts surrounding the case, along with the autopsy results."

"Simplify it for me, Bradley," I say.

"The coroner doesn't think it was a hunting accident anymore. He thinks it was murder."

I laugh once. It comes out awkward and sharp-edged. "Congratulations. They've finally realized how hard it is to accidentally shoot yourself with your own hunting rifle."

"I'm serious."

"So was the coroner. So was the forensic technician. Why are you telling me this now?"

"Because you're involved. And because you've been involved since the beginning." He pauses and glances up at the waitress carrying a tray of water glasses and coffee mugs.

"Good to see ya, Shari." The waitress, Cindy, drifts by and drops a mug in front of me without asking. She fills it with black coffee, then places a pile of creamers and a full sugar bowl next to it. Cindy knows me so well.

"Good to see you too, Cin."

Then she looks at me pityingly, says, "Hang in there, hon,"

and leaves.

Word travels fast in small towns. I push the mug aside. My stomach is no longer in the mood for coffee today.

"Back to what I was saying," Bradley picks right back up where he left off, "we need to gather all the evidence you have to prepare for this case. Shari, this is big. You'll finally get justice for your husband."

"I don't know, Bradley." I shake my head, uneasy about unearthing this. "You already represented me in the embezzlement case Ramsey Shenk pinned on me, and you lost. No, correction—*I lost*. I did three years and have a Class C felony charge pinned to my name for the rest of my life because you dropped the ball. What makes you think you'll win this time?"

Bradley balks. I know I'm being harsh on him, but I can't get those three years back and I'll never clear my name.

"This time I have a suspect," he pauses, then adds, "and a motive."

"I'm listening."

"Ramsey Shenk," he proudly states, like I should be impressed.

"Tell me something I don't know."

Back before my conviction, before Stew was murdered, we both worked for Ramsey Shenk's online newspaper *In the Margins Media*. Stew was an accountant, I was a photojournalist. I don't know what prompted my husband to go digging so deep into the financials of *In the Margins Media*, but his hunch turned out to be dead on when he discovered a million-dollar accounting error. Stew subsequently followed the missing money directly to Ramsey Shenk's personal bank account.

Before Stew could expose Ramsey, he was found dead after an alleged hunting accident. How does one accidentally turn a rifle on himself and drive a bullet point-blank in the back of the skull while hunting? After a too-brief investigation, officials declared it a "fatal hunting accident." Case closed.

But—and this is a huge but—I had proof otherwise. Trail cams were hidden all throughout our property where Stew had been hunting that morning. Video evidence showed Ramsey Shenk killing my husband. When I replayed the trail cam footage, I watched Ramsey wrestle the rifle from Stew, force my husband to his knees, then aim the barrel at Stew's chest. I witnessed the bullet ripping through him, sickened by the blood coating the earth beneath my beloved husband's fallen body. And I can never forget.

The day I found that footage and was about to present a copy of it to the police, I was arrested and charged for embezzlement. My video evidence was subsequently buried, along with my husband. I was already in jail by the time the funeral date was set. I wore a prison jumpsuit to the funeral, where I was granted a supervised one-hour release to say goodbye to my husband's grave.

"So you already know," Bradley realizes, and his eyes soften behind his wire-rimmed bifocals, "that Ramsey killed your husband to shut him up about the embezzlement scheme."

"Yes. It's why he framed me—to discredit me before I could expose him for murder. So he got away with the stolen cash *and* murder."

"How did you know?"

"I had trail cam footage."

"You don't happen to still have that footage, do you?" He squirms in his seat and rubs his hands together as if eager to touch it.

"Yep, and it's saved on an SD card," I confirm.

"Somewhere safe, I hope?"

"It's hidden where no one will ever find it, I can assure you."

Bradley slaps the table hard enough to rattle my mug. A couple at the counter turns. "Why am I only hearing about your evidence now?"

"Because Ramsey had no problem killing my husband. I wasn't about to hand him a reason to go after my mother or my brother next while I'm sitting in a jail cell unable to protect them."

His anger simmers, changes shape. "We could have built a case against Ramsey if you wouldn't have kept that secret."

"That's assuming he hadn't paid off everyone involved in my conviction, Bradley. I was an easy target and Ramsey's powerful and wealthy. There was no way Ramsey would have been found guilty. But it doesn't matter anymore. Stew's dead and I survived prison. And in the end my husband's killer got what he deserved."

Last year, *In the Margins Media*—and every other national news outlet—had reported that Ramsey Shenk's yacht caught on fire and sunk while he was deep-sea fishing. Although they never found a body, the charter log confirmed Ramsey had taken the boat out alone, and the harbor master at the marina had confirmed seeing Ramsey board the vessel. GPS showed Ramsey's last location out at sea in the same spot where deep divers located the sunken yacht. There was no doubt that

Ramsey would not have survived.

Bradley scrubs a hand over his face. "But what if Ramsey isn't dead?"

I don't like where this is going. "What makes you say that?"

"I know it's a stretch, but there were some details about the case that didn't sit right with me. For example, the lifeboat was missing when they recovered the yacht. And I know logically it probably burned up in the fire, along with Ramsey, but I can't shake this hunch that he's still out there."

He's going on a *hunch*? Everything pointed to Ramsey's death, and it was a relief to have him gone from the face of the earth. I can't go back to a world with my husband's killer in it roaming free all because my attorney has a hunch.

"You know a hunch is what got my husband killed," I remind him.

"That's why I hired a private investigator to keep an eye on his girlfriend Gillian. I figured if Ramsey's alive, she would know."

"Wait—did you say *girlfriend*? Gillian and Ramsey aren't married?"

Bradley shakes his head. "No, from what my PI discovered, he'd been married before and swore off ever marrying again. I don't know much more than that. But I think that's why Gillian was so devastated by his death. She inherited nothing from him, other than what he had already given her while he was alive."

Interesting. I wonder what happened to his wife. Divorce? Or death? My fingers tighten around the package I still haven't opened yet. "And?"

"Anyway, now that Gillian's bank account is drying up, she has suddenly made some interesting moves, in particular revisiting the details of the day Ramsey's boat sunk. And the biggest twist?" He pauses for effect. "She's moved here."

I didn't see that coming. Although I had never met Gillian in person while working at *In the Margins Media*, her reputation preceded her. You could hear her Manolo Blahnik heels tapping from a mile away. This is a martini and penthouse girl moving to a tequila shots and single-wide trailer world.

"Why do you think she's in Doomwood Falls?"

"I think Ramsey is hiding out here. Planning how to get that trail cam evidence back so he can rejoin the living without a murder charge."

A boat fire without a body means somewhere out there Ramsey could be among the living. It's not completely insane, I'll give Bradley that much. And I am the only person with the evidence that can put him where he belongs: behind bars for life. I stare at the package in my hands. Proof small enough to fit in a bubble-wrapped envelope but dangerous enough to kill for.

"Can I speak to your private investigator in person?" I ask.

"Unfortunately I've been unable to get ahold of Vick for the past couple days. But when I do, I'll set up a meeting."

For the first time in four years since I was hauled away in handcuffs I have hope that justice will prevail.

"So what's in the package?" I lift and shake it, listening for a hint at what's inside.

Bradley places his wrinkled hand on mine and pats it tenderly. Maybe after all of these years he thinks of me like a daughter—a daughter who can't seem to stay out of trouble and constantly needs saving.

"Let's just say it's a gift that might save your life… or ruin it. It all depends on how you use it.

Chapter 22

The moment I open the package Bradley Reese gave me, my life splits in two: before I know too much, and after it's too late. But I need answers before someone decides to make good on that death threat and turns me into a missing persons poster with an unflattering photo.

The padded envelope sits in the center of my dining room table begging to be opened. Leftover Chinese takeout reheating in the microwave sends a waft of soy sauce throughout the house, and the LED lights in the chandelier overhead blink like they're on the fritz. I can't sit still, and I can't stand either. Every muscle wants to move, to head for the horizon away from this whole mess. But running has never solved anything. It just postpones it.

I circle the table once, then twice. My bare feet stick slightly to the hardwood. Luca stands a few feet away, leaning against the china cabinet with his arms folded. His greasy hair is pulled back in a ponytail that I've offered to cut into a more grown-up style, but he prefers the garage band look. The sweater he's wearing that I salvaged from my garage storage bin of Stew's old clothes fits so snug it looks like it's one deep breath away from ripping like a Hulk reenactment.

"You don't have to open it," Luca says for the umpteenth time.

"Yes I do," I reply for the umpteenth time.

"Bradley didn't say what it was?"

"Nope." And Bradley never misses a chance to explain something, which tells me everything I don't want to know.

I pull out a chair and sit, bracing myself, while Luca pushes off the cabinet, then hovers over my shoulder. Long stray hairs tickle my cheek as he's leaning too close. He doesn't know better than to crowd me when I'm like this. There is a very specific kind of resolve that comes when knowing something is going to hurt you and choosing it anyway. My dentist relies on this same masochism to stay in business.

I slide my nail under the packaging seal and peel it open. I pour out the contents on the table. The first thing that drops out is a black pen drive.

"Is that all of it?"

"No." I gently squeeze the package and it crackles and bulges. There's something else inside. "That's just the appetizer."

I push the pen drive aside, not touching it any more than I have to. A folded sheet of paper slides out next. When I unfold it, I recognize the block handwriting immediately. It's Bradley Reese's neat lawyery script:

Someone sent this to me. Maybe you know what this is about.

I tilt the envelope again. A white plastic baggie slips out and lands on the table soundlessly. Written across it in thick black Sharpie, all caps, is my name:

SHARI CATALANO

It's the baggie the jewelry store had placed my repaired necklace in. I open it and turn it upside-down. The familiar necklace spills out onto the table, the two intertwined lilies with petals curled together like they're sharing a secret. Except it's not sparkling like it should.

Dark red stains the gold, caked into the grooves, smeared across the petals. It looks like the lilies are bleeding.

Luca recoils a step. "Is that—"

"Blood," I answer. "Someone stole this from my car and sent it to my lawyer."

"Covered in blood," Luca fills in the blanks. He looks at the necklace again, then at the pen drive. "Whose blood do you think it is?"

"I don't know, but I hope whatever is on this pen drive answers that question."

I already know whatever is on the pen drive won't solve everything because nothing is ever that simple. I pick it up, head to my laptop sitting on the coffee table in the living room, and plug the drive in. The computer hums, locating the files. There is only one folder saved:

Vick

Vick, I'm guessing short for Victor, must be Bradley's private investigator. I click on the folder and read the file names of half a dozen documents. Whatever is on it must be life-altering for Bradley to have come all the way to Doomwood Falls to hand deliver it to me in person. I just hope whatever he found is worth it.

Chapter 23

The place Luca picked for dinner with our mamma is called The Codfather. Nothing says comfort food like a fried seafood joint with cartoon fish in fedoras painted on the walls. But when you uncover a pen drive that reveals a person close to you has been lying to your face for months, pretending to be someone they're not, it's hard to find comfort, even in deep-fried oil-soaked seafood.

I can't resist the urge to twist my necklace around my index finger. The chain bites into my neck with each tightening loop, reminding me of what it looked like before I washed it in bleach—dark with blood.

Luca leans back in the booth, drumming his fingers on the table next to his empty fried seafood platter. "You're doing that thing again."

"What thing?" I ask.

"Necklace twirling. It's like clicking a pen but more annoying."

After losing my necklace the first time, I'm afraid that if I let go, it'll vanish and reappear someplace worse, like an evidence locker. I considered placing it in my hiding spot along with the pen drive, but it's not a risk I can take anymore. This necklace links directly to me and someone got to it once before, along with breaking into my home. As far as I'm concerned, there's no safer place for this other than on my neck.

"And you drumming your fingers on the table isn't equally annoying?" I shoot back at him.

"Kids, enough bickering!" Our mamma, Rosetta, presses her napkin to her lips with unnecessary force. A Scarlet Mischief pink imprint—her favorite lipstick she's worn since the 1990s—of her lips sticks to the napkin. The color is on par for our family history. "What is going on? What did you need so urgently that I had to miss Last Firsts Club to come here?"

"Last Firsts Club?" Luca looks to me as if I have any idea what that tongue twister is.

Mamma straightens up before answering, which means this is going to be a very detailed explanation. "It's a group of advanced-age people who meet at the community center once a month with a common goal: If it's your last chance to do something for the first time, you do it. It's kind of like a bucket list but more positive. No one wants to think about checking off a list before kicking the bucket, but if you look at it like it might be your last chance to do something, it feels less morbid."

Bucket list, Last Firsts list… the concept sounds like the same morbidity to me, but what do I know?

"Anyway," Mamma continues, "Luca, we haven't spoken in a while. Are you seeing anyone special?"

I snort a mouthful of soda out of my nose trying to withhold a laugh. "Yeah, Luca, tell Mamma about your girlfriend."

Luca passes me a look that could kill. "I'm not dating Freida anymore. I think she's ghosting me. I've tried everything to reach her, but she won't answer calls or texts."

"Who is Freida?" Mamma asks with a lilt in her voice.

"No one!" Luca answers before I can. "It's just a girl I was talking to. The lady Ivory Cobb who disappeared, it's her daughter. But it's over. She was too young for me anyway."

"Oh, well, probably best not to attach your cart to her horse." Mamma injects a wise old woman tone to the words. "So, you both invited me here. What do you need?"

What I need is to un-live the last week, but I should probably come up with something more doable than time travel.

"I need advice. Someone sent my attorney this necklace," I murmur so the waiter refilling our drinks won't hear. I slide my fingers along the chain. "Whoever it is stole it from my car."

Mamma blinks. "And…?"

"There was blood on it," I whisper.

She gawps at me with a not-so-subtle horror. "Don't tell me you washed it off," she chides.

"Well, what else was I supposed to do? If *my* necklace has blood on it, what do you think the police will think? Especially considering," I pause on the right word, "my history."

"If you explain it to them, I'm sure they'd understand." Mamma is of the generation where she still trusts in people to do the right thing.

Both Luca and I turn a baffled expression on her. "You mean like I tried to do last time and ended up serving time in prison for it?"

"Okay, you made your point." She raises her hands in surrender. "Do you think someone's trying to set you up again?"

"I don't know what to think." Except that yes, a setup is exactly what it feels like because I've been through it once before and this has an uncanny resemblance to that. When you have a record, people don't need evidence—just a good story. And someone is clearly writing one for me, leaving props around that could eventually pin Ivory's disappearance on me.

"Well, connect the dots for me," Mamma suggests, and for the first time I feel like I have guidance. A support system I've been lacking the last four years.

I explain to her how my lawyer hired a private investigator to tail Ramsey Shenk's girlfriend, and he thinks Ramsey might still be alive and wants to come out of hiding. When I get to the part that Ramsey can't resurrect himself while I have video evidence that could put him immediately behind bars for Stew's death, Mamma earnestly grabs my hand.

"Oh, you think Ramsey is behind Ivory's disappearance so he can frame you for murder. That way you can't use your evidence against him!"

Luca and I exchange a look that Mamma catches too easily.

She arcs her finger from me to Luca and back again. "What was that look about?"

"I don't think Ramsey abducted Ivory himself," I answer for the both of us, "but his people could have. A man who can get away with murder and frame an innocent woman for embezzlement has to have people."

"And even if he doesn't have people," Luca chimes in, "he has a tunnel-visioned girlfriend who wants her hands on Ramsey's money."

"The worst part is," I squeeze Mamma's hand and reach for Luca's, and for the first time in four years I feel like we're a family again, "if I'm in jail again," or *dead*, I think despondently, "my evidence stays suppressed."

I glance out the window at a playful Bernese mountain dog in my periphery, and something catches my eye. Actually, *someone*. Fred Cobb is walking along the sidewalk half a block down next to the dog. And the interesting part is he's not alone.

A dark-haired woman walks beside Fred holding the leash to the Berner. The two are perfectly in step and talking way too close. She touches Fred's arm, and he leans in as if she said something intimate. It's highly inappropriate behavior for a man whose wife vanished three days ago.

"Is that Fred?" I mutter.

Luca twists in the booth. "What the—it sure looks like it."

Mamma gasps like we're sharing gossip. "Who is the woman he's with?"

Good question, but I have theories. None of them charitable. Before either of them can lecture me about keeping a safe distance like my attorney advised, I'm already sliding out of the booth.

"Sit your buns back down," Mamma demands.

"I just want a better look."

Hope is a drumbeat pushing me forward. Maybe that is his mistress. Maybe I can finally figure out who she is and start piecing all of this together… All I need is a picture of her.

"Gianna Shari Catalano!" Mamma scolds, but I'm halfway to the door with no plans to stop now.

The evening sun is low and blinding as I step outside. Fred and the dark-haired woman are speed-walking down the sidewalk, now disappearing around a corner. I push my gait into a sprint while digging in my purse for my phone. My fingers catch on receipts, gum wrappers, the empty pepper spray I keep forgetting to replace—but not the phone. Of course the phone has lodged itself in the deepest possible pocket.

"Come on," I grumble. "Seriously?"

If that woman is his mistress, I can figure out who Z is,

though I'm still leaning toward Zala. After that, I can redirect the police in her direction, proving that Fred lied to them. *Bam*—obstruction of justice and hindering the investigation. While my past makes me an easy scapegoat, the perfect fall girl, if I can slide the puzzle pieces together in the right order, maybe I'll be able to give Detective Yankovic a new picture that doesn't make me look like a kidnapper.

My fingertips finally contact the smooth edge of the phone. I yank it up triumphantly and immediately step off the curb. Bad timing.

The sound impacts me first—an engine revving hard. The roar explodes from my left. It punches the air out of my lungs before I can think. I look up, but it's too late. High beams blow out my vision as the car charges toward me. Time jerks like someone hit pause. There's a fraction of a second where my brain tries to negotiate—maybe it'll stop, maybe I can jump back—but before my body can react the bumper slams into my hip.

The impact is brutal and intimate. Metal meets bone. I feel myself lift, weightless and crooked, the world tilting as pavement rushes up to claim me. Glimpses of color—gray concrete, blue sky, a flash of pink—invade my vision all at once in a kaleidoscopic blur. The phone flies from my hand, spinning away.

Then the ground slams into me. All the air leaves my body at once. Pain fractures through me in sharp, disconnected bursts—hip, ribs, shoulder, skull—my thoughts shattering with it. The world narrows to noise and light and the taste of coppery blood in my mouth. Somewhere nearby, tires screech. I lie there, stunned, staring at the empty stretch of road where the car should be, where it was a second ago. A fleeting thought fades away as I ponder that the car barreling away is one I've seen before.

As the edges of the world dissolve into abyss, my brain sparks with the familiar face of the driver through the windshield. The recognition hits me harder than the car did. And then there's nothing but dark rushing in, fast and merciless.

Chapter 24

The memory of the face behind the wheel is gone when I wake up, as if it never existed. My body feels like it's renegotiating the terms of its will to live. My throbbing skull, my broken bones, my weary spirit—it's anyone's guess which one will give up first. It takes several flutters of my eyelids before my consciousness becomes fully aware. I'm drowning in aggressively white light and beeping machines that I immediately know belong to a hospital. If this had been heaven, I was asking for a refund.

The room holds the intimate scent of unwashed hair and dry lips, along with the metallic pungency associated with open wounds. The faint echo of bodily fluids never quite leaves no matter how often the sheets are washed.

My brain feels encased in bubble wrap. I try to move my head. Bad idea. A worse pain detonates behind my eyes like a tiny atomic bomb.

"Hey," a voice to my left says, hoarse and relieved. "There she is."

My eyes peel open with a crunch of dry eye boogers. Luca is slumped in a plastic chair wearing a wrinkled version of yesterday's shirt—have I been here since yesterday? or a week? or, God forbid, longer?—and in this moment I love my brother more than ever before. My Patron Saint of Bad Decisions clearly hasn't left my side.

"What…" my throat scratches out the words, "happened?"

Luca sits up, brushing his disheveled hair off his forehead. "You don't remember?"

My eyelids drift closed and I try to dig backward through the fog. But it's like someone shook my memories in a snow globe and all the pieces are still floating. Luca holds out a cup of water with a straw angled toward my lips. I sip at first, then gulp. The iciness of it isn't doing my headache any favors.

"I remember," I swallow, "walking. In town. And… my purse."

A car. A face. An accident—but it doesn't feel like it was an accident. Then the images are gone before I can grab hold of them.

"It's okay." Luca squeezes my hand. He does it gently, which is rare for him. He's more of a pat on the back that cracks your spine kind of guy. "You were in a hit-and-run."

I blink at him. "I was hit?"

"And run," he confirms. "By a car."

"Thanks," I mutter. "In case I thought it was a bicycle."

He huffs a tired laugh. "You were out for almost twelve hours. I was starting to think you might wake up and start swearing in Italian again."

"I don't speak Italian."

"You do when you have a concussion." He leans back, stretching. "Mamma's at your place with Zoomie. The dog wouldn't stop howling at the front door, so she's with him until you get home."

Zoomie probably thinks I died. Then again, Zoomie also thinks the mailman is a demon who steals souls, so maybe he's not the best judge.

I rub my forehead, careful of the IV taped to my arm. "Did you see who hit me?"

"No. By the time the screaming started and I ran out, the car was gone."

"Did anyone else see it?"

"Only that it was a black sedan," he says. "And fast. That's it. The police are going to come take a statement from you at some point and hopefully find footage of the exact make and model."

I do remember a black sedan had been parked in front of my house, but I feel like there's more on the tip of my memory. I reach for the visual and it's like trying to grab smoke. My traitorous brain slides away from it and it's *poof*—gone.

"The doctor is concerned about your stress levels, sis. He wants to discharge you, but only if you can promise to eliminate stress." Luca watches me carefully. "You're not exactly coping well since Ivory's disappearance."

"Oh really?" I arch an eyebrow. "And what gave that away? The lack of appetite? Or the insomnia?"

"Shari—"

"You're right," I cut in. "I'm a wellness disaster."

"I just want you to deal with this in a healthier way."

I glance at his knuckles, scabbed and bruised. "Healthier way?" I echo. "Uh-huh. Luca, you look like the dictionary definition of unhealthy."

He follows my gaze and pulls his hand back. "This? This was out of necessity."

"Meaning?"

"Meaning if someone hurts you—or tries to bash you

online—I bash them. That's how it works when you're a brother."

"You think getting in fights with someone who posted a bad review about my business is necessary?"

"Absolutely," he snaps. "It was an indirect threat, Shari. Ever since Ramsey—"

"Don't." The word is stern. That name is a razor blade dragged across a scar I don't want to tear open anymore.

"After what Ramsey did to you," Luca continues anyway, because stubbornness is his love language, "I told myself I'd never let someone target you again. I promised."

"And look how well that turned out." I'm referring to the bloody necklace, to Ivory missing, and the car that definitely did not run me over by accident.

I stare at my fierce, loyal, infuriating brother. The one who once threw himself in front of a boy twice his size because the kid wouldn't stop calling me a baby. The one who believes it's his job to fix me, even when *fixing me* would probably require a lobotomy.

"I love you, Luca, but I'm not your responsibility."

"Yes you are," he fires back. "You're my sister. And I'm not losing you. We've already lost Dad and Stew…" He lets my husband's name linger and drops his gaze. "I'm done losing family, Shari."

We all saw my dad's end coming. After every type of Western medical treatment, we even tried a list of hopeful Eastern medicines, but nothing could fix advanced stage brain cancer. None of us were prepared to lose Stewart, though. On top of that, my own life was barely clinging to a thread after my sentencing.

"Yeah, I'm done losing too."

The painkillers make me sleepy, and I feel myself slipping away. Another flash pops behind my eyelids—

A windshield, and that familiar face behind it. It's someone I know.

Behind the memory, my heartrate monitor beeps urgently, and Luca calls for a nurse. Another presence enters my room, but I'm stuck in the dream forcing the face behind the windshield to materialize.

"I know—" I gasp. "I think I know who—"

As quickly as it came, the memory once again evaporates, leaving a void. I slam back into the present to a nurse checking my vitals.

"I can't remember," I whisper. "I know I saw the driver. But I can't—" My voice breaks. "Luca, I can't remember."

He cups my cheek and kisses my forehead. I really like this version of him. "Then don't try right now. Let your brain heal."

I nod, because fighting my brother takes more energy than I currently possess. But inside me, something dark uncoils. Someone wants me dead, someone close to me. And someone who knew where I'd be. Whether it's about Ivory's disappearance, or somehow connected to Ramsey Shenk, or it's something I have yet to understand… whoever is after me is not finished.

The worst part is I can't trust anyone.

Chapter 25

I'm released from the hospital a few hours later with a discharge packet thick enough to stop a bullet and a headache that feels like someone wedged a live grenade behind my left eye. The nurse tells me I "just need rest," which is hospital speak for *don't die on our watch.*

My left arm hangs helplessly in a sling, and a bandage sticks to a bald patch of stitched scalp that I'm worried may not grow hair back. I'm already planning ways to style my hair that would cover it up as Luca wheels me down to the lobby, then escorts me out into the parking lot.

"Remember, you've got to take it easy," he instructs me for the sixth time in thirty steps.

"I will. I'm basically a sentient marshmallow right now," I assure him.

He doesn't smile, not even a twitch. "I'm worried about you. You could have died."

"But I didn't." I inject a playfulness, but the undercurrent is dark. I'm lucky I'm not roadkill still stuck to the pavement. "And I'll be more careful going forward."

It's a downpour all the way home, and my post-traumatic stress is acting up with every jarring turn Luca makes and zero visibility. When we safely arrive at Hemlock Drive, Luca shoots me a withered look.

"I have something to tell you, and you're not going to be happy about it."

"What?" I dare ask.

Not much is worse than a brush with death and an emergency room visit. He pulls up to the curb of my house, but there's another car crookedly parked in the driveway, blocking us from pulling in.

"I asked Mamma to move in to help take care of you until you're fully on your feet. That way you can relax."

I stand corrected. Having my mother as my live-in nurse is way worse. I'm already stretched thin having my brother invading my space, worried he'll start questioning me about what's behind my bookshelf door and decide to admit me to a psych ward. Luca might be somewhat understanding, but my mother would have a meltdown.

Anyone who knows Rosetta Catalano would have to agree that being under her care is anything but relaxing. As any Italian can attest, there is no such thing as a *nurturing* Italian woman. My mamma doesn't speak, she shouts. Then there's the food. You are guaranteed to gain at least half your body weight under her care. Don't bother turning down that second serving of pasta, because according to Mamma Rosetta, you are always looking too thin.

Her midnight cleaning rampages are enough to drive anyone to the insane asylum. You don't realize it at first that things are missing. Linens here, cookware there… and soon you begin to wonder if you're losing your mind. It's only when she drags you to go thrift store shopping for the tenth time in one day that you start to recognize all those missing items on the shelves and realize you're not the crazy one—Rosetta is.

"Absolutely not. I'm fine taking care of myself." I'm not convincing, though, as I struggle to open the car door on my own.

"How about for one week?" Luca negotiates.

"Two days," I acquiesce.

"Deal."

Hemlock Drive looks emptier than usual. With Luca's help I ease myself out of the vehicle, spotting movement a couple doors down. It's Wren, and she's speed-walking toward me. How does she manage to always have the worst timing?

"I heard you died," she says in her blunt Wren way.

"Nope. I'm still here and kickin'."

"Want me to bring you over a healing smoothie?" she offers, but I know better than to accept it. I've learned firsthand that her food tastes as gross as it looks. "It's packed with antioxidants. You'll feel better in no time."

"Thanks, but I'll pass. Feeding me back to health is my mother's jurisdiction. Interfere, and a man named Tony might come after your kneecaps," I jest, though it probably holds more truth than I care to admit.

When I reach the front porch and see three suitcases neatly lined in my entryway, I sense Mamma is here to stay longer than the agreed-upon two days. Zoomie barrels through the open door toward me so fast he nearly knocks me over. After a couple laps splashing in puddles, he dashes back into the house, jumping and slobbering all over me.

"Zoomie, buddy," I greet him, now sharing his wet dog smell. "I get it, you missed me. But can we avoid recreating the scene of the crime?"

The scent of *porchetta* roasting in butter drifts from the

kitchen. Mamma is already cooking away her anxiety, while I feel mine spiking. Along with my cholesterol. She hovers so close I can smell the garlic on her breath from taste-testing every aspect of the meal.

"Shari, darling," she gives my slinged arm a once-over, "maybe you should lie down. Or sit. Or Luca can carry you."

"Mamma, I don't need to be carried."

My arm isn't broken and casted, just wrapped to prevent further injury. I appear more broken than I actually am.

"I don't want you overdoing it, honey," she says, inspecting the bald patch on my head.

She makes me vow to go straight to bed, after brushing my teeth, once we eat. Standing at the foot of the stairwell, I even point in my bedroom's general direction on the second story as I agree. But my feet betray me and take me through the living room and toward my photography studio, the way someone might autopilot toward the fridge after a traumatic breakup. Since finding my Leica camera destroyed, I worry my intruder might have come back to do more damage.

"I just want to check something first." It's pathetic that I'm more worried about my cameras than I am my bones.

Mamma silently shadows me, hands clasped like she's praying. Knowing her, she probably is.

The moment I step into the studio, something inside me goes still. The air feels the same, lingering with the scent of sulfur and ammonia from the developer and fixer stored in my darkroom. But something is off, and I can't tell what it is. Like someone moved things a few inches to the left just to be annoying.

I glide toward my *Wall of Exile* display. There's a blank

space where a framed photograph should be. The picture of the cabin near Doomwood Falls is missing. I drop to my knees, searching the floor for it, looking under furniture, because it must have fallen off the wall. But it's not on the floor, not under the furniture, not on the wall. It's nowhere in the room.

A wave of terror sweeps over me, followed by the kind of dread you get when an oncologist says, *Huh, that's interesting.* Stewart had gifted me the frame days before he died, showing me its secret compartment and telling me to put something precious in it. He meant the key to the safe deposit box where he stored the evidence he had on Ramsey's embezzlement. But I didn't listen. Instead I placed the key in a metal chest in my hidden room.

After I nearly lost the safe deposit key the night Marshall showed up drunk at my house, I put it in the secret compartment hidden inside the frame… a frame that has now been stolen. I suppose I can always get a replacement key for the safe deposit box, but what if whoever stole the frame gets to it first?

But the key isn't the only thing I hid in the compartment. I also hid the SD card containing all of the trail cam video footage that would take Ramsey Shenk down for murder. And now that's gone too.

This is the absolute worst thing that could possibly happen short of someone finding my secret room. No one knew about that frame's compartment but me and Stew, so who could have figured it out? It seems impossible…

"How?" I breathe. "How did they find it?"

Mom approaches behind me. "What's wrong? Who found what?"

"My picture frame with the photo of the cabin. It's gone."

Mom squints at the wall, but it's as clear as day that it's missing. The subtle outline of a faded rectangle proves it was once there. "Gone as in… you moved it? Or gone as in… gone gone?"

"Gone as in someone stole it."

It's a strange thing to steal, but everything in the past week has been strange. I mentally splice it all together, but I can't connect the dots to who would be behind *everything*. Marshall's cruel review. Fred cheating. Ivory going missing. Her strange text. The break-in to my darkroom and my missing photos. Then the note and hit-and-run… and now this. My chest tightens, like fingers are wrapping around my lungs and squeezing.

"Mamma, I need to tell you something."

She visibly goes rigid. "Shari, what did you do?"

"Nothing! I mean, I didn't do anything. Something was done to me."

"What do you mean?" Her eyes widen.

"I found a note in my darkroom. The threatening kind. It basically said not to go to the police or I'll be next. You know, your standard nightmare fuel."

Mamma's hand flies to her mouth. "Dear God." She stares at me in disbelief. "Why didn't you tell anyone?"

"Duh, because it said not to go to the police or I'd be next."

My first stalker suspect would have been Gillian, but whoever this is knows me well enough to pick my most precious possession to destroy—my Leica. And they know where my darkroom is, which means I probably gave lessons to this person. And they stole my evidence proving Ramsey Shenk is a murderer, which means they have some kind of connection to him. Or maybe they didn't know the evidence was in the frame at all and only knew of the frame's sentimental value. I had announced it in class, after all, which means it's probably someone from one of my classes.

If so, why am I so afraid of this person? I did time in prison! I can easily take on whoever's after me—whether it's Zala, Ali, Wren, Fred, or even Marshall. I just need to get one step ahead.

"Do you think this is a clue?" I point to the blank space. "They came in here and took that exact photo out of all of these."

Mom steps closer, slow and careful. "But why that one? Why the cabin?"

"I don't know. There's nothing particularly special about it other than that it's near the Doomwood Falls waterfall."

The waterfall is where I saw Fred cheating, though. The only conclusion I've come up with so far is that maybe Ivory isn't at the beach like the police think she is. Maybe she's in the cabin. Her and I used to hike there together all the time. But then why draw attention to it by stealing my framed picture of it?

"It could be a warning," Mamma suggests.

Warnings. Clues. Threats. Little breadcrumbs from the world's most passive-aggressive stalker.

At the glass studio door that leads outside Zoomie starts growling. His teeth are bared as he stares at a dark corner near my equipment shelf. It's the low rumble he makes during thunderstorms, or when a wild animal lingers on the edge of our yard at night, at things I can't see. I definitely won't be sleeping tonight.

I can almost sense someone else's presence in the room. Someone who stood in front of that wall, close enough to touch it. Mamma watches at me, but she's not really looking at me.

She's searching for a truth she doesn't want to see, that her daughter's life is in peril. Her hand finds mine, and it's warm and dry.

"Mamma, I think they're telling me they can get to me anytime they want."

And for the first time, I feel like someone else is here with us. Just out of sight. Waiting to destroy me permanently.

Chapter 26

This is a bad idea.

That's the first thing I think as I push past the thicket at the edge of the trail, branches snagging my sweater. The camera around my neck bumps against my boobs and slinged left arm, which makes the trek even harder as it throws off my balance. I slip my arm out of the sling, gently running my fingers up the ACE bandage that doesn't seem to offer much protection.

Although every muscle aches from the exertion so soon after my hospital stay, I remind myself that the cabin picture wasn't stolen off my studio wall for no reason. Someone wanted me to come here. Honestly, if the culprit could send me a memo clarifying their villainous intentions, that would be helpful. But until that happens, it's up to me to figure it out.

I reach the clearing where the trees thin out and the cabin appears, looking exactly the same as it did in the photograph. Although the lush green foliage backdrop has been replaced by bare skeletal branches, nothing else has changed. In fact, I had taken the picture from the spot where I now stand.

The two-room structure looks harmless enough: weather-beaten logs, moss crawling up one side, a roof that sags with depression. The front door is closed, the lock rusted. I jiggle the handle just to be thorough, then shove my good shoulder against the door. It won't budge, and it looks like it's been locked and sealed for generations.

Two windows flank the door, and I test each one, pushing up to see if either will slide open. My injured wrist immediately regrets it as pain shoots up my left arm. I peer through the dingy glass and my breath fogs my view inside. The cabin is hollowed out by age. Dust lies thick on the plank floor, dulling the wood to the color of bone. A table squats in the center of the room, its surface scarred with knife marks and dark rings where cups once sweated. A single chair has fallen sideways, as if it gave up waiting for someone to come back. Cobwebs stitch the corners together, trembling faintly in the stale air.

The light inside is thin and jaundiced, sunlight filtered through grime. A stone fireplace gapes at the far wall, cold and black, its mantel crowded with nothing but dust shadows where objects used to be. The walls smell like damp rot even through the glass. Everything looks paused mid-breath, abandoned in a hurry or forgotten on purpose. I can almost hear the echo of boots on wood, the ghost of heat from a fire that hasn't burned in decades. The cabin stares back at me, empty.

No Ivory. And no secret message carved into the wall reading: *Shari, you're getting warmer.* Just ancient artifacts and dust. For a moment, doubt slithers in. Maybe this cabin has nothing to do with Ivory's disappearance after all. I force myself to turn away, hiking back along the river.

The trail to the waterfall is no joke. Only the most stubborn nature lovers attempt the climb, and yesterday's downpour has turned the path into a slick, muddy deterrent. Shafts of sunlight pierce through the burgundy and gold leaves still clinging desperately to their branches. The narrow dirt trail snakes along Doomwood Falls, weaving around the thick, knotted roots of trees settling in for winter. I breathe in the damp, woodsy air, hoping it will calm me. It doesn't. The panic crawling under my skin refuses to ease.

Within a few minutes the rumble of rushing water grows louder, drowning out my thoughts, vibrating through my bones. Mist sprays my face, and I step closer to the shoreline to reset my expectations to hopeless.

I thought getting out in nature might loosen the knot between my shoulders, but after the week I've had, that feels laughable. Ivory's disappearance. Luca's fistfight. My home break-in. Detective Yankovic's grilling. The hit-and-run. It's all too much for one person.

And the package my attorney gave me with my blood-soaked necklace has me on edge. I have no idea what to do with the private investigator's collection of information that may or may not lead to Ramsey Shenk—a man I prefer stays gone. I can't shake the feeling that my past has finally caught up with me, and its claws are tearing me apart.

I'm nearing the edge of the river when something sizable drifts into view, instantly giving me the sense that my day is about to get worse. As if that's possible. Some people look at nature and see peace. I look at it and start rehearsing alibis.

The current nudges the object closer, knocking it against rocks as it bobs downstream. A sharp crack behind me pulls my focus away. The sound sends a chill up my spine, reminding me of the constant feeling that I'm being watched—a feeling that's followed me since Ivory went missing.

Another snap is followed by leaves rustling.

"Hello?" I call, hoping to scare off a malevolent animal… or a malevolent human. At this point, either seems possible.

No answer. The brush is too thick to see through, so I turn back to the water. The surface glitters harmlessly in the sunlight, all sparkly and cheerful. It's a lie. The shape drifts nearer and catches on a branch along the bank. For a second, I convince myself it's just a log. But it's the wrong shape and wrong color. The current frees it, coughing it up onto the pebbled shore downriver. Mud grips my boots as I slog closer. I don't understand what I'm seeing until I'm almost on top of it.

My breath stutters when the definitely not-a-log slowly turns in the water, spinning in a grotesque, lazy circle. It's a body. Face down, with hair floating around the head in dark, tangled ribbons. Her arms stretch outward, palms open, as if she's surrendering. Her clothes cling unnaturally, nearly transparent, and the skin beneath is a dull, horrifying gray.

I freeze. Then, against my better judgment, I inch forward, drawn by a sick curiosity. *Please don't be her. Please don't be Ivory.* I crouch, but her face is buried in the mud. Only the slope of her neck and the back of her head are visible. Her hair is the right inky color to be Ivory. Or the wrong color, if my worst fear is justified.

Squeezing my eyes shut, I refuse to let that scenario take shape. Silence rushes in to fill the space, swallowing everything except the frantic thud of my heart. *Lub-dub. Lub-dub. Lub-dub.* With a fragile spark of hope that this person might still be alive, I grip her shoulder and roll her over.

Nope. Very dead.

I kneel and brush debris from her face, only to find features so damaged she barely looks human. Fish—or something creepier lurking beneath the surface—have had their fill picking at her. Whoever she is, she's been in the river far too long.

Something catches the light. My focus shifts from her ruined face down to something that doesn't belong in this river, or on a stranger's body. The realization of what it is hits me so hard it knocks the breath from my lungs. My eyes trail down her neck, then her collarbone, landing on something so impossible I lose my balance and hit the ground.

It can't be real. Except it is. A golden chain clings to her neckline.

It's a necklace. *My* necklace, and Ivory's necklace. The two lilies woven together. Our delicate matching necklaces because Ivory was like the sister I always wanted. I touch my neck and mine is still there, which means this is Ivory's. It has to be. But this woman isn't. How did Ivory's necklace get on this stranger's neck?

A wave splashes the rocks, soaking my shoes. I straighten, hugging my arms around myself. My mind is spinning too fast to slow down now.

Call the police.

That's what a normal person would do. Someone with a clean record. Someone who doesn't have the kind of past that makes detectives get suspicious. I can already see Detective Yankovic's face when he finds out who reported the body. The little downward twitch of his mouth. The look that says, *You again? Really?*

I've been incarcerated once. I plead innocent, but try telling that to people who hear the word *ex-con* and stop listening after the hyphenation. To them, I'm a potential suspect with a history of being in the wrong place at the wrong time. And now here I am again. Wrong place. Worst possible time.

If I call this in, Detective Yankovic will surely look into my past. He'll trace the necklace. He'll ask questions I can't answer. He'll decide I'm lying even when I'm not. He'll decide I did this.

I scramble to unclasp it with trembling fingers, shoving it into my pocket as dread settles deep in my gut. This isn't a random body. This is a message for me. It's no coincidence that the package Bradley gave me had my necklace covered in blood, and now this body has Ivory's matching one. If anyone else finds her, my future is over. This woman's death was meant to put me behind bars—or in the ground.

Adrenaline kicks in with an urge to survive. I can't leave the evidence. Even if I swore I had nothing to do with her murder—and I'm now completely certain this was murder—I wouldn't stand a chance. Not with my record.

Suddenly I remember the noise I'd heard in the woods and I scan the trees. Did someone see me take the necklace? I strain for any sound—footsteps, breathing, a phone notification, anything. There's nothing. Just a heavy, unnatural quiet. Me and the dead woman. It's just us, I hope.

So what now?

I could run. Get back to my car. Disappear into another town, another state, another country. Indonesia pops into my head, sunny and extradition-free. I checked. But my feet won't move and I'm so tired of running. An awful idea forms, and before I can stop myself, I step toward the body. Then another. Then I do the worst thing possible.

I touch her.

First the sleeve, then her arm. Her flesh is rigid and far heavier than she looks. Her skin is swollen with water, and I picture flesh and muscle tearing loose as I grab hold and start dragging her into deeper water. Something animalistic takes over, and I don't question it until I'm already committed.

I scramble up the bank and grab a rock. Then another. And another. My body moves on instinct, disturbingly practiced. Covering tracks. Hiding proof. Apparently I'm good at this now.

My hands turn numb and raw, nails packed with mud as I gather stone after stone. When it feels like enough, I wade back in, hauling her farther into the river. My heart slams against my ribs. Icy water creeps through my clothes, seeps into my bones. I keep going anyway, boots slipping, balance wavering.

When I can't go any farther, the body makes a low, awful sound—a wet groan that bubbles to the surface. I yelp and jump back, half-expecting her eyes to fly open. They don't. The sound fades and she stays dead.

With water up to my chin now, I drop the biggest rock onto her chest. It splashes uselessly, sinking her barely an inch. It's not enough. I unload the stones stuffed into my pockets and shirt, cramming them into her waistband, her sleeves, wherever they'll fit. Slowly, grudgingly, she sinks, as if reconsidering.

I agonizingly go back for more again and again. Until finally she disappears beneath the surface. At last she's gone.

I drag myself onto the shore and collapse, lungs burning, muscles quaking. Relief doesn't come because someone will eventually find her. They always do. And when they do, they'll find me next. When that happens, I'll do what I've been doing since I arrived in Doomwood Falls.

I'll vanish. Hopefully not the same way she did.

The river looks calm again. That's the part that gets me, the way it smooths itself out so quickly, like nothing ever happened beneath the surface. Just water gliding past rocks, catching light, whispering over itself. I stand there longer than I should, staring at the place where she sunk and hoping the water won't reject what I've done and spit her back up.

By now the chill has burrowed deep in my bones, a damp ache that won't leave. My sleeves are soaked. My hands are numb, scraped raw, nails rimmed with mud and memory of her dead skin beneath mine that no amount of washing will ever remove. I wipe them uselessly on my jeans anyway, smearing brown streaks across the denim.

The footpath waits, narrow and winding back to my car. The sunlight has shifted and thinned out, turning the forest the color of bruises—purples and yellows. Leaves crunch under my boots, and every sound feels amplified now. A bird takes off, and wind combs through the branches. My own breathing is fast and uneven.

I'm tempted to look back but I don't. I keep moving, forcing one foot in front of the other, following the curve of the trail away from the waterfall. My car feels impossibly far away. The muck thickens as I climb, tugging at my boots with every step. I stumble and catch myself on a tree trunk, the bark roughly scraping my palm.

The clearing where I've parked is in view when I see footprints cut cleanly through the mud just off the trail, darker where water has pooled in the impressions. I stop so fast my stomach lurches. They're not mine from the trek up, because they're heading in the direction of my car ahead of me. Next to the footprints are paw prints from what looks like a large dog.

My pulse roars in my ears as I crouch, hovering over the prints without touching them. They're fresh. The edges haven't softened yet. The mud still holds their shape.

I track them with my eyes. An anxious feeling fills my chest, spreading fast. I straighten slowly, every muscle locked. They're heading into the parking area toward my car. I step forward, then hesitate, scanning the trees one last time. The forest stares back, silent and secretive. Then I follow the footprints until they disappear at my car door.

Chapter 27

Every hour brings a deeper sense of dread as I wait for the police to show up with an arrest warrant.

On the drive home from the woods yesterday, I couldn't take my eyes off the rearview mirror, expecting flashing red and blue lights to appear at every mile until I got home. Later that night I tried to ignore images of handcuffs snapping shut on my wrists by binge-watching every romantic comedy in my Netflix queue. And this morning was no better as I anticipated waking up to SWAT storming my house.

But none of those things happened. Until now. As if summoning them, I'm washing dishes, envisioning the decaying face of the woman in the suds of my dirty dish water, when Mamma calls me to the entryway.

"Shari, make yourself decent—we have guests!"

I'm not going to look decent no matter how much effort I put into it, so I pad into the hallway and collide with Luca, who is blearily wiping his eyes. His shirt is on backwards, and his hair looks like he was electrocuted in his sleep.

I tell myself it might not be me that they're here for. It has been six days since Ivory disappeared, and no one is closer to finding her—or hearing from her—than I was that day she sent me the text and beach picture. I've called and texted her countless times since, but all I've gotten back are crickets.

Maybe the police are just here to check in.

I gravitate toward the living room window, searching for a sign of whose house the cops are heading to this time.

Please be Fred, please be Fred.

It's gray and drizzling outside, the street draped in a ghostly mist. Partially hidden behind a tree is a woman standing at the corner of my yard, soaked under a black trench coat. For a moment it looks like her, the dead woman from the river, her face pale and gaunt. My body startles with a jump. Then I blink, and the face reforms into Zala's. I rub a hand over my eyes trying to calm myself, but I'm not sure seeing Zala there is any better.

"Uh, why are the cops here?" Luca sidles up to me at the window.

I open my mouth to answer, but something outside under the cover of my porch catches my eye. A small grocery bag sits on top of my welcome mat that says *If You Don't Like Dogs, This Is Gonna Be Awkward.*

"Did you order groceries to be delivered?" I turn to Luca.

"No. I've just gotten out of jail with no time to get a job. So I'm broke, remember?" He plucks at his backward shirt. "This is thrift store couture."

"Then what is that?" I point to the gray plastic bag.

He shrugs. "Maybe it's a care package because of your accident."

"Right, a care package arriving at the same time the cops do," I deadpan.

I can't begin to guess what would be inside it. It almost looks like something I'd scoop Zoomie's poop into during a walk. But considering I've received a bloody necklace and a dead body showed up on my last hike, I'm not taking any chances.

The cruiser door out front swings open and a man wearing a familiar leather jacket and jeans steps out. I absolutely cannot let Detective Yankovic—Mr. Human Lie Detector—see that bag. My front door is still broken, but Luca had crookedly installed a makeshift lock until the handyman makes it out here. I fiddle with the lock until it releases, then yank the door open and snatch up the bag.

It's triple knotted, and it appears to be double-bagged. Whatever is inside feels heavy. I clutch the bag to my chest while looking for someplace to hide it. When the doorbell rings, I shove it behind the couch—my emergency hiding place, usually reserved for stranded laundry and junk when an unexpected visitor pops by.

"Shari, aren't you going to open the bag first?" Luca asks.

"No time."

The doorbell chimes again, and barely a second later a knock rattles the front door. It feels urgent.

Luca mouths, *What did you do?*

If only he knew. I square my shoulders, open the door, and step outside. Detective Yankovic stands there, thumbs again hooked in his belt loops, while his gaze cuts through me.

"Ms. Catalano," he announces. "I need to ask you a few questions."

"Absolutely. Anything you need," I casually say in my best innocent law-abiding citizen voice. "Is everything okay?"

He studies me. "I was hoping you could answer that question."

"Is this about Ivory? Do you have an update?"

Detective Yankovic waits on my front porch like he's expecting an invitation inside. He lifts his badge, all official and shiny, as if I haven't already seen it once before.

"No, this isn't about Ivory. I'm here to ask you a few questions about the incident."

"Incident?" That could be any number of things, considering the week I've had since last time we spoke. My bloody necklace someone sent my attorney. The body I found—and submerged—at Doomwood Falls. Take your pick, Detective.

"The hit-and-run that nearly killed you," he elaborates.

Oh yeah, that *incident*.

"Mind if I come inside? I'd like to see if I can get more information about the accident. Hopefully we can figure out who did this to you."

Inside, where he'll pass by my secret room and where that mystery bag is poorly hidden. I'm one wrong move from a complete and devastating downfall.

"Of course," I say, stepping aside and letting him in, because apparently I am constitutionally incapable of telling law enforcement no. He comes in, slowly passes by the bookshelf, and stops to admire my Nancy Drew collection.

"My mom loved these books. Are these original copies?" he probes, reaching to pick one up from the third shelf, which is eye level at his height.

Of course it happens to be the one that will unlock and open the bookshelf door. I reflexively lunge to stop him.

"Yes, they're originals, so I'd appreciate it if you didn't touch them. They're delicate."

He takes the hint and moves along into the living room,

walking the perimeter like he expects bodies to be piled in the corners. There aren't any. As he picks a spot on the sofa, my attention slips toward where the bag is barely hidden. Luca loiters by the entryway and offers the detective a friendly wave before disappearing into the kitchen where someone is hovering just out of sight around the wall, but their shifty shadow gives them away.

"Mamma?" I call out.

She drifts out behind the wall with a warm smile and holding a plate of *pizzelle* cookies.

"I just wanted to offer our kind visitor a homemade Italian cookie." Mamma thrusts the plate at Detective Yankovic, who seems eager to accept several. "And coffee to go with your cookies?" Mamma adds.

With his mouth already full of a bite, Detective Yankovic nods. Crumbs catch in various places down his frizzy beard, which could really use some beard oil. Mamma disappears and returns with a tray of coffee, sugar, and cream, and he helps himself to all three. I really wish my mother wasn't helping an officer of the law get so comfortable and homey while I have an incriminating secret room a mere ten feet away from him.

Detective Yankovic takes up a full two cushions of my couch, so I sit pressed up against the opposite arm away from him, folding my hands neatly to hide the way they tremble as my gaze keeps gravitating toward where the plastic bag looks like it's leaking something onto the floor.

Please let it not be blood.

"Ms. Catalano," he begins. No one calls me that except bill collectors and court officials. "I'd like to know if you remember anything about the vehicle or the driver who hit you."

"No," I admit. "I can't remember anything at all. My brother told me it was a black sedan, but I don't even remember seeing the car."

He studies me. This is the part in movies where the cop leans in and says, *What aren't you telling me?* But he doesn't. He just watches, waiting for me to fill in more blanks, which is worse. Because the truth is I do remember something. Not enough to be helpful. Just enough to ruin my sleep. An object behind the windshield. A face I should know. The feeling of recognition sliding through my brain, chilling me like ice water. But no matter how hard I try to pull it up, nothing. It's just a blank space as wide as the curb I stepped off.

A familiar car. A familiar driver. A familiar terror. But I can't access any of it. Every time I try, my mind clamps shut like a steel trap, and the memory slinks away.

"Do you recall what you were doing when you got hit by the car?" Detective Yankovic asks, flipping open his notebook.

I smile. Or maybe I grimace. It's hard to know. "I do remember looking in my purse for my phone."

Detective Yankovic scribbles something down. I wonder if he wrote *suspicious* or *subject sweating excessively* or *liar liar pants on fire*.

Yankovic clears his throat. "Witnesses say the driver didn't even tap the brakes."

"I guess the driver really hated me."

"They were trying to kill you, Ms. Catalano. Do you have any enemies?"

Does most of my neighborhood count? "Not that I'm aware of."

"I just want to understand what happened," he says softly,

"and why you were targeted."

"So do I. But I can't remember anything after stepping off that curb."

And that part is true. Then I realize the truth is one thing I still have. My laptop remains humming on the coffee table where I last left it, the pen drive my attorney gave me jutting out from the side. It's time to show someone this information who can actually help me.

"Can I show you something, Detective?"

Chapter 28

The living room feels smaller with Detective Yankovic in it. At well over six feet tall, he's perched on the edge of my sofa, his long legs awkwardly angled to avoid hitting the coffee table with his notebook balanced on his knee. The light slants through the blinds, striping the wall and catching on dust I haven't had a chance to clean. Okay, that's not true. Since most of my clients have cancelled their lessons I have plenty of time, just not the motivation.

My couch smells faintly of Zoomie mixed with Stew's cologne, which I dab on myself when I'm feeling especially lonely. Since Ivory's disappearance I've gone through almost a quarter of the bottle. A throw blanket with a huge photo of Me, Stew, and Zoomie is folded neatly over the arm.

"I need to explain some things," I tell the detective, rubbing my damp palms on my jeans, "before I show you this."

Yankovic's gaze lifts from the notebook. He's patient in a way that isn't comforting. "You've already shown me a lot, Ms. Catalano."

"I know. But this is different."

I cross the room and grab my laptop. The pen drive is still plugged into the side of it, a little black rectangle jutting out. My attorney's warning echoes in my head, to only share this if I had to, and only with someone I trust. I'm not sure Yankovic qualifies, but I'm desperate and it's too late to stop now anyway.

Sitting beside him, I flip the laptop open. The fan whirs to life while I debate just how much to tell the detective, and where to begin. I have no idea what detail he'll latch on to, or what he'll do with it. I won't be shocked if he digs into my past to verify what I'm about to tell him, but I cannot let him dig into my present to find out what I'm hiding.

"These files came from my attorney. He hired a private investigator to look into a man named Ramsey Shenk and his girlfriend Gillian."

Yankovic doesn't interrupt as I click on the folder icon. Several images pop onto the screen. A woman with white-blonde hair and sharp cheekbones stares off-camera. In the first photo she's stepping out of a grocery store, keys in hand. In another, she's sitting at an outdoor café, sunglasses pushed into her hair. In all of them she looks unaware of being watched and completely unbothered by what her boyfriend did to my life.

"The woman in these pictures is Gillian," I clarify. "Ramsey Shenk's significant other."

"Ramsey Shenk… Why do I know that name?" Detective Yankovic asks.

"He was the owner of *In the Margins Media* and drowned in a boat fire last year."

"Oh, I recall seeing that on the news. They never found his body, right? He seemed like a shady guy."

"Shady is an understatement." I click through more photos. Different angles on different days, all of them capturing the same woman.

"What does any of this have to do with your hit-and-run?" the detective asks.

"Here's where it gets a little complicated. Four years ago

my husband found evidence of Ramsey stealing money from his company. When my husband was about to go public with it, Ramsey murdered him and made it look like a hunting accident. But when he found out I had evidence that could convict him of murder, he framed me for the larceny. Everyone bought it, and I even did jail time for a crime I didn't commit."

"Do you have any evidence to prove what you're saying?"

"Well," I lengthen the word to buy myself time to explain, "my husband put the embezzlement evidence in a safe deposit box, but the key to it was stolen along with an SD card that had trail cam footage showing Ramsey Shenk committing murder."

The process of getting a duplicate safe deposit key ended up becoming much more difficult than I anticipated when the original owner is dead. Since Stewart Dobson's name is the registered owner, the bank gave me a dozen hoops to jump through just to get a new key. Getting the certified death certificate along with a court-ordered probate takes time that I don't have, because whoever has the key could already be figuring out a way to get access before I can. Especially if that someone has access to Ramsey's money and network. Someone like Gillian.

"So that's a no. You can't prove this story you're telling me," he concludes.

"What Ramsey did to my family isn't what I want to show you. It's what his girlfriend Gillian is currently doing that's relevant. When Ramsey died in the boat fire last year, the world thought it was the end of him."

I glance up at him. He's watching me closely, like I'm sharing state secrets.

"But your attorney apparently didn't," Yankovic concludes

for me.

"Right. Because there was no body and no credible witness to his death," I explain. "Anyway, my attorney hired a PI to follow Gillian when she drained her bank account and suddenly showed up in Doomwood Falls." I gesture vaguely at the window and the town beyond it.

"What's the logic for why she would come here?" he asks.

"I think it's twofold. First, my attorney thinks Ramsey's still alive and hiding out somewhere. And I think Gillian is here to get the evidence I have—*had*—against Ramsey that proves he murdered my husband. If Ramsey's going to make a miraculous comeback, he needs a clean slate. And the best way to get a clean slate is to get rid of me."

"You think Gillian came to Doomwood Falls to kill you."

"I wouldn't put anything past that family," I answer.

"Is that why you came here to Doomwood Falls—to disappear?" he asks me.

I shrug. "Yeah, to start over. This town was supposed to be my phoenix moment. Rising from the ashes of losing my husband. Or so I thought."

The truth is that Doomwood Falls is a lot more than my phoenix moment. This small river-adjacent town nestled in the foothills of the mountains is also my chance for revenge.

"There's one more thing I need to show you."

I get up from the sofa and detour to the dining room where several photos are splayed across the table. Most are extra copies I had re-developed from the negatives I had taken. I pick up two pictures and bring them to Detective Yankovic, then hand them to him. The top photo is of the clothing at the waterfall.

Pointing at the water's reflection of the letter *Z* stitched onto the neon sweatshirt, I say, "This is who I think might be behind the hit-and-run."

"I don't understand. What does this shirt have to do with anything?"

"This might help clear it up."

I flip to the next picture. This photo was taken during a group photography class when we were working on individual portraits, and the woman smiling at the camera is Zala. She has the same platinum hair as the woman in the private investigator's candid photos. Same cheekbone structure. The striking resemblance can't be coincidence.

"This is one of my students," I say. "Zala, spelled with a Z. But I don't remember her last name. It was… exotic. Hard to pronounce. And she doesn't list it on Facebook. But look at her—the hair, the cheekbones, the eye shape. I think Zala is Gillian."

I angle the screen toward him, then position the images side by side. Gillian. Zala. Gillian. Zala.

Yankovic frowns. "Coincidence," he says immediately.

"No," I insist, "this looks like the same woman. Gillian is here in Doomwood Falls, and she's hiding behind a different name and living on my street. It's the perfect way to get close enough to me to carry out everything that's happened. I've been stalked, threatened, had a break-in, stolen from, and hit with a car! The person behind it is close to enough to watch my every move. It has to be her!"

The room feels too quiet after that. Yankovic straightens and his face hardens, all patience evaporating at once.

"That's enough." His tone has sharpened. "You're making

crazy assumptions that bare no truth, Ms. Catalano."

I blink. "What?"

"That *Z* is a reflection off the water, which means it's actually a backwards *S*, not a *Z*."

I hadn't considered that before now, but Zala's last name could very well start with an S. I have no idea, but it doesn't mean it's not her. The resemblance alone is enough…

"So you're saying these two women don't look alike?"

His jaw twitches. "From this grainy photo that PI took, sure, they appear to share features, but lots of people do. People constantly mistake me for Jason Momoa, but that doesn't make us twins."

My eyebrow involuntarily bolts up. Detective Yankovic looks as similar to the Aquaman actor as I do Margot Robbie.

"This is more than sharing features. They're, like, doppelgangers."

"You need to stop this," he barks. "You are spiraling and accusing innocent people without any proof."

"Gillian is not innocent—"

"But Zala is!" he cuts in. "And you're crossing a line. Zala is not Gillian. She's not terrorizing you. And you need to stop playing detective before you ruin someone's life. Or your own."

Heat floods my chest. "You're not listening to me."

"I am listening, but I've heard enough." He rises to his feet so abruptly that the sofa legs scrape against the floor. "And I'm telling you to back off. If you don't stop right now, I'll throw you in jail myself for obstruction of justice!"

He leaves, and the moment the door slams shut, I break down and cry. I fall into the sofa and rest my head on a throw pillow, letting out a long, shaky sob. Then I wrap myself in the blanket with Stew's picture next to my heart, while wiping my tears with Zoomie's face. Maybe this is the end of it.

My phone buzzes next to the laptop where Gillian's face still fills the screen. My auto-response to any communication is panic, but I try to convince myself it's probably a spam text. Or one of those cheerful alerts from my bank informing me that my balance is low, as if I don't already know. I pick up my phone and see a text bubble from an unknown number.

And the message is only four words and a link.

Chapter 29

I know you're involved.

Normally I would never click a link from someone I don't know, but this time I have no choice. The moment I tap the screen, a website pops open and my throat constricts as the page loads, the spinning circle taunting me. An article from the Doomwood Falls Daily materializes.

The headline in fat, bold letters lets me know I'm absolutely not sleeping tonight:

BODY RECOVERED AT DOOMWOOD FALLS — FOUL PLAY SUSPECTED

Below those words a video auto-plays of police at the base of the waterfall. Yellow caution tape flutters in the foreground as a reporter talks into a microphone, gesturing back at the waterfall behind her. Flashlights cut through the inky background, which means the body must have been found last night.

Detective Yankovic would have asked me about it if I was a suspect, which he didn't. Yet.

The anchor's voice gives way to rushing water. The camera wobbles and then steadies, focusing on the falls in the background as white water tears itself apart over gray rock. The reporter steps back into frame, her jacket zipped up to her chin and makeup impossibly perfect for the late hour.

"Good evening," she says, solemn as a church bell. "Authorities confirmed this evening that the body of an adult woman was recovered earlier today from Doomwood Falls. Police have identified the victim's identity as Janet Vick."

The name Janet Vick sounds familiar, but I can't place where or why. This woman is obviously connected to me, since her killer put Ivory's necklace on her. Or maybe her death has nothing to do with me and I stupidly bumbled my way into it anyway. I lean closer, the proximity to my phone sharpening the reality of this. The camera pans to the falls again and the spray catches the floodlights.

"We're here at the river where she was found speaking with a witness," the reporter continues, turning to a man standing just off-frame. Only part of him is visible with a baseball cap pulled low and red curls poking out from the brim. His hands are jammed into the pockets of a flannel jacket.

"Sir, can you tell us how you came across the body this evening?" the reporter asks matter-of-factly.

The man shifts his weight. He doesn't look at the camera but stares somewhere over the reporter's shoulder. "I was hiking and noticed something down by the rocks. Near the base of the falls. At first I thought it was trash. You know, a jacket or a bag. Stuff washes up there."

My thumb hovers over the volume button. I turn it up.

"What made you realize it wasn't?" The reporter verbally nudges him for more delicious details to feed the masses.

He clears his throat. "The color. And, uh, the way it didn't move right. With the water. So I went closer. I shouldn't have, probably." He laughs once. "That's when I saw hair."

"Did you touch anything?"

"No," he says quickly. "No. I backed up and called 9-1-1 and waited for the EMTs to show up." He rubs his hands together, like he can scrub the memory off. "I didn't see… I mean, I didn't see any injuries. I wasn't looking for that."

The reporter nods respectfully. "Police have indicated the death is being investigated as suspicious," she says, turning back to the camera. "If anyone has information—"

I mute it. The sound of the falls drops out, replaced by the hum of my refrigerator and my own breathing. Suspicious is just a placeholder for a deeper investigation that I fear will lead to me. The man shifts closer to the reporter, his face finally turning to the camera, and I scream.

"What the fu—!"

"Gianna Shari Catalano!" Mamma rebukes me from the kitchen doorway. "No cussing!" I wonder how much she's heard so far today.

"What's going on?" Luca chimes in, because there is no privacy in my home anymore. He's scooping mouthfuls of cereal from a bowl and I realize it's been days since I've eaten anything of substance.

I slam my phone screen-down onto the table and think I hear a crack. "Nothing is going on."

Mamma raises an eyebrow. "It sure doesn't sound like nothing."

"Can you please just give me space?" I wave a hand to dismiss them both.

I can't let them find out about what happened at the waterfall. Mamma would order me to go to the police, and I don't trust my brother not to hold it over me how stupid I am for putting my DNA all over a murder victim.

Luca obliges and wanders upstairs slurping milk from his cereal bowl, but Mamma is more stubborn than me, Luca, and Zoomie combined. "I'm not giving you space until you tell me what's going on. Are you in some kind of trouble?"

It occurs to me that if my DNA does turn up on Janet Vick's body, I need to get ahead of it. Maybe telling Mamma is the only way out. With all of the secrets I've been hiding for so long, this is one I can't keep in anymore.

"Yes, if you count falling behind on bills, losing my business, and a becoming the suspect in a murder investigation. You know, the usual trouble."

The gap of skin between her gray eyebrows furrows. "What are you talking about?"

I suddenly rethink telling her. I don't want to drag my mother into the hole I keep digging deeper and deeper. There's no point burying us both. "Don't worry about it."

I snatch the phone up and hold it out of her sight, which of course she finds suspicious. But she keeps staring at me, as mothers seem to have that sixth sense when their children are in distress. During my teen rebellion years she put this unnerving skill to use, looking at me until my secrets spilled out on their own. I grip the phone tighter so it doesn't leap from my hand and confess.

"Why did you just say murder investigation?" she asks quietly. "Did you hear something about Ivory?"

"No, it's not about her."

"Then what, Shari? I'm your mother. You can trust me."

She's right, I can. And Luca too, who proved himself

trustworthy to the point of doing something highly illegal for me right after I got out of prison. Although we never spoke of it after that day, he proved himself more than just a brother. He became my confidante.

"I'm afraid you're going to never speak to me again once I tell you, Mamma, like how you stopped talking to me after my embezzlement conviction."

My mother pulls me into a hug, and her chest heaves. Her tears mix with mine as she apologizes over and over. "I'm so sorry, bambina. That was cruel of me. Please forgive me."

The truth pulses in my mind, a flashing warning sign that I can't die with this secret. I can't be the only one who knows that I sank Janet Vick's body under the water. Did I kill her? No, of course not. I never saw the woman in my life. But my hands were all over her. I swallow, and it tastes like guilt.

"There's something I need to tell you. But I don't want you to say anything until I'm finished."

"I promise I won't," she says, drawing an invisible cross over herself from her forehead to her chin, then from shoulder to shoulder.

"Last night a woman's body was found—it wasn't Ivory— but I may have accidentally left my DNA on her after she was already dead and covered up the murder."

Mamma doesn't reply for a moment. I can't tell if she understands what I'm saying at first, until she yells, "What in the heavens, Shari? Even your brother wouldn't do something so… irresponsible!"

Irresponsible is Mamma's version of a cuss word, and apparently I'm officially worse than Luca, who sets the bar pretty low. She sucks in a calming breath, sits down on the sofa, and pats the cushion next to me. "Sit, dear."

I obey.

"Let's figure it out together. First, did you know the woman?"

I shake my head. "No, I have no clue who she is." But I do have an idea of how she might be connected to everything, and it could be why she's dead.

"You're going to need to explain the whole DNA situation to me. Why on earth were you anywhere near a dead woman?"

"I saw Ivory's necklace on her and thought it was her. By the time I realized it wasn't Ivory, I had already removed the necklace. I was trying to protect my friend, because if the police saw her necklace on that dead woman, they would have blamed her for the murder."

Mamma stands up and heads to the kitchen. I follow her, already predicting exactly where she's going. "We need biscotti for this conversation." She hands me a cookie and I nibble a bite. I'm not hungry, but something about food is comforting.

"Anyway, I think she was Fred's mistress. And I bet he killed her and planted Ivory's necklace on her to frame Ivory so that the cops will think she murdered the mistress and ran."

"So a little of your DNA may or may not be on her body. There's no motive for you to kill her, right?"

"It gets worse, Mamma. Someone saw me tampering with the body, and this person is dead set on destroying my life…"

I turn my phone screen toward Mamma, replaying the news video for her. At the end of it, the interviewee turns to the screen and it's Macho Marshall.

Chapter 30

I replay the news interview video for my mother, and the moment Marshall's face emerges near the end, my entire nervous system feels like it's shutting down, followed by explosive anger. Marshall converses with the reporter wearing an expression of saintly concern, like he didn't spend the better part of the last two weeks singlehandedly destroying my business and my life.

Mamma fills a plate with two more biscotti and a mug with freshly brewed coffee and hands both to me. This is her way of saying it's going to be a long night.

She taps her fingernail on Marshall's face and frowns. "Is that the young man who assaulted your brother?"

Apparently Luca made up his own version of the events, but I nod anyway. "Yeah, that's him."

"So he's back in our lives again, huh?"

Again. As if Marshall is a recurring sinus infection instead of the man I am ninety-nine percent sure has been torturing me. Police always talk about motive, and Marshall has plenty: First my rejection, which spurred his retaliation by posting the cruel review. Then Luca kicking his ass added fuel to the vindictive fire. But he's taken it way too far. It's time to put a stop to this.

"What was he doing at the waterfall in the first place?" Mamma asks.

My skin prickles. "Stalking me, I guess. I was there right before he *happened* to find the dead woman."

"Any idea who she is?" she asks at the same time I'm thinking it.

After double-checking the woman's name on the news video, I open up another web browser and start typing into my search engine:

Janet Vick, Doomwood Falls

A dozen search results fill up the screen, along with photos of various Janet Vicks. But only one link associates her with Doomwood Falls, along with a picture of her when she was alive and smiling. She's standing in front of an office building with a dog at her hip. The dog in particular leaves me with an odd sense of familiarity—it's a Bernese mountain dog.

I follow that link, and the headline tells me everything I need to know:

JANET VICK, PRIVATE INVESTIGATOR, FOUND DEAD

Our mystery woman isn't Fred's mistress but a full-on, licensed, business-card-carrying private investigator. Mamma's eyebrows shoot up her forehead. My laptop with my attorney's pen drive is still open, and I navigate back to the main folder name: *Vick*

"She wasn't Fred's mistress," I deduce slowly. "She was the private investigator my attorney hired to look into Gillian."

In addition to the dog, there is something strangely familiar about Janet Vick, like I've seen her before. I can't quite pull up her face, but my memory is stuck on her dark hair and I have no idea why.

"I feel like I know her," Mamma murmurs.

"Me too…"

We stare at each other until it clicks. At the exact same time.

"She was at the hit-and-run accident," Mamma says right before I say, "With Fred!"

By now I've eaten three biscotti and drank two cups of coffee. It's the most calories I've consumed in days, and the sugar rush coupled with caffeine are doing wonders for my energy.

"But why would an investigator hired to look into Gillian be talking to Fred? There is no connection between the two that I'm aware of."

"Unless you're right that Zala is Gillian," Mamma suggests, "in which case the private investigator might have wanted to talk to Fred since he lives next door to her."

I turn on my mother, because I haven't told anyone about my suspicion over the connection between Zala and Gillian—that I believe they are one and the same. "Were you eavesdropping on my conversation with Detective Yankovic?"

"The walls are thin!" she defends herself, her arms lifting in a full-body shrug. "It's kind of hard to ignore a police officer interrogating my daughter in the living room."

I'm trying to put all of the various events in some kind of logical order, like a mental conspiracy board with the red yarn linking private investigator Janet Vick to Gillian to Zala to Fred to Ivory to Marshall to me. My brain hurts just imagining the convoluted knotted mess.

While Marshall is the one who found Janet Vick's body, do I think he is capable of killing her? I don't know him well enough to peg him as a killer, and there's no motive that I know of. That leaves me with Fred next in line as the murderer, since I saw Janet Vick speaking with him out on the sidewalk in town when I got hit by the car. And I'm pretty sure Janet was who Ivory saw when we were at the coffee shop, because I'd recognize a Bernese mountain dog anywhere. It seems Janet was making the rounds and it got her killed.

Mamma adds a fourth cookie to my plate, and even though I know I shouldn't, I take a bite. So who murdered Janet? And why? What did she undercover that was worth killing her over? Whoever murdered her would be the person with the most to lose. I think I know who it is, and the knowledge makes my stomach twist.

"Fred killed Janet," I blurt. "He's the most logical suspect because they were seen together at least twice."

"What's the motive?" Mamma asks grimly.

"Well, Janet was tailing Gillian before Ivory disappeared. I'm sure Gillian was here on Hemlock Drive watching me. It wouldn't be unrealistic for her to see what the other neighbors are up to. Maybe she caught Fred cheating during her reconnaissance and threatened to tell Ivory. Then he wanted her quiet. Permanently."

My theory still feels like it's missing something big. It wasn't part of Janet's job to investigate Fred. He has no connection to Ramsey or Gillian. There's a hole in my puzzle, and no piece seems to fit quite right. Then something even worse than Ivory's disappearance and Janet's death occurs to me.

"Oh no…" The words fall out before I can stop them. "What if—what if Fred killed both Ivory *and* Janet Vick?"

Mamma stiffens. "Honey, that's unlikely to be the case—"

"No, listen." I can already picture the events, a deadly domino effect. "Fred cheats on Ivory, and when Ivory finds out," and I don't mention that it's all my fault she found out, "he kills her in a heated argument. Then while Janet investigates Gillian—or Zala—while visiting our quiet little street, she witnesses the murder and confronts Fred. Maybe she wants paid to be quiet. Or maybe she cares about justice. Either way, the cheating bastard kills the PI to cover up his first murder. Then to cover up his second murder he plants Ivory's necklace on her to make it look like Ivory did it." I finally take a breath, and I almost think I've solved the case. "What do you think—am I brilliant or am I crazy?"

Mamma chuckles, and any excitement I had wheezes out of me like a deflated balloon.

"You're probably a little of each," she answers. "But if what you speculate is true…" she gulps audibly and her voice trembles, "and Fred killed more than one woman…"

She pauses, and I fill in the gaping hush. "We have a serial killer living across the street."

I head toward the window. The blinds are half-open, slanted so anyone can peer inside if they want to. I step so close I can feel the cold outside air penetrating the glass as I nudge a larger gap between the slats.

Fred's house sits directly opposite mine. And behind his living room window—and I know this because our floor plans are almost identical and I've spent countless hours sitting in the very spot I'm looking at—Fred stands completely still, watching me. His face is blank, and his eyes are locked directly on mine.

I yelp and flick my blinds shut, jumping back from the window. Fred doesn't look surprised. He looks like he's been waiting for me. And the creepiest part? He doesn't look away.

Chapter 31

It's a solid ten minutes before my pulse returns to normal, but Mamma ruins that short reprieve as she turns on the television, picking a docuseries featuring a police hunt for a notorious serial killer. I can't help but keep glancing at the street beyond the safety of my walls where my very own neighborhood serial killer lives.

"Solve the murder yet?" Luca jokes as he tromps casually down the stairs.

Mamma glares with a look that tells him this is no laughing matter, but Luca is immune to Mamma's opinion by now.

"I'm going to cook a meal. Something hearty. We can't figure this out on an empty stomach." Mamma returns to the kitchen and makes a point of clattering pans and dishes.

Luca wanders into the living room, loitering near the edge of the sofa with his gaze glazed over watching the TV show. He picks up the bag I had hidden behind the sofa and forgot about.

"You ever going to open this?"

My hands feel clammy. "I'm not sure I want to."

"Oh, stop being scared. I'll open it for you," he offers, curiosity scribbled all over his face. "It's probably a grocery delivery."

Except that there is no receipt pinned to this bag. And it was dropped off right before Detective Yankovic arrived this morning. It's pretty convenient if Fred only had to walk across the street to drop it off.

"Wait!" I dart forward, snatching it out of Luca's hands before he rips it open and destroys any fingerprints. Just in case it's something I feel safe turning over to the police.

"Just open it already."

I untie the first bag's knot. The bag flaps open, revealing one more inside. I unknot that one next and reach in. Something wet sloshes inside. A piece of bloody flesh? I pull my shirt sleeves down over my hands and slowly pull the object out, careful to keep my skin from touching it. When I realize what it is, I instantly feel nauseous. An organ would have been better than this.

"What is it?" Luca asks.

It's the shirt Janet Vick was wearing when I found her in the water. But dead women can't package and drop off their clothes from the grave. I hold it up with my sleeve-covered hands, inspecting it to see if there's a message somewhere among the folds of wet fabric.

"What are those stains?"

Stains is too domestic of a word to describe what's covering the front of the shirt. It's soaked with mud and blood. Pinned to the collar is a note on a slip of paper that is halfway disintegrated from the bloody river water. It's a single line printed in a blocky font and all caps:

YOU MISSED SOMETHING.

My heart stops, flips, then swan-dives into panic.

Luca takes the shirt from me, rubbing all kinds of his skin cells on it while examining it. "Interesting."

"Don't touch it!" I scream. "You're going to mess up the DNA evidence or whatever."

He scoffs at me. "Uh, I'm pretty sure that ship has sailed, sis. There's no way your DNA isn't already all over this… and I'm sure whoever sent this knows that."

My brain tries to generate answers like a dying printer spitting ink blobs. Fred, or Marshall? Or are they working together? They are close friends, after all.

"Shari, what are you going to do?"

I wish my brother would stop staring at me like I'm already booked for a life sentence. I stare at the shirt, at the note, at the evidence someone holds over me.

"I, I don't know," I manage to say.

"You can't turn this in to the police," he reminds me, as if I don't already know this.

"Then what the heck am I supposed to do with it?"

My skin feels icky and wet, crawling with the sensation like I'm wearing the soaked blood-stained shirt myself. I storm through the kitchen toward the bathroom, because my bladder is about to explode from all the coffee, and I might possibly throw up while I'm at it.

Mamma hovers behind me, holding a plate full of spaghetti carbonara out toward me. "Eat. Then after you've got a full stomach, let's tell Detective Yankovic everything, including how you sunk the body. If you explain it all, the worst you'd get charged with is tampering with evidence, which is a lot better than first-degree murder."

What my mother is suggesting has to be a joke. "I was innocent last time and ended up in jail. Unless you've forgotten? Or do you think I was guilty…"

"You're acting like you killed someone! And we both know you didn't, Shari."

I stiffen and Mamma notices.

"Oh, Shari," she whispers. "You didn't, did you?"

"Of course not," I hiss.

But there's something my mother doesn't know about me, and if she found out, well, she'd think I'm capable of anything. Even murder.

Chapter 32

By the time the handyman finishes fixing the door frame, adding a multi-point locking system, and installing a door cam—one can never be too secure—darkness has settled in for an early night. My porch feels like the opening scene of a true-crime reenactment, minus the dramatic foreboding music. He wipes his hands on his cargo pants and steps back, admiring his work like he just performed heart surgery instead of sticking a camera above my door.

"There," he declares proudly. "All installed."

His voice is too chipper for the hour. Or for anyone working customer service past eight o'clock at night.

"Thanks," I say, hugging my arms to my chest. The evening air bites harder than usual as Doomwood Falls is heading deeper into autumn.

The handyman doesn't leave. Instead, he lingers on the porch, his eyes darting over my house the way someone looks for security before robbing a store blind. "Quiet neighborhood," he comments.

"That's what the brochure said," I reply.

There's another awkward pause. He shifts his weight and his boots squeak. And then casually he asks, "So, have you heard anything new about that Ivory Cobb disappearance? She lived across the street, didn't she?"

How does he know that I know Ivory? Or that I know anything about her disappearance?

I force my expression into something neutral, probably failing miserably. "Why would I know anything about that?"

"Small town. People talk." But his eyes stay locked on mine, which makes me squirm.

"Oh, well, I don't know anything that the news hasn't already told us."

"Huh, is that so?" He backs away finally, giving me a little two-finger salute. "Well, you take care. Keep an eye on that feed. You never know who's out there."

Oh great. I love when random handymen drop vague horror movie warnings before sprinting off into the night. Nothing says *sleep well* like a stranger implying I'm being watched. The minute his work van disappears down the road, I hurry inside.

Luca's sprawled on my couch, one sock on, one sock halfway through losing a fight with gravity. The TV casts a bluish glow over the room as he absently watches some action movie. Guns. Explosions. Men screaming. Typical soothing background noise.

I flop down beside him, opening the door cam app to get familiar with the settings.

"You get it working?" Luca asks without looking away from the TV.

"Yeah. But the guy who installed it was weird."

"Everyone's weird. Especially around here. I swear something's off about this neighborhood. Can't trust anyone."

I let out a nervous laugh. "Says the man who's done jail time for robbing his own roommate."

Luca doesn't smile. That's when I know he's about to say

something sobering.

"Seriously, Shari. I think it's time to move on."

"Again? I'm tired of running. There's a point when my parole officer is going to start asking questions or telling me no. Besides, soon there will be nowhere left to go."

"Running is better than dead."

The video feed refreshes on my phone. That's odd. The handyman's van is parked out front, and I watch the image on my screen with an unsettling sensation… not fear, but dread. I watched him leave, so why is he back? There's no movement in his van's interior, no human shape at the steering wheel. In fact, there's no sign of him at all.

"Where the heck are you?" I mutter to myself, and Luca glances at me like chatting with my phone is something I do all the time. Though with people dating their AI these days, maybe I'm not as crazy as I think.

The curve of a head draws my attention to the corner of the video, where the handyman comes into view. He's lingering somewhere near my windows, most of his body out of sight, but I catch the occasional glimpse of a body part moving in and out of the screen. When he does come fully into the door cam's view, he's holding something up, aiming it at the house.

Is he *video recording* my home? I tap the image to enlarge it, and sure enough, he is! Behind him the street is an eerie, foggy dark, and the streetlamp smears him with pale, spectral light. Luca leans over my shoulder, watching this unfold.

"Why is he just standing there?" Luca growls.

It's a terrible new normal I'll have to get used to. I did it once before, I can do it again. I'm reminded of the news crews scrambling for an interview when I was dealing with the embezzlement trial. People love a good show, and suddenly I'm once again in the spotlight.

"He'll go away soon, once he gets his footage," I try to convince myself. I mean, he can't stand out in our yard all night.

"Like hell he will!" Luca jumps up from the sofa, readjusts his fallen sock, and storms to the front door.

"Please don't engage!" I beg, dreading the price tag of another bail bond to get my brother out of jail for assault a second time this week. "You will only make it worse."

My pulse trip-hammers in my neck as the anxiety of more chaos rushes through me. I can't handle anything more.

Luca swings open the door to yell at the handyman a moment too late. The guy is already traipsing across the lawn toward Fred's house now, probably hoping to use this in his next podcast, because even handymen probably have podcasts. I can already envision this week's topic:

Serial Killers Hate This One Upgrade (Handymen don't catch killers, we disappoint them)

From my screen I watch him stand in front of Fred's house for a minute doing exactly the same thing, videotaping whatever boring footage he thinks viewers will want to see. Fred isn't quite as accommodating as I am. He almost immediately confronts him, which means he's one step ahead and probably already has a door cam. The handyman wisely dashes off, and I'm relieved when his van turns the corner and doesn't U-turn to come back.

But Fred is still standing there as if inspecting his property. All I can think is that he's taken lives—first Ivory, then Janet.

Two women, two disappearances. Two unsolved cases. And Fred, somehow, is still living his normal life across the street with his daughter like his senior superlative isn't Most Likely to Have a Body in His Freezer.

And then there's the mistress—the mysterious unknown woman no one's been able to identify. The one who might be missing. Or dead.

Then something unthinkable occurs to me. I haven't seen Freida since the day I confronted Fred.

"Luca," I block the television with my body to demand his undivided attention, "have you seen Freida lately?"

He barely glances up at me. "No, I tried calling but she won't answer. All she did was send me a text that she needs space. You know, because of her mom."

"So you haven't spoken to her or seen her in person?"

Luca shuts off the television. "What are you trying to say, Shari? Spit it out."

"I haven't seen Freida, and neither have you—her boyfriend. Do you think Fred would do something to her?"

Luca's eyes widen with horror, and I can read his thoughts because they're the same as mine: There's nothing a serial killer wouldn't do.

Chapter 33

I'm wearing all black in order to blend in better with the night. Zala's house sits next door to Fred and Ivory's, so it only takes me a couple minutes to reach the curb hugging her yard, although it feels as long as a Death Row walk. The sky is a black velvet sheet suffocating the stars. Her porch light glows like a single interrogating eye.

When I reach her mailbox, I check for obvious signs of someone tracking me—the crunch of frosted grass beneath feet, puffs of cloudy breath rising in the frigid air—but it's hard to carve out people lurking in the shadows when it's this dark out.

The mailbox door opens with a metallic *pop*, and I slide my arm in, reaching from corner to corner hoping to touch paper. Anything with Zala's name will do. But it's empty, and now I face another decision. I need to get inside her house.

Squaring my shoulders, I remind myself that this is a casual, sociable visit. Zala—or Gillian, or whoever she is—won't murder me in her home. That would arouse way too much suspicion and make a heck of a mess to clean up. So I choose to present this as a totally normal visit between friends with a shared concern over their murderous neighbor. Just two women chatting about a missing woman and a homicide. If I'm lucky, I'll figure out Zala's real name and if she has any connection to it. Hallmark material, really.

In one hand—my injured left one—I clutch a pocketknife tucked into my coat pocket. While I don't think Zala would overpower me or risk killing me, I can't take any chances.

With my free hand I knock. Beyond her closed door I hear faint mumbling, and a minute later Zala opens the door wearing massive fluffy slippers and a robe so thick she could survive in the Arctic. Her expression is cautious, like she's expecting a salesman or a cult recruiter, which makes sense considering the late hour. My palm reassuringly grasps the cool metal of the hidden knife.

"Oh, it's you, Shari." Her voice is flat, and she scans the street, then lifts her gaze to the night sky. "It's awfully late. Did we have plans?"

"Not exactly. I've just been worried that the police haven't updated the media with anything new about Ivory. I was hoping maybe you heard something and we could talk. As friends."

She looks skeptical as she hesitates but then steps aside. "Sure. Come in."

Her living room is tidy in that *don't touch anything* way. I search for a sign of where she might keep a piece of mail, a magazine, anything with her full name on it, but this woman's house looks as sterile and impersonal as a model house.

She gestures to the couch but doesn't sit herself, which is an effective way to make a guest feel like a defendant. There is no offer of tea or coffee or a refreshment of any kind, which is fine by me. I'd be cautious of consuming anything Zala offered me.

"It's been crazy what's going on in Doomwood Falls," she comments, breaking the ice. "First Ivory going missing, and then a woman's body found at the waterfall. It's a little terrifying, if you think about it, our small town so plagued with murder."

"Speaking of Ivory," I clear my throat, "have you heard anything new about her case?"

Her arms fold tightly across her chest. "Why?"

"Because it doesn't seem like the police are doing anything to search for her. They supposedly tracked her cell phone's last location to some beach resort, but that was a week ago and no one's laid eyes on her since she went missing. I'm starting to worry that she might not be missing but is…"

"Dead?" Zala finishes for me because I can't utter that awful, horrible, definitive word. "You and everyone else in the neighborhood are thinking the same thing."

We're both quiet for a moment, so I take the opportunity to peruse the space. I spot a magazine across the living room on a table next to a plush armchair. I'm mulling over the most inconspicuous way to go over there when I almost forget the other reason I came here, which is to ask, "Have you happened to see Freida in the past week?"

Zala thinks for a moment, or at least she pretends to. "No, I can't say I have."

"I'm worried about her. No one has seen her for days."

"Her mother is missing. She's probably afraid to leave her house," Zala suggests, and it actually does make sense.

"Do you think we should go check on her to make sure she's okay?"

"I wouldn't worry too much." She waves me off. "Kids are more resilient than you think, especially a girl like Freida. She's as tough as nails. I'm more concerned about the dead woman they found in Doomwood Falls. And that unusual detail about that case. So odd."

"What unusual detail?"

I don't recall reading anything that stuck out to me as odd. Unless you count the fact that a woman was murdered in a town that ranked as one of America's Top Ten Safest Place to Live list. Two women gone in a week is pretty unusual for a town with a zero percent homicide rate.

She continues, almost carelessly, "Didn't you hear? The poor woman was found without a shirt on! How mortifying!"

That detail wasn't made public. I would know, because I researched the heck out of the case after I opened up that bag with my wet shirt souvenir. I checked every source to make sure my name wasn't attached in any way. Then I double-checked. No article, no rumor mill, no neighbor gossip ever mentioned anything about Janet Vick being shirtless when Marshall found her.

Only one person—the person who sent me the shirt—could have known that detail. Did Zala send it to me? I reach into my pocket and feel the edge of the blade folded into its metal vessel. My fingertip traces the indentation in the handle, ready to pry it open if needed.

"Where did you hear that?" I ask.

Zala's eyes snap to mine, confused. "Hear what?"

I unfold the blade.

"How do you know she was missing her shirt? Nothing in the news mentioned that." I'm not going to let this go without an answer, and if she goes on the offensive, I'm prepared to fight back. "Who told you that?"

Realization of her mistake distorts her expression from a kindly grin to an annoyed frown. "I don't recall where I heard it."

Her slippers swish against the carpet as Zala steps to the side of the sofa where I'm sitting and she sighs loudly, mentioning something about the late hour. When I don't instantly rise to my feet, she gestures to the door.

"I hate to be rude, Shari, but I was in the middle of getting ready for bed. It's late and time for you to go."

I'm running out of time and conversation, which means my window to discovering a clue to Zala's real identity is narrowing. If only I could get a look at that magazine, or access an office or desk of some kind. I wonder if she keeps magazines in her bathroom like my own mother does.

"Do you mind if I use your restroom before I walk home?" I smile sweetly. "Weak bladder."

"Of course." She nods like she completely understands my dilemma. "It's right through that hallway."

I open my mouth to thank her, but the walls suddenly erupt in red and blue lights flashing violently. They strobe through her gauzy curtains, turning her living room into a deranged night club.

Zala's head whips toward the window. "What the heck is going on out there?"

I jump up from the sofa and rush to the window where Zala is already standing, pulling the curtains aside. One patrol car turns the corner. Then another. And a third. All of them are barreling straight toward my house. The law enforcement mood lighting washes my lawn in patriotic panic.

"Come on," Zala urges me to follow her. "Let's see what's going on."

From her front yard we watch three police cruisers park in the street, blocking my driveway, their lights bouncing off every mailbox and windowpane. Several officers climb out with their hands on radios, static crackling in the air.

Along the entire block my neighbors appear like paparazzi drawn to a celebrity. Curtains twitch open. Front doors swing wide. People emerge onto their porches wrapped in blankets with phones aimed and recording. And all those eyes—and every phone—are fixed on my home.

"Why are the police at my house?" I wonder aloud, because it could be any number of things, from the discovery of what's behind my bookshelf door, to sinking Janet Vick's body.

My worst fears rise to the surface. Did they find my DNA on Janet Vick? Would that be enough to ensure my arrest?

Zala pivots to me sharply. "That's a very good question, Shari. Why *are* they at your house?"

I can't answer, because I don't want to incriminate myself. "I don't know…" I mutter, but what I do know is that tonight is not going to end well for me.

With that realization, I sprint home, hoping to head off the police before Mamma or Luca attempt to inject themselves in my defense and land in jail alongside me. Ready or not, I'm about to face whatever disaster is waiting for me on my own turf.

My shoes slam against the pavement, and the cold bites my fingertips numb. I linger on the edge of my driveway, waiting for a policeman to escort me to the back of a cruiser when a scream slices through the chaos of crackling radios and babbling speculations. It's a high-pitched, panicked shriek, and every neck in sight turns toward the wailing.

Chapter 34

"Stop!" The shrieking takes form into a single word, and it thrusts me back to the waterfall when I witnessed Fred with the other woman whose similar panicked "*stop!*" still reverberates in my nightmares.

I'm dragged back to the present as the screams get closer, louder, and the voice more familiar. "No! No, you can't take my dad!"

Bursting through her front door is Freida Cobb, trailing Detective Yankovic who hauls Fred out of the house in handcuffs. The police are not here for me after all. My brain stutters to life. The cops… they're not swarming my driveway. They're arresting *Fred.*

"Please stop!" Freida's begging and sobbing and yanking on the detective's arms, pulling at him with all her might.

Her elbow connects with his chin as she pries at his massive chest, clawing to release her father. Using his shoulder, Detective Yankovic partially covers his face from her blows, then shields himself by turning his back on her, which also swings Fred around like a rag doll in his arms. This whole time Fred remains calm, compliant even, not trying to break free.

"Get 'er off me!" the detective yells, and another officer intercedes by wrapping his arms around Freida's chest to restrain her.

"Freida, please don't!" Fred glances back at her mournfully, shaking his head for her stay back, to stay safe. "Everything will be fine. I promise."

It's a paternal love you can't fake, and this makes me question all the evil I assumed about Fred. He's protecting his daughter, and she's protecting her father. How could I ever think Fred would hurt Freida? But then what are they arresting him for?

"Just tell me what's happening!" Freida cries, wriggling and attempting to free herself from the officer's grip.

The crowd on the curb thickens—neighbors wearing pajamas, bathrobes, one woman holding a mixing bowl like she sprinted out mid-brownie prep. Doomwood Falls loves drama. They might as well sell tickets to this.

I, too, gravitate toward the disorder, desperately wanting answers. Does Fred's arrest mean they found Ivory's body? Has Fred been the one stalking me, planting evidence against me? And most importantly, does this mean it's all over?

Fred shouts something, but I can't hear it over Freida's wails and the growing crowd and police radio chatter. As Detective Yankovic leads Fred toward his car, Freida's face twists with fury.

Zala appears beside me, then exhales sharply at the crowd of looky-loos out on the street. "I always thought there was something odd about Fred."

Of course everyone says that after the fact, but I never saw Fred as anything but a decent husband and loving father until just recently. But clearly my judge of character is wrong. Fred Cobb is not the good guy we all thought he was. He is a—a what? A killer? Because I still don't know what happened to

Ivory.

"I'll be back," I tell Zala before sprinting across the street, shoving through the wall of rubberneckers.

Fingertips catch my shoulder, barely holding me back from Detective Yankovic, who is wrestling Fred into a squad car. I squirm until I break free of the officer's light grip, coming face to face with Detective Yankovic himself. He waves another officer to stand guard over Fred and turns to me, his cheek already bruising from where Freida's elbow made contact.

"Detective," I gasp, catching my breath, "what's going on? Did you find Ivory? Is she—"

He raises a hand sharply. "Ms. Catalano, stand back please."

"No!" I shout, my defiance surprising even myself. "I just want to know about Ivory. Did Fred kill her?"

Yankovic stares at me, then sighs the tired sigh of a man who hasn't slept since his last big bust in the nineties.

"We're arresting Frederick Cobb," he says, "for the murder of private investigator Janet Vick."

I stagger back a step. Poor, relentless Janet met her demise. I still don't know why Fred would kill her, but I honestly don't care. All I care about is Ivory.

"I knew it," I say. "Fred killed her, and probably his mistress too. Wait, did you find the mistress? And Ivory—" My voice cracks. "Have you found Ivory yet? You have to make Fred talk!"

My whole body is shaking as I'm pleading for just an ounce of mercy, that I'll finally know what happened to my best friend.

Detective Yankovic's expression hardens. "I can't answer your questions, Ms. Catalano."

"Can't or won't?"

"It's an active investigation," he reminds me, sounding like he's reciting it from a handbook. "I can't disclose anything else."

"But Detective—"

"There is, however," he cuts in, "one thing I can answer."

My hand involuntarily shoots out to grab his. "What?"

He turns and points toward the nearest police cruiser. "Go look."

The back door opens. A Bernese mountain dog hops out, tongue lolling and happy to be the center of all the excitement. Detective Yankovic leans down, patting his thighs and calling for the dog, who scampers toward him with the enthusiasm of a toddler getting candy. I recognize the pooch as Janet Vick's.

"The dog? I don't understand."

"No, the dog was Janet Vick's and now apparently my new partner. Just wait."

Then someone else steps out of the vehicle behind the dog, flanked by officers.

Chapter 35

The person who steps out of the police car parts the sea of people who are blinking into the flashing police lights angling for a better look. She's wrapped in a gray police-issued blanket like she was plucked straight out of a survival documentary. Her hair is tangled, her cheek is cut, and she is wearing the exact same clothes she wore the day she went missing.

My knees nearly buckle.

"Ivory?" I breathe.

Her head lifts. Her eyes—wide, stunned, haunted—lock on mine. And then she cries out, "Shari?"

Everything inside me erupts. I bolt toward her, nearly tripping over someone's foot and slamming into a shoulder or two on my way through the pressed-in bodies.

"You're alive!" I throw my arms around her, and I don't care if it's too hard or if I'm technically hugging evidence.

She folds into me with a choked sob that vibrates through both of us. She's shivering and filthy, but she hugs me back, gripping me like she's terrified someone might pull her away again.

"I can't believe you're okay," I choke out. "Thank God. I thought you were dead."

Her voice cracks. "I thought so too."

When I pull back, tears drip down my cheeks and she offers

me a weak smile of comfort. Of course Ivory would try to comfort *me* when she's the one who just went through unspeakable trauma. Detective Yankovic stands near us holding a leash as the Bernese mountain dog strains against it, eager to greet every single person individually.

There are so many questions, I don't know where to start. "So, what happened?"

Ivory swallows before she answers, and I can only imagine how hard it must be for her to relive it. "I left that night after we spoke to get away from Fred. I needed space. Time to clear my head. That's when I texted you from the beach."

So it *was* actually her. Ivory clasps my hand, and I squeeze it gently. I'm almost afraid to let go.

"But then Fred tracked me down," she continues, voice shaking. "He… he found me and took me to a cabin near Doomwood Falls. That old hunter cabin we used to hike up to. He bound my wrists up with zip ties and nearly starved me."

I want to hug her again, but I'm afraid she might crumble. How had I not seen her there? "But I went to the cabin to look for you yesterday. No one was there."

"You did?" She cocks her head curiously. "How did you even know to look there?"

"Someone left me a clue. Well, I guess it was Fred. So I hiked up there and checked it out and it was empty."

"*Fred* left you a clue? Why would he do that?" she murmurs, sounding as confused as I am. Then she takes a shuddering breath. "Well, it doesn't matter. I managed to break through the zip ties and escape. After that I ran through the woods, but it was so cold and I was weak from the hunger… I didn't think I would make it out of the woods. That's when

Marshall found me and took me straight to the hospital."

What an interesting coincidence. Of all people, Marshall found her—also known as Fred's close friend. And on the same day he found Janet Vick. That means I must have just missed finding Ivory in the cabin. She had probably escaped right before I got there.

But something about the details pokes a hole that I can't reconcile. How had Ivory broken out of the cabin, then locked the door and sealed the windows behind her? Because the place was sealed tight. I swallow the questions down, because it's not important. What's important is that Ivory is alive. Besides, I have a more pressing question begging to come out.

"Do you know if Fred killed Janet Vick?"

Ivory's hand tenses within mine, slowly constricting so hard it actually hurts. I attempt to pull away, but she won't let go.

"Ivory…" I whisper. "You're hurting me."

I lift our conjoined hands, and that's when I see a long, bloody gash across her wrist. Picking up her other arm, I find another indented slash of split skin where she had been bound. My heart breaks for her, seeing a glimpse of the trauma she went through.

Her hands slip out of mine and her mouth drops open. "I'm so sorry. I didn't mean to—"

"It's okay," I quickly say.

"The police asked me the same thing about Janet Vick, but I know nothing about that. I assumed that she was Fred's mistress and he killed her to hide what he'd done."

Other than Janet and Fred being seen in public together, nothing points to them having an affair. Besides, she was hired to track Gillian, not start a side romance.

"No, I don't think that's it. Janet was working here as a private investigator."

Curiosity hazes over Ivory's eyes. "Who was she investigating?"

"A woman named Gillian. She's the girlfriend of my former boss Ramsey Shenk."

"Did you say Ramsey Shenk?"

"Yeah, you probably recognize the name from the news. He owned *In the Margins Media* and died in a boat fire last year."

Ivory lets out a contemplative "ohhh" and wraps the blanket tighter around her shoulders. The crowd is closing in, and I can tell it's making her anxious. I follow her toward the curb where Freida sits on the ground, creating distance between us and the neighbors. Freida gives us a brief glance before turning her attention to a news van that approaches. I gather a strange awkwardness between mother and daughter. Freida has yet to acknowledge that her mom is home safe. I would have expected a much more enthusiastic reunion.

"Why would someone be investigating Gillian Szabo?" Ivory asks.

Szabo? Why does that sound familiar? I hadn't mentioned Gillian's last name, because I never knew it before now. "How do you know about Gillian—or her last name?"

Ivory stares at me dumbly, and I can't tell if she's forcing a memory or creating a lie. "The police told me when they asked me about her."

"And you're sure they said *Gillian Szabo*?" I reiterate.

Why does that last name slam into me like a brick? I heard it recently. Multiple times. I even read it, and I can almost drudge up the visual imprint of it on the tip of my mind... And there it is, on Luca's assault record.

Marshall Szabo.

That's too unique of a name for him not to be related to Gillian. He looks too young to be her brother, but he's about the right age to be her son. And his steel-gray eyes are all Ramsey Shenk's. Marshall must be the son of Gillian and Ramsey.

All at once, a nasty tangle of questions and answers knots itself in my head. But before I can start mentally unraveling them, Detective Yankovic steps between me and Ivory, a human blockage separating us. It feels strangely metaphoric for what's happening.

"It's time," he states. "Mrs. Cobb, we're going to need to head inside so we can get a formal statement from you."

As he ushers her toward her house, Ivory glances back at me. For barely a moment, her eyes look like someone carrying a dangerous secret.

An officer lingers next to the back door of the cruiser where Fred is yelling something at Ivory about being framed, and how he "didn't do anything," which is exactly what guilty people say right before the handcuffs click. I would know because I lived with those same types of people for three years.

When a second news van rounds the corner, I recognize what's about to happen. Hemlock Drive is about to witness a media frenzy. I twist around looking for Luca and my mother, skimming the outskirts of the crowd. Spotting them across the street, I start to head over when a whisper floats above the chatter:

"Gianna…"

No one in Doomwood Falls knows me as Gianna. That name belongs to my past life.

"*I know what you're hiding.*" It's a *he* who says this, and he sounds just like my husband's killer.

I glance at the faces surrounding me, but everyone's focus is directed elsewhere. At the officer standing by Fred in the cruiser. At Ivory being escorted into her house. At the reporter and her cameraman prepping to film. But not me. I'm focused on my whispered name pulling me back, but I'm too short and the horde is too big for me to find him.

When I lift myself up on tiptoes, I think I spot him, a ballcapped man shoving and angling away through the mass of people. The crowd is so dense that bodies are jockeying for position behind the news crews, making it difficult to navigate. By time I break through the wall of people he's gone.

Only one thought breaks through the screams inside my head:

I have to kill him before he kills me.

Chapter 36

The scandal-soaked excitement is finally over. Once again the street is empty, the bystanders tucked away in their homes, and the solitude is returned to Hemlock Drive. I stand on the sidewalk gripping my arms, pretending I'm not two seconds from passing out or going on the run. Or both. I'm a multitasker like that.

I can't shake the sensation of his slippery voice in my ear: *I know what you're hiding.* But what's most terrifying is that Marshall Szabo is getting bolder and more confrontational, just like his father. And as Gillian Szabo's son, I have a terrible premonition that they plan to kill me.

The way the words slithered from his lips is burned into my memory. In fact, every detail about him is, from our first video chat up through his news interview when he found Janet's body. He and Gillian have become a parasite in my brain chewing its way into every thought. He thought a baseball cap pulled down low and his five o'clock shadow could hide him amid the crowd, but that arrogant, self-satisfied curve of his mouth sets off a fire of hatred inside me.

I'm completely immobile in self-defeat and self-loathing as I step inside my house. Mamma stands near the dining table, her purse still on her arm, keys clenched in her fist. Luca is by the window with his arms crossed and jaw tight. They both look at me the same way. Stern, wary, and braced for some horrible truth.

"What?" I nudge the front door shut behind me and engage the triple lock that still doesn't feel like enough. "Why are you both staring at me like that?"

Neither of them answers. They share a silent exchange, then their eyes shift to the bookshelf. It's not fully open—just a crack. An inch, maybe two. Enough to reveal the dark seam where the wall shouldn't give way. It's enough to tell me I'm screwed.

Heat rushes up my neck, and my cheeks sting with mortification. "Mamma," I say, my words carefully chosen, "why is the bookshelf open?"

Her mouth tightens. She steps toward it, her heels sharp clicks against the hardwood. "I was dusting. When I saw your Nancy Drew book, it brought back memories, so I went to pick it up. Instead of bringing me delightful childhood nostalgia, it opened up a horror story, Shari. Care to explain?"

My lungs forget how to work. Silence slams my lips shut. I look at Luca, but he doesn't look surprised. In fact, he looks resigned to whatever wrath our mother is about to dish out.

"Oh my goodness," Mamma gapes at Luca, then me, "Luca, you knew about this?"

Luca exhales through his nose, and it makes a little whistle. "Yes."

"And you let your sister do this?" Her voice jumps an octave.

"Yes, Mamma."

"And you didn't think to tell me?" She gestures wildly at the bookshelf, at the open wound in my hallway wall. "There is a room back there, Luca. A hidden room in your sister's house with—" She shudders, because there is no way to explain what's back there or make any sense of it.

"I know."

"And you've both been leaving it there like this is normal?" Mamma's gaze snaps back to me. "Explain. Right now."

I open my mouth but the words feel flimsy. Anything I say to justify it would be like trying to dam a flood with paper.

"I didn't want you to find out like this," I say finally.

Her laugh is humorless. "Oh, you think?"

She walks to the bookshelf and yanks it open the rest of the way. Dust and unventilated air spill out, tinged with a dank stench that's impossible to pinpoint. Mamma stops short of stepping inside.

I plant my feet between her and the doorway. "Mamma, listen to me. Please."

Her shoulders sag just a fraction, and her anger cracks, revealing something raw and sad underneath. "Why?" she begs. "Why would you do this, Shari? Is it my fault? Because you felt abandoned by me?"

I meet her gaze and don't look away. I've spent too much of my life deflecting. "There was no other way."

"There is always another way."

"No." My voice is steady, even if my insides aren't. "There isn't, not for me."

"And your brother supported this?"

"Yes," Luca says without hesitation.

"Why, Luca?"

I know my brother's answer, and I know why he won't tell her. It's because he has always and will always choose to believe in my goodness, no matter how many nights I've spent in prison or what the courts rule against me. Especially when my own mother chose to instead give up on me.

Mamma sinks into a chair like her legs have finally given out. She presses her fingers to her temple. "*Madonna mia*, I raised you both better than this."

"I know, and I'm sorry to disappoint you." Then I add without hesitation, "But I'd do it again."

The admission shocks even me. She studies my face like she's searching for the daughter she knows, the one who cried over broken cameras and believed the world could be beautiful if you just took the right picture.

"You're in danger," she concludes.

"I already was."

At last she straightens her back and squares her shoulders decisively. "I won't tell anyone. But I will warn you that secrets rot. They poison everything around them."

"I know."

"So then tell me, to what end do you plan to keep this one?"

I don't answer because I don't know. And somehow, that's the most terrifying revelation of all.

Chapter 37

I've never seen a book club turnout like this before. It's almost as active as the Psychological Thriller Readers FB group I'm a member of.

Wren's house is packed tighter than a clown car, except instead of clowns, most of Hemlock Drive has shown up, which is arguably worse. Everyone's perched on assorted folding chairs she dragged out of her garage, all of them in a circle around her like she's hosting a timeshare pitch. I have a feeling there will be very little discussion about the serial killer thriller Wren selected for this month's read, and more gossip about the actual real-life serial killer living on our street.

With my paperback copy on my lap, I'm seated on a rigid futon in between Ivory and Freida, who looks like she hasn't slept since the cops arrested her father. The teen resembles the cover image of my book—a lady's face appearing to melt as she screams against a black, drippy backdrop. Very Edvard Munch-like and understandable for a girl who has endured an ordeal that will haunt her forever. My own insomnia has had a similar effect on my appearance, too. Trauma twins.

Wren claps her hands. "Okay, neighbors! Let's get started. We all know why we're here."

"To stuff ourselves into a fire hazard?" Zala mutters from the love seat catty-corner to me. An interesting choice of seating, given how she's cozying up to Ali, their thighs pressed together.

Wren shoots Zala a silencing glare, then puts on a chipper voice that would be perfect for a kindergarten art class. "No, Zala, we're all here to discuss books! I hope everyone read this month's book club pick—"

Another groan from Zala interrupts her. "Are we really not going to talk about the fact that I have a serial killer living next door to me?" She flings her arm dramatically toward Ivory. "In poor Ivory's home!"

Freida flinches. "My dad is not a serial killer," she says quietly.

"Oh, sweetie, yes he is," Zala argues, voice dripping with condescension. "The police would not have charged him with murder if he wasn't."

"Are we really doing this?" Wren grumbles. "It's book club, people. We're supposed to talk about the book—"

"He only killed one person," now Luca is chiming in, and book club is officially replaced with armchair detective club. "Since he didn't kill Ivory, he's not technically a serial killer, just a regular murderer."

"I stand corrected," Zala admits.

"Ug, I guess we're doing this." Wren admits surrender and tosses her book on the table in the center of the room.

"I can't believe cops release a serial killer back on streets." Ali squeezes Zala's shoulder, hugging her close. "On one-hundred-thousand-dollar bond. Who has money like that?"

"A *regular* killer," Luca reminds him.

"Small detail," Ali states.

"Killing anyone is not a small detail," I interrupt.

"Before I forget," Wren slips into her kitchen, then returns with a package of dried seaweed and individual cans of energy drinks, "I have snacks. We can discuss books or murder or whatever it is we're discussing while we eat."

Wren passes the food around, and people pick at and examine the seaweed, taking tiny nibbles before setting it back down. No one seems to be picking their seaweed up for a second nibble. The energy drinks, while more popular with this crowd, I am pretty sure had been taken off the market due to causing heart attacks in children. I pass on the energy drink but indulge in a flake of seaweed. It tastes fishy.

"Aren't we supposed to have wine at these things?" Luca grumbles, noticeably staying as far away from Freida as possible.

"This is healthier for you," Wren explains, though I highly doubt that discontinued energy drinks are healthier than wine.

"The point is, none of us feel safe," Zala brings the conversation back to our local killer.

"You act like he's contagious," Ivory snaps back, and I find it odd that she would come to Fred's defense.

"He might be!" Wren says. "Murder *is* contagious. In fact, I just did a killer podcast about it—"

Zala snorts. "That's not how epidemiology works, Wren."

"My dad didn't do anything!" Freida shouts. "You're all acting like he's some kind of monster. He would never hurt anyone."

"Freida, he abducted and hurt your mom." Wren idles behind her and pats her shoulder. "Denial is very common in the children of killers."

"He's *not* a killer!"

I reach over and give Freida's knee an affectionate squeeze. A lot has happened since Fred's arrest and subsequent release on a hundred-thousand-dollar bond that I can't figure out how they afforded to pay. When Fred was released back into the house, Ivory moved in with her parents. But Freida refused, insisting on staying at home with her dad. She keeps saying he's innocent, and the worst part? She believes it with her whole fractured heart. Part of me trusts her intuition, because even I have to admit that something about her mother's abduction and the connection to Janet Vick's murder baffles me.

"I just can't believe it," Ivory's whisper reaches my ear as the rest of the group debates what types of traits are imprinted on children of killers, and how to identify a killer. "I lived with Fred for two decades. If he was a murderer, I think I'd know, right?"

Would she, though? I want to say, but I don't. Because she's friends with *me*, and if she knew what I was capable of… well, Ivory apparently is a bad judge of character.

Wren clears her throat, forcing the attention back on her. "We need a plan. A neighborhood safety protocol. Something to keep us protected while the killer is still lurking around."

"*Alleged* killer," I correct her because I see the toll this conversation, this judgement of Fred, is taking on Freida.

"Whatever." Wren turns to me suddenly. "Shari, you've been quiet. What do *you* think—did Fred kill Janet Vick or not?"

"How would I know?"

Something about Fred being the killer feels like trying to force a puzzle piece into a game of Connect Four. It might kind of fit if you jam it hard enough, but that doesn't make it right. But the alternative—that another killer is still running around

Doomwood Falls—is worse.

"Are you saying you think he's innocent?" Wren demands.

"No, I'm saying…" What am I saying? "I'm saying maybe we don't have all the facts yet."

Freida squeezes my knee gratefully while Ivory exhales shakily. Wren opens her mouth with another retort, but suddenly the front door swings open so hard that the doorknob smashes a welt in the drywall behind it. A crumble of white wallboard chunks plummet to the floor.

I'm about to owe Zala a huge apology.

Chapter 38

Most of the book club energy drinks are sweating on the coffee table untouched. The seaweed flakes are even less popular. A dozen neighbors are packed into Wren's home, with knees knocking and voices stacked on top of one another like kindling. Wren's front door bangs open with a violence that rattles a piece of abstract art hanging in the hallway, and imprints the plaster with the doorknob.

"I'm here! Don't start without me!"

Ivory bolts up from her seat. Wren spills purple energy drink on her erratically patterned carpet, so she grabs a paper towel to dab up the liquid. The rest of us are too occupied staring at the stranger standing in the entryway whose glare locks directly on me.

She is a blinding splash of color, wearing a hot pink pantsuit that looks like it belongs in an eighties movie. But it's not the outfit that makes the air leave my lungs. It's her face, and the way she isn't blinking as she stares at me. I don't know her, but she seems to know—and hate—me.

I look at the stranger, then I swivel to look at Zala sitting next to me. Then back to the stranger. It's like looking at a split screen. Same high cheekbones. Same almond-shaped eyes. Even the same perfect little nose.

"What the—" I'm too confused to notice the dry seaweed

crumbling in my hand.

Leaving the front door open behind her, the woman in pink carelessly kicks off her heels—also pink—and struts into the circle, beaming. "Hi, everyone. Sorry I'm late. Traffic was a nightmare."

"Who are you?" Zala asks on behalf of the whole room, because no one appears to know her.

"Hi, I am Gillian."

And I am mortified.

Gillian Szabo—Ramsey's girlfriend and Zala's doppelgänger. The woman Janet Vick was following is here in the flesh, and she isn't Zala after all. How could I be so thoughtless to tell Detective Yankovic that Zala was Gillian Szabo and possibly connected to Ivory's disappearance and Janet's murder? All because I thought they look so much alike. And yet when I really examine them—Gillian's pink heels compared to Zala's thick-soled comfort shoes, or Gillian's high-maintenance makeup compared to Zala's fresh-faced woke-up-like-this look—they are nothing alike.

Gillian tilts her head. "And wow, do you have a mirror? Because I feel like I'm looking at one." Her gaze drifts down Zala's body and she reassesses. "Well, an older poorly-dressed version."

Zala doesn't seem to notice the dig as she steps forward, one eyebrow cocked as she scans Gillian's body. "I'm Zala," she holds out her hand, which Gillian limply shakes, "Zala Yankovic."

Yankovic. You've got to be kidding me. Zala must be Detective Yankovic's sister. No wonder she knew about the missing shirt detail from Janet Vick's murder investigation. Her brother must have leaked it to her. And now it makes sense, the disdain he showered me with when I laid out my theory of Zala being Gillian.

I thought he was just being a dismissive cop, but he wasn't. He was pissed off because I was accusing his sister of sleeping with a married man and then murdering someone. I am an absolute, colossal idiot.

"Yankovic?" Gillian repeats, ignoring the tension radiating off the rest of us. She looks Zala up and down, then points a manicured finger at her face. "Wait a second. You have the Szabo cheekbones. Are you from Piešťany?"

Zala's defensive posture melts instantly. "Yes, in fact I was born on Spa Island! I used to explore the underground treatment corridors… well, before they were sealed shut. We moved to the United States when I was a teenager."

"*The* Spa Island?" Gillian shrieks, clapping her hands together. "My father—my *tatko*—wouldn't shut up about it. He said the mud cured his gout."

"Do you know my aunt, Magda Yankovic?"

"Aunt Magda!" Gillian screams. She lunges forward and wraps Zala in a hug that looks like it might crack a rib. "What a small world. My dad is her cousin, Jozef. That would make us… second cousins?"

Zala laughs and wraps her arm around the hot pink back of Gillian Szabo, then draws her into the circle of seats. "I haven't seen Jozef since I was a child. That explains it. The resemblance… it's uncanny."

"We Slovaks have strong genes. Look at us!" Gillian pulls back, holding Zala by the shoulders. "We look like a before-and-after photo for a makeover show!"

No one but me seems to notice the drop in temperature from the open front door sucking the heat out, or the wind whipping inside, ruffling the coats hanging on a coat rack in the entry. Instead, the room erupts into confused but inviting greetings aimed at our newest book club member who has taken an intense interest in watching me. In a way, I'm relieved to finally put a face to the name of my newest enemy.

Wren asks if anyone needs an energy drink refill. Zala and Gillian hijack the conversation, prattling away in a mix of English and what sounds like Slovak, bonding over a place called Spa Island and their shared cheekbones that women would kill for.

But I can't smile. I can't join in this warm welcome. Gillian is here for an agenda, and I know it revolves around me.

A prick of unease starts at the base of my neck and works its way up. I watch Gillian laughing, her sleeve brushing against Zala's arm. The pink is strikingly familiar—in fact, it's the same blinding pink I'd seen at the waterfall. Another piece clicks into place when the letter that I thought was a *Z* in the water's reflection was actually an *S*… for *Szabo*.

Gillian Szabo has to be Fred's mistress, and she shouldn't be here. Not just in this house, but here, in this moment. Ivory needs the truth, and I'm going to get it for her. So I stand up, though my legs feel heavy. The commotion dies down as I step into the center of the room.

"Gillian," I demand her attention.

She turns to me, her smile bright and vacuous. "You must be Shari. I've heard so much about you."

"We didn't invite you," I say flatly. Zala's expression turns stern, because of course she thinks I'm being rude. But I'm not.

I'm being protective and proactive. "This is a private book club. Zala didn't know you were coming. I didn't know you were coming. Wren didn't know you were coming."

Gillian's smile falters, just a fraction. With a flip of her hair she steps toward me.

"So," then I take a matching step toward her, because I will not back down—not now, not ever again, "how did you know we were meeting here tonight? Who told you about it?"

No one posted about this book club meeting outside of our private Facebook group. And beyond that, Wren only invited the neighbors verbally, in person because she insists texting "spreads misinformation," like she's chairwoman of some HOA version of the CIA.

The room goes dead silent except for the crunch of shoes on leaves somewhere outside. The joy of the Slovak family reunion evaporates, replaced by the suffocating weight of suspicion. Gillian stares at me, and for a second her bubbly exterior slips. Her gaze darts to the window, where the darkness presses against the glass.

"I…" she starts, but stops.

"Why are you *really* here in Doomwood Falls, Gillian?"

Before Gillian can answer, a heavy thud comes across the front porch. The front door slams shut, followed by the distinct sound of a deadbolt sliding home.

Chapter 39

The lock clicking is a mechanical, claustrophobic sound, sealing us in. Every head whips toward the hallway as a chorus of "what was that?" ripples through Wren's living room.

"Do you want to know why I'm here in Doomwood Falls?" Gillian sits and perches stiffly on a dining chair, her ankles crossed and spine straight. Her lipstick is too cheerful of a pink for the frown on her face. "Or why I'm here at your book club?"

"Both," I answer.

"Well," she twists her blonde hair around a finger, then looks directly at Ivory and says, "I came here to set the record straight about someone."

The thud of footsteps I'd just heard is much closer now. They echo across the entryway, then stop under the archway that leads into the living room. We're looking at where Fred Cobb has materialized from behind the hallway partition. I move to the arm of the sofa, and my paperback slips from my thigh to the floor.

"Fred?" the word jumps from mouth to mouth around the room, along with a lone "Dad!" from Freida.

Ivory scurries behind the futon as if using it as a shield. "What are you doing here, Fred?"

"He's here to kill us!" Zala screams.

A glass shatters. Wren yelps and backs into a cabinet to

avoid getting cut by the shards of glass. I slide off the arm of the sofa, already mapping exits in case of emergency.

"Don't panic," Fred says quickly. "Please. I'm not here to hurt anyone. I'm here to explain."

"Get out of my house!" Wren shrieks. "Someone call the police!"

"Enough!" I yell over the rising hysteria. Ivory reaches over and grabs my hand, and when I glance over at her, she's shaking her head. *Don't*, she mouths. But I need answers, and Fred is the only one who has them. "I want to hear what he has to say."

"You want to know about Janet Vick's murder, right?" Fred dangles that carrot in front of us, then winces at the curses erupting around him as the wording lands wrong. "Please just listen. Five minutes. That's all I'm asking."

"Why would we listen to *you*?" Zala spits.

"Because I didn't kill Janet Vick. And if you don't hear me out, you're going to blame the wrong person."

Silence drops hard, and the shattered glass and spilled energy drink are forgotten about.

I hear my voice before I realize I'm using it. "Then talk."

Fred looks at me, relief and gratitude touching his wet eyes and trembling lips. He steps forward slowly, like he's approaching a wild animal. "Yes," he finally says, his eyes tearing up as he first meets Ivory's gaze, then Freida's, "it's true that I had an affair with Gillian."

The room explodes again with gasps, expletives, and someone actually laughing like it's a punchline. I think I recognize Luca's voice, and sure enough, when I turn around he throws his hand in front of his mouth to muffle his inappropriate amusement.

Gillian shoots to her feet. "How dare you say that! That is *not* what we agreed you would say—"

"But it's the truth! And I'm not proud of it," Fred cuts in. "We met a few weeks ago through her son Marshall, who is a friend of mine."

"Wait a minute! Let me get this straight." Wren steps out from the corner of the room where she had abandoned broken glass cleanup. "Gillian is Marshall's *mother*?"

Fred nods. "Yeah, why?"

Wren humphs. "He never mentioned that to me."

I'm about to ask how Wren knows Marshall, because this is all suddenly getting very convoluted and confusing, but Fred bulldozes right along.

"Anyway, Gillian and I had gotten a drink at Dirty Dan's after a bad day at work. She suggested we go for a hike to clear our heads and get some fresh air. So we did… and the next thing I know we're drunk at the waterfall and she's flirting and undressing me and we're both buzzed. But I swear it was a one-time, stupid moment of weakness."

He swallows and turns to Ivory, a pleading in his gaze.

"I hate that I have to admit what I did—publicly, no less— but I'm willing to do anything to prove how sorry I am. Even humiliating myself in front of all these people." Fred drops to one knee with his arms outstretched toward his wife and daughter. "You both deserve to know the truth because I love you and I deeply regret what I did."

Gillian's mouth bobs open and closed, but I can't let her derail this confession.

"Sit down," I snap at Gillian. She does, cheeks blazing. "And Janet Vick?" I probe. "Where does she fit into this?"

"She was investigating Gillian, but I have no idea why," Fred answers. "I didn't know who Janet was at first. While she was following Gillian she saw us together and confronted me about our affair. She told me she was a private investigator, and she asked a lot of questions about Gillian."

"What kinds of questions?"

"Things like where Gillian was staying. Who she was seeing. Why she was in Doomwood Falls. But as I told Janet, I hardly knew Gillian. It was a heat-of-the-moment connection, and Gillian was pretty tight-lipped about herself."

"Funny," Zala mutters under her breath. "She didn't seem to have that tight-lipped problem with you."

I feel the tide turning in this room. For the first time since my incarceration I'm holding the mic. Everyone believes me for once while I'm fighting for my life. I turn to Gillian, and we both know what question is coming next. There's nowhere for her to hide, no one to keep her secrets safe anymore.

"Why would a private investigator be investigating you, Gillian?"

She's publicly cornered and she knows it.

Her finger twirls her hair more roughly now, and her placid expression is unsettling. "I came here to spend time with my son Marshall. Janet must have thought I was involved in something else."

She's planned a reasonable excuse for everything, which makes her hard to trip up. I almost smile, because I know how to lie too. I've edited them, cropped them, and sold them to this town until it resembled just enough truth to trick everybody.

"You claimed to show up at this meeting to set the record straight, Gillian. So let's set it straight. You came to this town to avenge Ramsey Shenk, your boyfriend who stole money from his own company, framed me for it, then murdered my husband. When he died, you blamed me for it. *That's* why you're here."

"Ramsey never did any such thing," Gillian attempts to yell over the erupting conjecture that just keeps building. She pounds her fist on the coffee table and everyone's mouths shut at the sudden outrage. "That is a bold-faced lie!"

"Is it? Because I think Janet Vick was close to finding the truth and that's why you killed her—to protect Ramsey's reputation and secure your financial future."

Fred's head snaps toward Gillian. "What is she talking about? Is this true?"

Glancing around the circle of onlookers watching her every movement, Gillian shifts uncomfortably. She gets up and walks to Fred, then rests her hand on his arm in what appears to be a plea for an alliance. "Shari is just upset because she got caught stealing money from Ramsey's company. Now she's throwing baseless accusations against him because her husband died from a self-inflicted gunshot wound and she needs someone to blame."

"Stewart did *not* kill himself!" I scream. "He was *murdered!*"

"Tell yourself whatever helps you sleep at night." Gillian shakes her head at me while leaning into Fred.

"You know what helps me sleep at night?" I seethe. "That I have proof of what Ramsey did."

"What kind of proof?"

"The kind that would put Ramsey behind bars… if he was still alive."

Gillian huffs. "Well, Ramsey may have had some," she

fumbles the words, then says, "*questionable* business morals, but he never hurt anyone."

Gillian doesn't seem to realize what crime I have proof of, because she apparently thinks I'm referring to the embezzlement, not Stew's murder. So I keep going, and I'm not stopping until every sordid detail is out.

"There are only two options, Gillian. You should think carefully before you answer. The first option is that you're telling the truth that Ramsey is dead and he's never coming back. And you're only here to visit Marshall, then you'll go on your merry way." I take a steadying breath. "Or the second option is Ramsey is alive and hiding out somewhere, and you're here to find him so he can bankroll your lifestyle again. In which case, I have proof that Ramsey committed murder. So if he is in fact alive, he's heading straight to jail."

"Are you *sure* you have proof of that?" There's a lilt to her voice, and far too much confidence. Leaning over, she picks up her pink shoes and slides them on her feet. "Trust me, you don't want to wade in deep waters with me, *Gianna*, because I know a lot more about you than you think."

I don't like the way she says it, like she knows something I don't. Is it possible she's the one who stole the picture frame and got her hands on my evidence? The room buzzes with fear, excitement, the electric thrill of accusation.

Fred rises to his feet and yells, "Enough!"

We all shut up and turn to him.

"There is only one person in this room that I know for sure has been lying," he says slowly.

He scans the faces—Wren, Zala, Ali, Luca, Gillian, Freida, Ivory, then he lingers on me. He lifts his arm and points. I sense a terrible unraveling about to happen. Where his finger lands, I already feel it burn. The whole neighborhood missed seeing the real monster all along.

Chapter 40

The room inhales as one, hollowing out the oxygen and thinning it until I can't breathe. Fred knows what I've done, and the rest of Doomwood Falls is about to find out. I had thought three years in prison felt long, but that will be child's play compared to the sentence I'm about to get.

Stepping toward me, Fred's finger slices the air and lands—

not on me but on Ivory standing next to me, like a blade finding soft flesh.

"My wife lied," Fred states, his voice unwavering, "about the abduction."

Ivory shakes her head, willing everyone watching to side with her. But Fred's tears and the earnest way he's speaking is pretty convincing.

"I know my affair hurt you, Ivory, and I regret it more than anything, but I don't understand why you would fake an abduction to get back at me. Hate me, kick me out, tell everyone in town about my betrayal—those are normal responses. But to pretend I abducted you to get me charged with false imprisonment and kidnapping? Because of that the cops think I killed a woman. Your lie is destroying me! I want to know why you'd do that to me."

The futon beneath me scrapes back so hard it screeches as Ivory shoves her way around the obstacle course of chairs and tables. "You *did* abduct me, Fred. You're insane."

"Am I?" Fred locks in on her, and I feel like I'm eavesdropping on what should be a private conversation. "You told the police I took you. You told them I zip tied your wrists. You told them—"

"I *was* kidnapped," Ivory barks. "You don't get to rewrite that."

She yanks up her sleeves, both of them, exposing her wrists. Fresh scabs ring her skin with raw, uneven, angry half-moons where skin tried to heal and failed. The marks are thin, but they bit deep enough to testify what happened. The tips of her index fingers and thumbs are cracked and discolored.

"Could I fake these?" Ivory demands, shoving her arms out like weapons. "Could I?" Her voice cracks, then hardens. "I couldn't possibly put those on myself. Especially not tight enough to do this."

Silence slams down any argument Fred might have had. But I remember Ivory's fingers digging into my arm earlier, her breath hot against my ear. *Don't*, she mouthed when I pressed Fred to tell his side. As if to say, *Don't let him talk.*

At the time I thought she was scared. Traumatized. Protecting herself from hearing his voice again. Now it crawls under my skin. Why did she want him quiet so badly?

Fred exhales like he's been waiting for this excuse. "You didn't put them on yourself. I never said that. What I said was you lied about me doing it when you faked your abduction. There very well could be someone who helped you."

Wren breaks their conversation first. "Fred, if you didn't abduct her, then who did?"

Fred spreads his hands. "That's the question, isn't it?"

My thoughts trip over each other. If Fred is lying, he's doing it with terrifying calm and conviction. If Ivory is lying, why invent a story so horrible? Could his affair have really driven her to such extremes?

I recall the anger that her ex-husband had planted in her with his infidelity, the wrath that took root and her vow to never let anyone make a fool of her again. In retrospect, the way she had reacted so calmly after I told her what I saw fit the bill for someone plotting revenge. As they say, it's best served cold… or with a cold heart, in this case.

"This is unbelievable. You're all just going to let him stand there and accuse me of making it up?" Ivory's laugh is harsh.

"No," I say. "We're not letting anything happen. We're just listening to both sides."

A subtle twitch shifts her expression from anger to hurt. "Shari, you saw me after I got back. You saw what I looked like. You actually think I could stage that?"

I do remember, and it was awful. She was shaking and bruised, a battered woman who barely escaped. But all of that can be manufactured. I know better than anyone just how skilled we are at pretending.

"Ivory, I understand why you were mad at me about the affair." Fred steps closer and the floor creaks under his weight. "And I know your ex hurt you badly. But what I didn't know until just recently," he glances at Gillian, and I wonder what that look is saying, "was how badly you needed a villain. Because if you told the truth, your whole story falls apart."

"And what truth is that?" Ivory's hands curl into fists.

Fred's gaze travels from her wrists then to her face where a cut still mars her cheek. "You weren't abducted by a stranger.

And you weren't abducted by me."

My mouth goes dry.

Ivory waves her arms violently. "No. No, don't—"

There it is again—*Don't*. What is my best friend hiding?

"I'm not going to tell your story for you, Ivory, because I love you and I'm sorry I betrayed you." Fred steps backward toward the door, hands raised in surrender. "But I'm not going to let you portray me as a monster who would abduct you or kill someone. My daughter should not have to grow up believing that lie about her own dad. Freida needs to know the truth. That you were with someone she knew," he concludes. "Someone you trusted enough to go with willingly."

My thoughts spiral. If she went willingly, why the restraints? Why the injuries? Unless the restraint came later. Unless something went wrong. Unless she needed the story to end a certain way.

"Who did this to you?" I ask her quietly.

She looks at me like I've punched her. "You think I'd protect my abductor? I'm telling you, it was Fred."

I don't answer, because I don't know if I believe her. Every certainty I had an hour ago is dissolving. If Fred is telling the truth and didn't abduct Ivory, someone else did—or Ivory staged just enough damage to sell a lie everyone, even the police, would believe. Either way, we all have proven to be world-class liars.

My gaze drops back to her wrists. The scabs are real. The pain had to be real. But pain doesn't tell the whole truth. It just proves that someone suffered. The question gnawing at me now is sharper than fear: What really happened, and who is Ivory protecting?

Gillian is uncharacteristically silent this whole time, and I suddenly realize why. She's gone. She must have slipped out unnoticed, but I catch a flash of pink fast-walking toward a black luxury car. I rush to the window in time to watch her open the door and step into the vehicle. Something about the fissure of pink at the steering wheel makes my whole body subconsciously react.

It's the same black Mercedes I'd seen idling outside of my house. And again, it's familiar from somewhere else, but where? My brain can't force the memory, even though it clings to the edge of it. Was it in town? Yes, that feels right, but it's not the whole picture.

She's backing the car down the driveway when the remainder of faint golden sunlight hits the front bumper crookedly, making the fender appear bent. Or maybe it's not a trick of the light. A deep, ugly dent cuts the symmetry of the front hood, right near the hood ornament. Like she rammed into something. Or *someone*.

I know that dent. I *felt* that dent. A flash sears across my vision—headlights blinding, a car lunging forward, my own scream swallowed by impact as the world flips sideways. It's the same car that hit me.

My mind vomits horrible images and sounds. The glisten of waxed black metal, the crunch of a fender into flesh, a flash of neon pink behind the window, bone cracking on cement. It aligns the dots perfectly. I try to picture the driver's face, but it's the same blur as always, like someone painted over the memory with watercolors. The flashback hazily completes itself enough that I can confidently conclude that Gillian Szabo *must* have been driving the car that ran me over.

Gillian Szabo is going to kill me.

Chapter 41

After Fred leaves and Gillian rides her hit-and-run evidence off into the sunset, Wren insists we all decompress in the kitchen. This apparently means being force-fed a bowl of something green, lumpy, and steaming that smells like a witch's brew and tastes like sewage—not that I've eaten sewage in order to know. She calls it Wren's Comfort Stew, her own take on the more flavorful Moroccan Comfort Stew. It looks more like something she scraped out of a defunct aquarium.

Zala pokes hers with a spoon. "Is it supposed to move?"

"It's quinoa and some other stuff," Wren snaps, though she won't make eye contact with the bowl. "It's packed with superfoods."

"It's alive," Zala corrects.

Freida refuses to eat anything, still sniffling and refusing to be comforted. Luca tentatively nudges her shoulder, then playfully pokes her rib cage, almost cracking a smile on Freida's lips. Ivory stares blankly at her spoon as if hoping to astral-project out of this conversation entirely. And the conversation? It's not even about Fred anymore. Somehow it devolved into a heated argument over the proper way to fold fitted sheets.

Wren claims she has a patented method. Zala claims Wren is a compulsive liar. They may both be right. I pretend to be listening, but my body is buzzing with everything I saw, everything that feels wrong, every off note in this supposed peaceful suburban symphony.

"I'm heading home get dinner started," Luca announces, though no one seems to be listening.

Checking the time, I realize how late it is and I'm eager to get home. Luca promised Ivory and Freida homemade authentic Italian pasta tonight, which means I have to make sure he and my mother don't destroy the kitchen in the process. I slip away from Wren's center island and look for my coat, which isn't hanging on the coat rack.

"Where'd you put the coats, Wren?"

"Aw, are you heading home already?" she says, then before I can confirm adds, "I put the coats in the upstairs spare bedroom."

"I wish I could stay longer," I lie out of politeness, even though it's the absolute last thing I would wish for, "but I'm exhausted. It's been a… day."

A traumatic day? An eye-opening day? There are too many adjectives I could fill in that blank with. No one responds or seems to care that I'm leaving except maybe the sentient quinoa blob.

I climb the staircase of Wren's recently renovated open-concept house that makes the second floor seem cavernous. I walk lightly in my socks, and glide up the stairs. The sounds of bickering float up behind me.

"You don't tuck the corners first, Wren," Zala is arguing. "What kind of sociopath—"

"It's called structure, Zala!"

"You want to talk structure? This mush needs some structure!"

The upstairs hallway blooms with bright bohemian color. A floral-patterned runner rug stretches its length, reds and indigos softened by footsteps. Tapestries drape the walls in layered textures and symbols. I open the first door I come to and find a heap of more clashing colors and patterns, clothes strewn all over the floor, the covers on the bed a rumpled mess, and an incense stick burning that makes me think of cinnamon snickerdoodles. This must be Wren's bedroom. It's the type of room where you might go blind if you stare too hard.

Behind the second door is an equally messy bathroom.

The bedroom behind the third door doesn't appear quite as messy, though it's still cluttered with balls of yarn and crafting supplies and a wall-length desk holding a microphone, several computer screens, selfie ring lights, and enough equipment to host a podcast and full-feature movie production.

Along with her podcast, her self-proclaimed fashion design empire—if you call an Etsy store an empire—appears to live here. Bolts of fabric hang from the walls. A mannequin stands in the corner wearing something that looks like a prom dress mated with a disco ball. Sketches cover every surface. Sequins litter the floor like cheap glitter snow.

I step inside, listening to the voices downstairs. These women do not give up.

I find my coat on the bed next to a pile of fabric swatches, then linger near her desk doing some good old-fashioned snooping. Several binders line the table labeled: *Client Sizing*, *Color Theory*, and *Confidential: For Wren's Eyes Only*. Obviously I reach for that binder first.

Inside? Podcast concepts in detail. Nothing illegal or thrilling. But then something catches my eye on the corkboard above the desk. A photograph.

A recent one, it looks like. She's even wearing the same shoes she'd worn when I first met her. Wren stands next to a man, his arm looped around her shoulders, and he's kissing her cheek. The girl is unmistakably Wren but sweeter, with softer eyes and a smile that looks genuine instead of the strained, tight-lipped thing she wears nowadays.

The man kissing her, however, intrigues me. I pull the photo down.

His profile looks insanely familiar. Not in a vague, *Oh, he could be someone I passed in the grocery store* way. He is someone I met. Just recently. Someone whose presence sends cold needles down my spine. I draw the picture closer. The curly red hair, the double-chin, the pale eyes… it looks just like—

"Shari?" Wren calls from downstairs.

Footsteps mount the steps. Someone's coming, so I hurry to pin the photo back to the corkboard then jerk upright just as Wren's familiar boots clunk down the hallway. I yank my coat off the bed as Wren walks in.

"Get lost up here?" she asks me with a stiff, straight mouth. There's not even a hint of kindness in her tone.

"Oh, I was just admiring your sketches." I glance at the papers strewn all over the place offering an array of revolting fashion creations.

She takes a long look at me before she says, "Thanks." She stands way too close. Her lips are stretched thin, like someone pulled them taut with fishing line. "Well?"

She waits for me to answer, but I don't know what the question is. "Well what?"

"What do you think of the sketches?"

"Oh, they're great!" I exclaim, trying to sidestep her. "I admit I don't know what the cool kids are wearing these days, but your style is… innovative. I've never seen anything like it." I'm actually being honest.

She doesn't move, but her eyes narrow by a millimeter. "I thought I saw my *Confidential* binder moved. Did you look inside it?"

My stomach drops so hard it hits my ankles. How the heck did she notice that amid all of the mess? I laugh a little too loudly.

"Oh, you got me! I was just curious."

"In some modern societies we call that nosy."

"Sorry. I wasn't trying to be nebby. I genuinely admire your work." I feel panicky over getting caught, but she seems to soften at my compliments. Seeing Gillian and confronting Fred has piled more anxiety on my already frazzled psyche. "I should probably head home. I have to feed Zoomie."

I follow her downstairs, tasting bile rising in my throat. I can't push the gross visual out of my head of Macho Marshall kissing Wren. I thought Wren was odd, but I didn't peg her as desperate enough to date someone like him. Though, since the beginning of time, some girls prefer a guy who drives a flashy sports car over having good character.

When I reach the entry, I bolt past her before she can interrogate me any further, nearly tripping over my own feet as I sprint to the door. The moment I'm outside, the fresh air welcomes me like freedom. I keep running until I'm halfway down the driveway, when I have no choice but to stop.

Chapter 42

I hustle out of Wren's house like it's on fire—which, frankly, it might be soon if my nerves spontaneously combust. Nighttime melts the sun away early this time of year, but Wren's got enough spotlights in her yard to illuminate a stadium. I'm thankful for them, considering we're back to square one with Janet Vick's killer, who could be lurking in any shadow or behind any corner at any time.

Even if there was an ax murderer behind me, there is no way I'm not pausing to pay my respect to what's parked in Wren's driveway. A 1967 Corvette convertible T-top sports car looks oxblood red in the dusk. This car is a collector's dream, and in mint condition. Sleek and classic and expensive, it's the quality of car that screams money, which I am pretty sure Wren doesn't have.

Hadn't she been complaining about the cost of my photography class when I first met her? But she casually mentioned "coming into money," which I had assumed meant she'd gotten a job. It appears she meant *real* money, like a rich uncle died and left her his inheritance kind of money.

But what stops me cold isn't the enviable car or the silver exhaust pipes running down each side, which I kneel to admire. What concerns me is what's sitting in the tan leather passenger seat.

Even through the frosted glass I would recognize that color neon pink anywhere. With my sleeve pulled over my hand I wipe at the icy glaze until the passenger side window reveals the eye-blinding shirt. How did Wren get it? I consider several options, like maybe Marshall or Gillian planted it in Wren's car. Or maybe there are more than one of this specific sweatshirt out there. There's no way to know without directly asking Wren, and after she caught me snooping in her spare bedroom, I will certainly *not* be doing that.

What I *do* know is that Fred already confessed to Gillian being his mistress at the waterfall, so I know that wasn't Wren. Plus Wren is young enough to be Fred's daughter, so it would be downright gross.

Assessing the collection of junk inside, I wonder how she could treat this beautiful vehicle specimen with such carelessness. Apparently it's become a storage room for all of the clutter she doesn't have space for in her house. I need to get a better look at that sweatshirt.

My instincts tingle dangerously. I glide closer until my fingers find their way to the door handle. The door is unlocked. Of course it is, because kids her age assume locks are for "old people" like me.

I tug the door open and pick up the sweatshirt. The color is right, but the embroidered letter is wrong. This one has a *W*, presumably personalized for Wren. Tossing it aside, I'm pretty sure Wren won't notice a difference if I rifle through fast food wrappers hidden beneath discarded clothes.

The original glove box has the key hole removed and replaced with a knob. Upon popping it open, the sleek half-moon door falls down revealing a stack of papers inside. I pick up the top page, which is a purchase contract for this car. The purchase date is especially noteworthy. It's the same day Ivory went missing.

"Okay, that's convenient," I say aloud.

Beneath the purchase agreement are half a dozen amateur printed photographs, definitely the poor quality I would expect of Wren. What's more terrifying than the awful angles and poor resolution is that every photo is of *me*.

Me at my mailbox. Me hiking to Doomwood Falls waterfall. Me in my *Juicy*-butt-emblazoned sweatpants that Ivory teased me about. My throat tightens. Is Wren the one who has been stalking me?

Another picture shows me and Luca and my mother eating at *The Codfather*. We've only been out together once in the past four years, the day I got hit by Gillian's car. These photos show that Wren had spent a week surveilling me, the pictures of which seem to start the day I met with Ivory for coffee and end on the day of my accident.

A vague piece of a memory slams into me from that day. The black car careening toward me… but I can't pull anything more from the image. Closing my eyes, I force the rest of the picture to congeal as I search for the face behind the wheel. It's still a grainy blur of dark hair. The flash of that damn neon pink. But there's something more forming as the pink shirt bleeds into the dark hair. Just like the pink tips of Wren's hair.

"Wren was supposed to kill me…" I sputter.

It explains why she was so surprised to see me after I was released from the hospital. It was Wren watching me from outside the restaurant window right before the hit-and-run. The neon pink sweatshirt matching Gillian's is in Wren's car. While

Gillian's car is dented, I think Wren was behind the wheel. But Wren seemed genuinely surprised to meet Gillian. Could she be that good of an actress? Or maybe her beau Marshall set the whole thing up.

I don't have concrete evidence against Wren, but I do have an exorbitant car purchase receipt from the day Ivory disappeared and photos tracking my whereabouts for days afterward. If I were to follow the money—which most crimes revolve around—I'd conclude that Wren got paid a pretty sum to run me over and used Gillian's car to do it.

I worked as a photojournalist for years, so I know a feature scoop when I see one. I also know how to harvest the facts and weed out the fiction. My gut was rarely wrong when I was in the field, and I know what it's telling me now: Wren is hired to hurt me. Maybe even kill me, though I don't think Wren has the stomach for that.

If I were to guess, I'd say Gillian asked Marshall to find a girl financially desperate enough to help him. Enter Wren, willing to do almost anything for a quick buck, as long as the risk was minimal. But I need concrete proof if I'm going to put a stop to their plans, which I'll find soon enough because I have something they want. And I'll use it as collateral for my life if I have to.

"Shari?" Luca calls from the end of the driveway. "What are you doing?"

I bolt up while inside Wren's Corvette, smacking my head on the roof of the car.

"Nothing!" I squeak, grabbing the entire pile of photos and frantically shoving it under my armpit. "I, just, uh, dropped my house keys."

How long has my brother been standing there watching me pillage Wren's car?

"You mean the keys you're holding?"

"Yep. These ones." I dangle them in the air. "Found 'em!"

I close the door shut so gently that the velvety *thunk* is barely audible as the latch catches, but there's no hiding from Luca what I've been doing. Let's face it, this is nothing compared to what else he knows about me.

Hurrying down the street toward home, the glossy photos begin slipping free from under my armpit. A stray picture flutters mid-air, then gracefully lands at my feet before the wind can steal it away. I pick it up, horrified by what I see. Staring at the print, I don't know how to make sense of it. The story I just built about Gillian and Wren and Marshall tumbles down like a house of cards.

"Ivory and Freida are at the house. We're all waiting on you so we can eat," Luca says.

He waves me on, but I can't tear my eyes—or fingers—away from the photo. The paper sticks to my fingertips with a bizarre tackiness. I certainly won't be eating tonight.

"Hey, what's wrong?"

I swallow, unable to speak. Instead, I lift up the picture to show my brother, and the moment he sees it, he also knows this is bigger than us.

"We've got to turn this in to the police."

Chapter 43

The loaf of Italian bread is eaten down to a crusty nub. Next to it sits a chef's knife Luca used to cut the bread because Mamma *accidentally* donated my bread knife to Goodwill. The serving bowl of Luca's Legendary Linguine sits mostly empty in the middle of the dining room table, although I couldn't stomach a single noodle. Not because Luca can't cook—he's an idiot in the real world but a genius in the kitchen—but because the photograph has made me lose my appetite.

Mamma begins clearing the table while Luca, Freida, Ivory, and I gather in the dining room, the plates licked clean and wine glasses topped off. I leave the corkscrew and extra bottle of unopened wine in case we need it. After the past few days I've had, I'm not convinced two glasses of wine are enough to dull my nerves.

Ivory sits next to me on one side, and Freida sits stiffly beside my brother, arms wrapped around herself while he rubs his hand in circles on her back. While Mamma collects empty plates and silverware, I grab the small pile of Wren's photos and dump them onto the table. The stack fans out in a creepy collage of my past couple weeks, like a serial killer scrapbook made just for me. This might be exactly what it is.

Sliding the top photo into the center of the table, I draw it out from the rest. The photo captures the day Wren came for her private photography lesson, where both of us are standing on my porch. Obviously Wren didn't take this picture. But that's not the strangest part of it.

"Okay, if you look closely," I try to sound calm but instead sound like someone who should never be in charge of a hostage negotiation, "what do you notice about this picture?"

I point out a subtle glare that reflects a faint face hidden behind the camera in the foreground of the picture. In the background behind the face is the image of Wren and I standing on my porch talking moments before she came inside.

"It wasn't taken from right outside this house," Luca answers. "It was taken from behind a window. Up there."

He stands and walks to the living room window, then points across the street. Not at my mother's car crookedly parked in front of the house, but at the house across the street. Fred and Ivory's house.

"Specifically," he adds, "that second-story window."

"That's my bedroom," Ivory says. "Are you sure?"

I pick up the picture, examining it carefully. "I'm pretty sure. You can even see a smudge on the windowpane in the picture. And the downward angle definitely is from higher up, Ivory."

Freida shakes her head, insistent. "No, that's impossible. My dad would never do that. He doesn't even like photography."

"I agree," I say. "That's the weird part. Whoever took this didn't use their phone. This was taken with a professional zoom lens."

"But why *you*?" Ivory motions to the whole chronological collection of photos featuring me. "Why would someone be watching you specifically?"

"I don't know." As I say it, I can't help but glance at the bookshelf.

"Maybe someone broke into our house to frame Dad for taking these?" Freida suggests, and I catch her gaze shifting to Ivory. "Obviously someone is out to get him since they already tried to pin that lady's murder on him."

"Maybe," I waver, "but then there's this." I slide the Corvette purchase contract across the table toward Ivory.

"This is Wren's car." Ivory glances at me questioningly.

"Look at the date of purchase."

She reads it aloud. "The same day I went missing."

"So Wren bought a new car the same day Mom disappeared." Freida gets up from the table, pacing as she's thinking aloud. "And then someone used Dad's bedroom to spy on you. But none of this makes sense…"

Not yet it doesn't, but my gut feeling is that I'm close to unlocking the identity of Janet's killer and my stalker. One detail could be the key to finding out who exactly is behind it all. I just need to root out that detail. And soon. But even if I figured it out, the bigger question is how do I deal with it?

I'm convinced that my suspect list has narrowed considerably. Zala and Ali don't have any motive, so I've crossed them off my list. Fred's only crime was cheating on his wife and disappointing his daughter, which they only found out about because of me. Is that enough reason to stalk and harass me? People have killed for less, so I can't rule him out for at least some of what's happened.

Simpleminded Wren is an unlikely mastermind, probably blindly coerced by ex-boyfriend Marshall for a big payday. But

Gillian has plenty of reason to come after me for the evidence I have against Ramsey, and to kill Janet, who was investigating her. Plus her car is the one that hit me. Her son Marshall could have easily been persuaded to aid and abet her, since I am the reason his father is dead.

There's still the matter of the professional quality picture taken from Fred's bedroom. I know Marshall was in Fred's house, and Gillian could have slipped inside at some point too. But I'm forced to rule them out as I pick up the photograph, noting its tacky residue that reveals it was developed in a darkroom, but rushed and sloppily. This photo was underwashed and air-dried without proper rinsing. An amateur mistake by someone who knew what they were doing but didn't have the time to finish.

I rub my temples. My head feels like a computer overheating.

"Someone wants to pin that private investigator's murder on my dad," Freida says, covering her face with her sleeve, "but I know he would never do this. He just wouldn't."

I exchange a glance with Luca.

"Then we'll figure out a way to prove his innocence." I want to promise her this, but ultimately getting involved only puts me at greater risk of getting caught for my own crimes. "Something is happening around him, maybe involving him, maybe not. But someone is using your dad for something bigger."

"Bigger?" Ivory echoes. "How much bigger?"

I stare down at the photos. At my face. At my windows. At the angle from Fred's bedroom.

Then I consider the dent in Gillian's car, along with Gillian and Wren's matching sweatshirts. But most importantly, I dwell on the largest piece of evidence I still have that I know Gillian wants.

Chapter 44

I collect the photos into a neat stack and set them aside, unable to look at them any longer. Freida props her hands on his hips, and Ivory exhales a long, exhausted sigh.

"Okay," Luca says, slapping his thighs before stretching his lanky arms upward. "My brain is fried. I'm going to go grab some dessert before we all lose our minds completely. Freida, want to come with me? Some fresh air might help."

Freida nods, shaky but seemingly relieved at any excuse to escape. She glances at Ivory—seeking permission, maybe.

Ivory strokes her daughter's hair. "Go with Luca, sweetie. Bring back whatever doesn't look like Wren baked it."

Freida manages a weak grin and follows Luca out the door, and I notice their hands brushing against each other, then clasping together. I hope to God this doesn't rekindle their forbidden romance. My mother offers to take Zoomie on an overdue walk, since he's spent the better part of the past hour resting his slobbery jowls on every lap hoping someone would drop food.

Now it's just me and Ivory, like the good ol' days before her disappearance and my constant state of dread. Except it doesn't feel like the good ol' days at all. It feels like I'm with a stranger.

I lean back in my chair, folding my arms. "Okay. It just you and me now. Do you want to tell me what's really going on?"

Ivory trains her eyes on her hands in her lap. "Shar, I'm as confused as you are."

"Don't lie to me, Ivory. I know it's you who took the picture of me from your bedroom, and who broke into my darkroom and left that note."

She's sitting close enough for me to grab her hand and flip it over. I'm not focusing on her wrists, though. I'm more concerned with her cracked and discolored fingertips.

"Your fingers tell me everything I need to know."

Only Ivory could have shot the photo from her bedroom, and not just because of the skill level needed to execute this type of long-distance shot. But because of her cracked fingertips.

"That photo was waxy, Ivory, which is a telltale sign of rushing the development process. You're the only one who knows how to develop film, though you should know better than to rush. That's why your fingertips are messed up—the fixer solution damaged your skin."

"I swear it wasn't me." Ivory closes her eyes, and a tear slides down her cheek.

"You're still going to deflect? If it wasn't you, then who?"

"You don't know what he's capable of," she insists.

"Stop with all of the vague excuses and lies! This picture proves you were watching me, Ivory. Hardly anyone else in my classes knows the difference between a camera lens and a paperweight. But you do."

Her head snaps up.

"But somehow Wren ended up with that photo. So when I start to connect the dots, Ivory, you are at the center of everything that's been happening. First you disappear, then someone stalks me, and Janet Vick ends up murdered. But what I don't know is why you're after me. What did I do to piss you off?"

Her hands grip and tighten on the edge of the table.

"Shar—" Her voice is too controlled. I feel something shift, like a blade sliding out of its sheath.

"Was it all about revenge?" I'm a runaway train who can't stop talking. "Were you angry with Fred about the affair and blamed me for telling you?"

"Stop." Her voice deepens with a dark warning.

"I know you. You're someone who hates being underestimated. And I know you were still angry about your ex's betrayal. But that had nothing to do with me. So why target me?"

Ivory stares at something on the table. Her jaw twitches and her hands slowly move from the table's edge to resting flat on its surface.

"You know what? If you're not going to tell me, let's let Detective Yankovic sort it out." I pick up my cell phone and start dialing. First the 9, then the 1, then—

A stupid move, I realize too late.

Ivory jumps up suddenly, the chair grating violently across the floor. Her hands are reaching for something—it happens too fast—but I'm too slow. Two different weapons are within her grasp, and within less than a second she'll be holding either a knife or a corkscrew. Or if she's a quick draw, both.

"Iv—" I begin to plead, but her hand is already grabbing the knife without hesitation. For one suspended second we stare at each other before she lunges. The knife slices through the air, and the overhead light flashes against the blade.

"What are you doing?" I scream, stumbling backward as the pointed metal arcs toward me, catching on my sleeve and shredding a hole in it.

Her face is not scared but desperate, and her desperation is fierce.

"You don't understand!" she cries, propelling the knife forward again.

And I realize that no, I don't understand. Not yet, but I'm about to. If I survive the next three seconds.

Chapter 45

Ivory springs at me again, and the blade whistles past my cheek so close I feel the air shift. My phone drops to the floor as I blindly scramble along the table, smacking my hand on the surface until it lands on the heavy ceramic serving bowl. I raise it in front of me like a shield. Thanks to my time in the slammer, I know how to handle a knife fight.

She slashes again, and I block her with the bowl. The impact rings up my arms like I've just absorbed a lightning strike. Rushing me with her full body weight, her extra inches of height give her the advantage over my extra belly weight as she easily overpowers me. She rips the bowl from my grip and shatters it against the wall.

I'm empty-handed against her wild swings while the blade arcs back and forth in front of me, missing me by mere inches as I duck around the table. Her eyes are wild, wet, burning with something that isn't just anger. It's devotion. Obsession. But fighting is more exhausting than most realize. Within a couple minutes Ivory's arms are spent, and she pulls back, chest heaving.

I have barely a moment to dart past her while she catches her breath, but I succeed in reaching the other side of the dining room before she catches up. I'm left with a choice between my phone or the corkscrew as my last resort. Ivory's rounding the table, leaving me with the corkscrew as my best defense. Placing it between my index and middle finger, I aim the twisty point at my friend, wondering how we got to this point.

"Please stop!" I beg, and Ivory pauses just long enough for me to jab at her, forcing her a step back. "What is going on?"

We're in a faceoff, but she has momentarily stopped swinging. "None of this was ever about Fred. You think this is about his affair?"

"If it's not about Fred, then what's it about?"

Ivory's sucking in frantic breaths. "You have to promise not to tell the police."

I shake my head. "It's too late for that."

I really should think before I speak. We both swing almost simultaneously, her knife slicing across my arm while my corkscrew grazes her chest. She reels back, hunched over, and I grab my fileted skin and cover it with the shredded sleeve of my shirt. Our friendship vanishes in an instant, and we've become rival animals fighting for survival.

Taking only a moment to assess her wound, she comes at me again, charging after me as I dart into the kitchen. I throw myself sideways as her knife stabs into the cupboard door behind me. She yanks at it furiously, but the blade sticks. I kick her shin hard enough to knock her off balance. She stumbles, crashing into the center island.

The knife falls on the tile. I dive for it. So does she. We collide, both of us scrambling for the handle. Her nails rake across my wrist, but her hesitation gives me enough time to reach it first. My fingers close around the knife, and without looking, I stab it in her direction. It sinks into her stomach, then I pull it out and fling it across the room. It skitters under a barstool.

Ivory's breath breaks, but she chases after the knife, me clumsily trailing. My body hasn't had a workout like this in months, and I'm feeling every bleeding cut, every muscle shaking, my adrenaline fading. Ivory collapses against the barstool leg, grabbing her bleeding abdomen with one hand and the knife with the other, sobbing so hard she quivers.

I crawl backward facing her, panting like my lungs are about to explode. We stare at each other, her holding out the knife, me holding out the corkscrew, but neither of us wanting to engage.

Every cell in my body vibrates with the urge to attack, but I don't. My body is too fatigued, and it's not about winning a battle. I just need to know the truth.

"You said it's not about Fred. Then what's it about? We're best friends. What is going on?"

Her face twists with pain, and she clutches her stomach. "We weren't supposed to be friends, Shar."

How could she say this? From the moment we met, friendship was our destiny. "What do you mean?"

"Oh, Shar," she sighs, "I knew Gillian way before I met you. We've been planning your downfall since before you arrived in Doomwood Falls."

I slump against the cabinet as the gashes across my arms start to burn and my hit-and-run injuries catch up with me.

"Why?" is all I have the energy to ask.

"She knew about my cybersecurity and police work background. She hired me as a headhunter to seek you out, offer you a job when no one else would, and convince you to move here to Doomwood Falls with the intent to ruin your life. From the moment I reached out to you on that headhunter website, it was so I could play you. I even used an old police case as inspiration for my own abduction."

No, this can't be true. "So you *did* fake it."

"Initially, yes."

I can understand Gillian hating me, but I had never met Ivory before moving here. "What did I ever do to you that made you dead set on ruining my life?"

"You ruined my life first."

My arm dips slightly. Ivory's bleeding too much, and I'm worried it could be fatal. "I need to call 9-1-1 before you lose too much blood."

"Wait!" She raises her hand with the knife to stop me. "Not until I tell you everything. In case I don't get another chance. Please."

I wave my corkscrew for her to hurry up. "You were about to tell me how I ruined your life. Though I didn't even know you. And about Gillian... how did you know her before all this?"

"Ramsey Shenk." The name shoves a pick in my eardrum. "Ram is dead because of you."

The house tilts around me, or maybe I'm the one tilting. My sense of balance shifts drastically. "How do you know Ramsey?"

"He was my husband, Shari," she says, lowering the blade slightly. It might be enough that I can grab it out of her hand. Or maybe kick it, if I had any aim left in me, which I don't.

"Ramsey Shenk is the man who broke your heart?" *Twice,* I want to remind her, but I don't for the sake of self-preservation. "That's how you know Gillian—through

Ramsey."

"Yes, she stole him from me but you killed him." She sobs, releasing the knife to clatter to the floor. "Gillian saw your brother Luca boarding Ram's boat on the same day the boat sunk and Ram died. Gillian figured out that you had your brother kill Ramsey in an act of revenge."

"That's not—that's not what happened," Well, not exactly. I hope she'll listen to each breathless word I need to say. "Ramsey lied about the embezzlement, and Gillian helped cover it up. Gillian is just as much of a liar as Ramsey is. Why do you think Gillian never told the police about Luca? Because it's a lie!"

I think she's actually believing me, but then she launches into a whole new direction. "I was so angry with you when Gillian told me what you did to Ram, she begged for my help. That's why she's here."

"That doesn't explain why she seduced Fred. Or why she killed Janet Vick," I remind her. "Gillian is here to cover up something worse."

I swallow down the memory that invades me. I recall every word of my last conversation with Stewart, on the night before he died, when he admitted he'd made a terrible mistake investigating Ramsey. Stew sensed Ramsey caught wind that he was about to be exposed. Hours later a supposed hunting accident took my husband's life. The next think I knew, evidence against me was planted and I found myself on trial.

"Ramsey killed my husband, but he needed to discredit me so no one would believe a word I said when I turned him over to the police. And he won. But I had evidence that proves what he did—the embezzlement, the murder, everything. And Gillian doesn't want it leaked. *That's* why she's here, and *that's* why she's using you to get to me."

"I know." Pain rips through Ivory's expression, distorting her features. "That's why I came back."

"Came back?" I echo.

"Gillian and I initially planned for me to disappear with the intent to frame you for my abduction, but then Freida found me. She was convinced I had it wrong about you, that you were a loyal friend. And she was right."

"So why didn't you tell all this to the police?"

Ivory's head drops and her chin meets her collarbone. "Gillian threatened to frame me for Janet Vick's murder if I came clean."

"But you still told the police that Fred kidnapped you! He's going to jail for a crime he didn't commit."

"The asshole should have thought twice before he cheated on me! I expect no less from Gillian—she stole Ram from me twice, after all. So it's not a surprise that she would attempt to seduce my husband. But Fred vowed never to betray me and he did it anyway. I was furious, Shar. And hurt." Her eyes flutter closed, and her breaths grow shallow. "But this conversation isn't about Fred. It's about you and me."

She goes still, and for a moment I wonder if she's dead. I shuffle across the tile beside her, wrapping my arm around her. Her body is warm, her lungs rising and falling, but I don't think she has much time left.

"I need to call for help."

Grabbing my wrist, she shakes her head. "Not yet. I need you to know I'm sorry, Shar, for everything. If it's any consolation, I love you like a sister. And I'll tell the police the truth about everything. Even Fred's innocence."

Although I now know the truth, it brings me no comfort. Ram didn't just destroy my life while he was alive. He's still destroying it from beyond the grave. Piece by piece. Person by person. Friend by friend.

He turned my best friend against me and destroyed Ivory's marriage. He created a murderer out of Gillian and a liar out of Ivory. And now that I know the truth, I have no idea what to do with it. I've been behind bars and I don't want to do that to my best friend.

But that's the least of my worries. The blood isn't just seeping anymore, it's pooling around her. A flashback of Stew's mortal injury fills me with trauma all over again. This is far too similar. She needs emergency medical attention, like five minutes ago.

"Ivory…" I whisper, watching the bloodstain spreading across her shirt. "I'm calling 9-1-1."

But she doesn't move. I jerk up to my feet, squat beside her, and press my fingers to her neck. I can't feel a pulse or anything, but I don't know if I'm even doing it right. I grab the hand towel from off of the counter and press it to her abdomen, unsure if I'm even in the right spot. There's too much blood to see the wound.

My phone—I need to find my phone. I last remember having it in the dining room, and I search the floor until I spot it. The phone case slips in my palm, and the screen can't detect my blood-covered fingers. I wipe my hands on my pants and try again, this time bringing my phone to life.

The 9-1-1 operator asks me what my emergency is, but when I return to the kitchen where Ivory had been laying at the foot of the barstool, the space is empty except for a bloody trail that smears across the floor toward my open back door. The gate along the fence creaks closed, which is where I assume Ivory has already headed.

I run to the backyard screaming, "Ivory? Wait!"

She's long gone. I sink to the cold hard patio, hand pressed to my heart. I'm alive, but I'm worried Ivory won't make it through the night.

Chapter 46

A car door slams just as I finish washing the blood—Ivory's, mine, who knows—off my hands. My arms vehemently shake. My breath feels stuck in my lungs. I'm trying to scrub away the appearance of someone who just stabbed her best friend.

The front door opens, and I'm standing at the kitchen sink when Luca enters, smiling cheerfully with Freida's hand in his. "Hey, we picked up dessert! And Freida stopped by her house to grab some clothes. She's going to spend the ni—"

His smile vanishes when he sees my face, then he lowers the grocery bag when his gaze flicks over my shirt. Freida steps in behind him carrying a stuffed bookbag, her eyes widening the instant they pass over my torn sleeve, then behind me at the kitchen floor that resembles a butcher shop. I pivot around to see what devastation I left in the wake of battle—the shattered bowl, blood everywhere, the corkscrew on the floor… but no knife. Ivory must have taken it with her.

"Where's my mom?"

I swallow hard as I glance down at my clothes. "She took off."

Freida's face breaks as her eyes skim over my bloody shirt. "What do you mean she took off? Where did she go? Is she okay?"

"I don't know." I'm trying to sound soothing, but it's

coming out shrill because I'm panicking on the inside and don't know what to do. "She's hurt and needs urgent medical attention. But she ran off and I don't know where she went."

"Why didn't you call the cops?" Freida shrieks.

"She told me not to." It sounds lame coming out of my mouth, but it's all I can offer.

Dropping her bookbag at her feet, Freida turns to the door—probably to go in search of her mom—and I rest my hand on her shoulder. I need to warn her so she doesn't make things worse for Ivory.

"What your mom told me is bad, Freida. Really bad. Your mom would go to jail for it. That's why she ran off, and I don't know what to do to help her."

Freida's lip trembles. She glances up at Luca for reassurance, but he's staring at me like I'm about to detonate.

"What exactly did she do?" he asks.

Freida suddenly blurts, "I already know that she faked her kidnapping and lied about my dad. She was helping the crazy rich lady—Gillian—who killed that private investigator. I saw my mom meeting with her right before she *'disappeared.'*" Freida air quotes the word with both index and middle fingers. "Initially Mom went to a beach resort, which is where I found her."

So Ivory *was* at the resort where Detective Yankovic had pinged her phone and where she had texted me from. At least that part of her story is true.

Luca's head snaps toward Freida. "You knew where your mom was the whole time?"

"Yes, and I'm sorry I lied." She hangs her head, swiping at tears that dribble down her chin. "I had no other choice…"

"It's okay, honey. You were trying to protect your mom." I shake my head, a mixture of frustration and despair for this young girl put in an impossible situation.

"No, it's not okay!" Luca spits. "You let the police and the whole town—and my sister, *her best friend*—think she was abducted and hurt… or that she was dead!"

I still don't understand how Ivory could have pretended it all. The scars on her wrists, the bruises on her face, they were real. I can't imagine her inflicting those on herself in a make-believe abduction. But I can envision Gillian helping with that…

"I didn't know what to do," Freida pleads with me, the only one left on her mom's side. "Gillian was after you. She even got her son in on it—that Marshall guy. He paid Wren to hit you with Gillian's car! That's how psychotic that lady is."

Luca turns to me. "Wait, are you saying Ivory didn't just 'find' you? She—"

"Lured me to Doomwood Falls," I finish the sentence for him. "Gillian sought Ivory out after I got out of jail because she blamed me for Ramsey's death. Apparently Ivory was married to Ramsey before Gillian met him—"

"*Stole* him," Freida corrects me. "Gillian stole him from my mom. It really messed her up for years, even after she married my dad. But I guess I should thank Gillian for that, because otherwise I never would have been born."

Luca wanders into the kitchen, picking up the bloody corkscrew and tossing it in the sink. "So now what do we do? Do we call the cops to sort it out?"

"I think we have to. She'll bleed to death if we don't find her."

"But she'll go to jail!" Freida wails. "They'll save her life then throw her in jail for helping Gillian murder that private investigator. And probably for faking her abduction too. My mom would rather *die* than go to jail."

"I don't think that's true, Freida." I've been to jail, and while it wasn't a picnic, I came out of it maybe not wiser but definitely stronger.

The poor girl's lips are a pale blue and she's shivering. A maternal instinct I didn't know I have kicks in. "How about I make you some hot tea and I'll go search for your mom? You look like you're freezing."

She nods weakly and reaches for her bookbag. I do a double-take at what she pulls out.

"Where did you get that?" I demand.

Chapter 47

I grab the neon pink sweatshirt from Freida, and she attempts to yank it back when I hold it up and read the embroidered *I*.

"Who gave this to you?"

"It's my mom's. Someone at my dad's work was selling customized sweatshirts for a Kick Breast Cancer's Ass fundraiser and he bought her one. The *I* is for *Ivory* since they could only pick one letter for the embroidering. Everyone is supposed to wear them this month for the fundraiser."

I for Ivory Cobb. *W* for Wren. *S* for Szabo. Pink for breast cancer awareness. What I thought was a case-cracking clue turns out to be a coincidence.

Fred had bought one for Ivory, and Marshall had probably bought one for Wren—his girlfriend at the time—and his mom Gillian. Ironically, all of them are involved in some way, and I have a sweatshirt to thank for tying the bow that holds them together.

I hand the sweatshirt back to Freida. "I have to find your mom. Any idea where she might be?"

Freida's mouth tightens when I ask about her mother. Not in anger, but in that careful way people get when they're choosing which truth to serve and which to hide under a napkin. "I have no idea."

That's not an answer. It's a door closed firmly.

"Was there anywhere special you two would go?" If Ivory is dying, there's a good chance she'd go somewhere sentimental.

"Not anywhere within walking distance." Freida shakes her head and her ponytail swishes like punctuation. *Period.* "Maybe my dad would know."

I remind my brother to make Freida some tea before crossing the street, my shoes scuffing along the asphalt. The houses sit in their neat suburban rows with windows gawping like unblinking eyes. Everything looks normal right up until it isn't.

I'm halfway to Fred's front door when something catches my peripheral vision. A light. A thin, moving blade of white slicing through the trees in Fred's backyard. I stop walking and the light disappears. Then it reappears, weaker this time, darting in and out of view.

I cut along the side of the house through the fence gate, pushing it slowly enough not to let it creak. The backyard is deeper than it looks from the street. Beyond Ivory's well-tended garden beds the yard is overgrown. Untamed. Bushes press in on each other, and the grass is wild, swallowing my legs whole.

The light flickers again. It's coming from the far corner near the shed, buried behind wild blackberry vines and thorny brush. It's a crumbling structure that used to be beige and is now a moldy black. The roof sags in the middle like it's tired of holding itself up. One window is gone entirely, just a dark, jagged mouth.

The light pulses unsteadily from inside then blinks off. Shrub limbs grab at my jeans. A thorn catches my sleeve and tears a thread loose. The shed emerges from the thicket, its broken door hanging open just enough for a person to slip through—so I do. The wood is soft under my palm, splintering slightly, like it's been waiting to give up. I head in.

The scent of wood rot and gasoline infiltrate me. My reflection stares back in a cracked window, fracturing my face into pieces I barely recognize.

"Ivory?" I call out but receive no answer except for the rustle of leaves either outside the shed or somewhere within.

Along one wall shelves sag under the weight of forgotten junk. Rakes, empty paint cans, a broken lawn chair folded in on itself. Then I hear movement. I realize I'm unarmed, and if Ivory's here, the knife she had taken makes me question how stupid I'm being.

"Ivory, I just want to help you," I tell the darkness in case Ivory is listening.

I'm going in blind, so I hold out my phone and turn on the flashlight. The beam skims the corners of the room, and I expect it to land on Ivory hiding in shadows, knife poised and ready to strike. But what the light lands on isn't Ivory. It's so much worse.

Chapter 48

My flashlight passes over something so sickening my stomach squeezes. I kneel down for a closer look, unable to process what I'm looking at.

Two zip ties lie coiled on the wooden floor like two dead worms, the teeth marks revealing the smaller one had been chewed in half and the larger one smoothly cut. Probably from a tool Ivory had found lying around. The smaller one for her wrists, the larger one for her ankles. The visual of her wounded wrists comes back to me uninvited.

A shelf of paint cans lines the wall, and one sits crookedly on the floor next to the zip ties. The paint rimming the lid is white, but there is a clear spot of red along the edge of the base. Like it had been used as a weapon on someone's face. Specifically Ivory's face, where I saw a cut and bruises.

Dried blood is smeared in uneven strokes across the plywood floor, up the rotting walls. Ivory's initial story about the abduction was never made up after all—this proves she had been bound. Through the broken window I catch a lamp illuminating Fred's window as his silhouette passes back and forth across the room. Fred effortlessly lied to my face about not having an affair. And I fell for it again when he lied about not abducting Ivory.

I step in something wet that sticks my shoe to the floor. For a second I hold my breath as I shine my light downward. A fresh, glistening trail of blood leads toward a floor-to-ceiling garden tool bin in the corner.

"I know you're in here," I whisper. "Are you okay?"

I follow the bloody trail, every step feeling like I'm walking into a nightmare. When I reach the plastic door, my hand shakes so badly I have to grip the rusted metal handle with both hands just to keep hold of it. I pull it open and skim the tiny space with my flashlight. Ivory is there, huddled but unmoving inside, arms loosely wrapped around her knees, braids hanging over her face. Blood drenches her shirt in a wide red bloom.

"Ivory!" I drop down beside her, pressing my hand to her cheek. It's wet—thankfully not with blood but tears. Her skin feels unnaturally cold. "We need to get you to a hospital."

She flinches at my touch, then blinks up at me like she's not certain I'm real. "I have you to thank for that…" She grins weakly, and her voice is barely a sound.

"I'm so sorry, Ivory. I never wanted to hurt you! I thought you were trying to kill me."

She presses her finger to my lips and lets out a long, "Shhh. It's okay, Shar. I know you didn't mean to. We both messed up. But that's not why I'm here. I have to give something to you."

She weakly shifts around, patting her hand on the floor finding nothing but empty space.

"Don't worry about that right now." I reach down, trying to squeeze my arm under her legs. "I'm going to lift you up and get you to the house."

"No!" Her hand clamps onto my wrist, surprisingly strong.

I'm worried I'm hurting her, making it worse. "Then I'll call 9-1-1. They should be here in a couple minutes. Just hang on, okay?"

She grabs my phone before I can dial and tosses it across the shed. "No doctors. No police. I have to find it."

"Find what?" I stare at her, stunned. But she's fading. Fast. "Ivory, you'll die if we don't get you to a hospital. It'll be okay. I'll be there for you."

Her lips tremble. A fresh tear slips down her cheek, streaking through the dirt. "I can't."

"You can't what?"

"I can't go to the police," she mutters weakly. Her eyes flutter and I'm terrified I'm losing her.

"You won't go to jail. I know Fred actually did abduct you. I saw the zip ties. And the bruises on your face—"

"It wasn't Fred," she states firmly. "A paint can fell on my head. Go look for yourself."

Maybe that part is true, but those zip ties don't lie. "You don't need to cover for him, Ivory. He can't hurt you anymore. But we need to make sure the police know what he did to you."

She shakes her head, but it's barely a movement. "I don't deserve your compassion." She swallows hard, eyes shifting to the shadows behind me.

"I stabbed you, girl. It's the least I can do."

"Well, I stabbed you first, Shar. Give credit where credit is due," she says with a fragile chuckle. "But that's not what I mean." Her breaths are coming out wet and wheezy now. It's going to be too late to save her if we don't leave now. "I need to give you something important."

I nod, hoping this will be quick because we're running out of time.

"When Ram broke my heart for the second time," her eyes

open, then drift shut again as if her life force is being sucked out of her, "I never recovered from the heartbreak. Ram knew it too, because he kept tabs on me just to keep my life intertwined in his. He stayed in contact with me for years, and while I was happy with Fred and never betrayed my husband, I couldn't just shut Ram out. He knew this and used it against me."

I had always known Ivory was fettered to her past, but I wish it had been to someone more worthy of her affection.

"Ram told me you stole money from him, and when I looked you up and saw your criminal record," her voice breaks, "I assumed it was true. I was so stupid to believe him. So when Gillian asked me to help her avenge his death, I was willing to do anything to hurt the woman who killed my first love."

My chest feels as hollow as her voice.

"But then as I got to know you over the past year, I started to doubt what I knew. I should never have trusted Gillian or gone along with her original plan to frame you for abducting me. Unfortunately it got a little out of hand…"

A little out of hand is the biggest understatement of the century. A woman was murdered, Fred was charged with kidnapping, and I nearly died in a hit-and-run.

"…but I had tunnel vision. I wanted to hurt you like you hurt me when you killed Ram."

"But I didn't kill Ram!" I tell her.

"Of course I know that *now*. But I didn't back then, Shar."

"And what exactly were you planning to tell the police my motive was for abducting you? Because they'd never believe I'd abduct you without a reason."

"Oh, Shar." She laughs at this, and it sounds like her laugh. The one she used every day with me when I'd say something silly or wear ridiculous thrift store sweatpants with *Juicy* across the butt. "It was actually a pretty good motive I had created for you. I was going to paint you as a jealous best friend who went crazy when I started distancing myself from you and making other friends. With your criminal background I figured it'd be pretty believable."

Considering the secret I've been hiding from her, Ivory might know me better than I know myself.

"How very *Single White Female*. So what made you decide not to go through with it and to blame Fred instead?"

Ivory scoffs. "The bastard cheated on me, so he kind of sealed his own fate. But the nail in the plan's coffin was Gillian turning into an actual psychopath. When she killed that private investigator I knew I had to end this whole charade. I'm so sorry for all of it, Shar. I thought I was angry with you for killing Ram, but really I was angry at him for hurting me and outsourcing my misery to you." Her breath hitches sharply, and I finally understand. Really understand.

Hurt doesn't disappear. It relocates.

She had said this to me right before this all started. How true it was.

Her breaths are becoming shallower, her eyes barely able to stay open. At the rate she's bleeding, I'm worried she won't live long enough for me to find my phone she tossed amid all the junk.

"Ivory." I reach for her hand and interlock her fingers between mine. "It's time. I have to go get help."

"First I need to give you this." She twists around, reaching for something behind her and pulls it out. "Found it!"

She holds my hand open, palm up, and places the object in

my hand. Looking down at it, I know what it means, what my friend who is like a sister—a dysfunctional somewhat crazy sister—is trying to tell me.

Chapter 49

The cold seeps into my palm as Ivory presses a picture frame into my hand. Behind the glass rests a faded photograph of a cabin. Sunlight streams through the trees, dappling the porch. I remember Ivory and I hiking to this place together chatting about growing old together, a dream we held close. Now it just feels like another ache.

The cabin wavers, blurring under my tears. With the wood worn smooth from age and tender care, it's the thick frame Stewart found in an antique shop and whittled a secret compartment in it to blend with the wood grain. Inside that compartment I had hid the safe deposit box key that held all of Stewart's embezzlement evidence against Ramsey Shenk, along with the SD card with video footage of him killing my husband. And now I have it all back.

"I saw you opening the compartment once, when you didn't know I was watching," Ivory says, her voice draining into the silence snuffing her out.

"Did you look at what was inside?"

"Yes," she continues, a strange mix of sorrow and determination in her eyes. "I know everything Ramsey did to Stewart… and to you."

My grasp tightens at Ramsey's name that has become a stone that sinks in my chest. Memories flood back, unwelcome and brutal, images I've fought so hard to keep locked away.

"You and Stewart deserve justice, Shari. I want to give that to you." The offer is nothing but a breathy whisper.

Justice. The word echoes even though it feels distant, unattainable, a cruel joke. I want to scream, to lash out, to tell her there's no such thing as justice if she dies, because that feels inevitable now that she's clinging to a thread of life. I look at the picture of the cabin, at the promise of peace it holds, a promise that was stolen from us both.

Ivory stubbornly waits, patiently letting time stop. Each moment is a weighty burden that she's taking from me as she holds me in place, one hand clutching mine and refusing to release me.

I close my eyes, and for the first time, I consider what she's telling me to do. Expose the truth. Release the pain. Surrender the fight. And give Stewart a little bit of peace. It will finally be over.

"I'm ready." Ivory releases her grip on me, and I rush to where I think I saw her toss the phone. I search for the glossy reflection of glass on the floor.

"We'll get you fixed up, Ivory. You're strong. I know you'll be okay," I reassure her, myself, both of us.

I finally find my phone hidden under a broken bucket and start to dial, but Ivory's softspoken words stop me. It takes every ounce of my focus to hear her.

"Shar," she rasps. "When the cops ask, tell them it was me."

"Tell them what was you? I don't understand."

"The abduction. It was me."

But that doesn't make sense. In fact, the more I think about it, the less sense all of it makes. Ivory is holding something back.

Someone did take her. Someone did bind and torture her. And I stepped into their crime scene when I followed Ivory in here.

"No," I argue, "I know you were actually abducted. I saw the bondage marks on your wrists. You didn't do that to yourself. Who? Was it Fred?"

Her head lolls weakly. "I already told you it wasn't Fred."

My pulse pounds in my ears. "Then who? Was it Gillian? Or Marshall? Ivory, please—who?"

She opens her mouth, but only a gurgle comes out. Her eyes roll back.

"Ivory!" I shake her shoulders. "Ivory, stay with me!"

She slumps forward limply, but she's already gone. I feel her soul depart as if it was my own. I fumble my phone with trembling fingers and dial 9-1-1. I'm barely able to choke out the address before the operator dispatches emergency services. When I hang up, her stillness smothers me and the questions that will never be answered haunt me.

Ivory wasn't lying. She was abducted. Someone bound her up. Hurt her. Left her to die. My throat tightens as I stare at the open garden shed door. If it wasn't Fred… then who?

And then there's the biggest mystery of all. While Ivory was bound up in this garden shed, who was running around breaking my camera, developing pictures in my darkroom, and stealing my cabin photo? I may never know, and I'm not sure I'm okay with that.

Chapter 50

Funerals aren't supposed to be this bright.

The sun hangs high over Doomwood Falls Cemetery, glaring down on us like it's offended that we gathered for something as dark as death. It feels wrong. My best friend is about to be lowered into the ground, and the sky is offering a perfect, cloudless blue. As if the world has the audacity to keep going.

My knees threaten to give out as I approach the open casket. I don't want to look, but I need to. A woman who doesn't look like Ivory lies inside, too still, her fake eyelashes brushing her cheeks like delicate shadows. Her mother unbraided her hair—Ivory would've hated that. Her lips have been painted a soft rose, not the red lipstick I'm used to. And around her neck, glowing gold against her skin like a cruel joke, is her necklace that matches mine.

Two tiny interlocking lilies. One for her. One for me.

I clamp a hand over my mouth, but the sob breaks out anyway—raw, ugly, and loud. A few people turn. I don't care. My chest feels like it's collapsing, bone by bone. Because this is my fault.

If I hadn't come to Doomwood Falls, if my mess hadn't followed me here, if I hadn't stabbed her, even if I'd found her in the garden shed sooner, maybe her body wouldn't be lying in a casket. My best friend is dead because of me.

"Shari," someone whispers behind me, but I can't look away from Ivory's face. I memorize every line, every softness, knowing this is the last time. When the funeral director approaches to close the lid, I almost scream for him to stop.

"No, wait." My fingers brush Ivory's arm. She's not warm like the Ivory I need her to be. My voice cracks. "I—I just… I can't. Please—"

"Shari." It's Fred's voice this time, thick and trembling. "It's time to say goodbye."

He's crying. Seeing tears on his cheeks—real ones—nearly sends me spiraling again. But it's Freida, Ivory's daughter, who hugs me and places a hand on my shoulder. A light touch. Gentle, but firm.

"We'll make sure she's safe," she murmurs.

Safe? She's about to be buried six feet underground. She's never going to be safe again. None of us will.

When the lid finally lowers with a heavy, final creak, something inside my chest fractures. I choke on a sob so violent I double over. Fred catches my elbow, steadying me, and I don't even have the strength to pull away.

Being a pallbearer feels surreal, like my body is moving while my mind is still kneeling beside her in the shed. Ivory bleeding. Ivory fading. Ivory whispering secrets I'll never get answers to.

We lift her. The weight knocks the air from my lungs—not because the casket is heavy, but because I am holding what's left of her. My best friend. My soul sister. I don't let go. Even when we reach the gravesite. Even when they tell me my part is done. Even when people begin drifting away, whispering condolences I can't hear. I stay rooted beside the casket, staring at the polished wood as if I can will it to open again, as if I can force time to rewind.

Freida steps up to the mound of ready dirt. Her black dress flutters in the unseasonably warm breeze, and red veins run across the whites of her eyes. She grips Fred's arm with both hands like she needs him in order to keep standing.

"My mother, Ivory Cobb…" Her voice wobbles at first, then strengthens. "What can I say about her? My mother loved deeply. Too deeply. She gave parts of herself to the world that she should've kept protected. She wanted to save people. Even when they didn't deserve to be saved."

Her gaze flicks to Fred. He bows his head, shoulders shaking as he sobs.

Then her eyes slide to me. "I always felt like it was my job," Freida continues, "to protect her from herself. From her big heart. From the way she trusted too easily."

My throat tightens. I know the words are for the crowd, not for me, but I feel them like unforgiving fingers wrapping around my throat. Because that's exactly what Ivory did. She trusted the wrong people—me, Ramsey Shenk, and Gillian. And now she's dead.

Freida inhales shakily. "But even though I couldn't protect her in the end, I know she loved us. All of us. And she wouldn't want us to fall apart because she's gone."

Her voice breaks at the last word. People sniffle. Someone behind me weeps openly. But all I can hear is Ivory's voice in that shed:

It wasn't Fred.

Then who held her captive, bound her wrists so tight they

cut and bled? The question drills into my skull like a parasite. Because I still don't have the answer and never will.

Freida closes her speech with a trembling smile and Fred guides her to the casket and hands her a white lily—so perfectly suited to Ivory—to toss onto her casket with a handful of dirt. I watch them through a haze, my heartbeat too loud, my vision misting. Because as I stand here beside my best friend's grave, guilt soaking into my bones like poison, I realize something terrifying.

Everyone believes Ivory's story ended here. But I know the truth. It didn't. And whoever abducted Ivory isn't finished.

Chapter 51

By the time I pull into my driveway, my dress is damp with tears. My legs ache from standing graveside for hours, refusing to move, refusing to let myself accept that Ivory is gone. The air in the neighborhood feels heavier than the cemetery, like it's suffocating me with Ivory's ghost.

Ever since I gave Stew's evidence and my trail cam footage to the BBPD, all of Hemlock Drive treats me differently. Almost reverential. And maybe a little scared of me too. I was exonerated of the embezzlement crimes, but Ivory still died at my hand, and that's all anyone remembers. Although it was ruled self-defense, there are always doubters out there. Some of them even live on my street.

Two doors down from me, Zala pauses while raking her leaves, staring at me the way someone might look at a car crash. She quickly pretends she wasn't. Helping her corral the leaves into piles to mulch is Ali, who lifts a hand in silent greeting. Fred has been staying out of the spotlight for the time being, and I can't decide if he's acting suspicious or wary. But Wren's house remains dark and empty ever since she was arrested for assault with a deadly weapon and solicitation to commit felony assault. She'll never drive again.

Marshall didn't get off easy when he was charged with solicitation of a violent crime. When he finishes his sentence he'll still be young enough to sleaze his way into a new girl's heart, but at least he won't have the big bank account and fancy car to help him. As for Gillian, she'll be doing life behind bars. I even made sure to let my *friends* on the inside know all about her in case they wanted to tell her I said hi.

On a positive note, everyone in Doomwood Falls now knows Gillian killed Janet Vick once her mugshot hit the *Doomwood Falls Daily*. But they still believe Ivory faked her own abduction and Fred was cleared of all charges. It doesn't matter what I tell them, that there had to be someone else involved because Ivory would not have zip tied herself. It doesn't matter that all the evidence points to Ivory being a victim. Some people look straight through the truth, as if it were made of glass.

I shut my car door too hard, and the sound startles a flock of sparrows from the telephone line. The silence afterward is fragile, like everything around me is one breath away from shattering.

When I turn toward my house, I spot Freida in her driveway, shoving suitcases into the trunk of her hatchback. She keeps glancing around like she's afraid someone's watching. Everyone has been a little jumpy since Janet's murder.

"Freida!" I call after her on my way across the street. The autumn weather is kindly warm, but I can't shake the nonstop chill. I meet her at the trunk of her car. "Going on a trip?"

She slams the trunk shut. Her face is streaked with dried mascara, but she forces a smile that looks more like a frown. "Yeah. My mom is gone and I just need to start over. There's too much trauma here."

My heart contracts painfully with empathy. "Did you say

goodbye to Luca?"

Freida shakes her head. "No, can you tell your brother for me? And please tell him I'm sorry. I just can't be a girlfriend right now. Not with everything that's happened."

"I understand." I really do. I don't know how long it will be until I can be a friend to anyone after losing Ivory so tragically.

There is something I need to ask her before she's gone, but I'm terrified to speak the words. More terrified to hear what she'll say.

"Can I ask you something?" I venture tentatively, hoping I don't regret this.

"Sure." She opens her driver's side door, tapping her fingers impatiently on the hood of the car.

Freida isn't giving me much time to word it properly, so I just shove the question from my mouth: "Do you blame me for what happened to your mom? What I mean is, do you hate me?"

A tear slides down her cheek, and Freida clasps my hand. "No, you were her best friend and tried to help her, even after you found out she had been plotting against you. I know it wasn't your fault."

"I appreciate that. I just wish I could have done everything differently."

"Yeah, well, I'm sure my mom wished that too. You know, I hope I find a friend like you and my mom were. Someone who will keep my heart's secrets like you guys did." She looks at the ground like she's avoiding me.

Something in the way she says it—soft, careful, almost rehearsed—pricks the back of my neck. Freida steps toward me, arms open for a hug. I force myself to move into her embrace, but my whole body goes rigid. Her grip tightens, just a second too long, and something cool and hard brushes the side of my neck—metal. I pull back, startled. And that's when I see it.

The necklace. Two small gold lilies glinting against Freida's collarbone. My lungs seize.

That's Ivory's necklace. Except it can't be, because I placed it on her in the casket. I saw it resting against Ivory's skin when they closed the lid. I carried her to the grave with that necklace inside the box.

Before Freida releases me, she whispers something in my ear that has the effect of an ice bath.

"What do you mean?" I ask, but she's already slid into her car.

Wiping her cheeks one last time, she tries to hide the emotion on her face but she can't hide it from her voice. "Goodbye, Shari."

She shuts the door. The engine roars to life. My eyes dart from her face to the necklace again, exactly like mine. Except—

My hand flies to my neck. It's bare.

"No," I whisper. "How did she—?"

Then her car peels away from the curb. I don't wait around to watch her drive off before I bolt into my house so fast I nearly slip on the welcome mat. Once upstairs, I run straight into my bedroom where I had last put my necklace. My nightstand drawer jerks open under my shaking hand.

The little velvet box where I keep my necklace is empty and in its place sits a photograph. I pick it up with trembling fingers. With our arms linked, it's a picture of me and Ivory at the fair last spring after a near-death experience on the Salt and Pepper Shaker carnival ride. She's smiling, wide and bright, and I'm laughing beside her because every conversation with her had laughter.

On the back of the photo, in black ink, are the handwritten words:

If my heart's a secret, you're the keeper.

I've heard that phrase before. No, not heard it but *read* it. It's what Ivory and I had engraved on our matching necklaces. My pulse spikes, because I read it somewhere else too. The text I received supposedly from Ivory—rather, her phone—after she disappeared, claiming she was fine. Apparently she wasn't.

The room tilts. I almost collapse. It was Freida who abducted Ivory, not Fred, and I know now why.

After all the details about Gillian came out, I had assumed she had sent the text and taken part in the abduction, but Ivory never admitted to it. I couldn't understand why Ivory didn't blame Gillian for her abduction, when she confessed to everything else. Ivory had no reason to protect her. But for Freida, whose words echo in perfect alignment with the text, Ivory would do anything to protect. Even if it meant taking the identity of her kidnapper daughter to the grave so Freida wouldn't pay the price for her crime.

It wasn't Marshall or Fred or Gillian who staged Ivory's disappearance or abducted and tortured her. It was Freida, and a fragment of her funeral speech explains why.

I always had to protect her from herself… from how deeply she loved… from the ways she trusted too easily.

Freida's last words suddenly make sense. "*I did it to protect you too,*" she had whispered in my ear.

I didn't understand it at the funeral, but now I do. Freida

was trying to protect both of us—me from Ivory, and both of us from Gillian. She had known what her mother was plotting and didn't want my life ruined over Ramsey's mysterious death, or her mother thrown in jail over a man who never loved her. So she zip tied her mother in the garden shed to give her an alibi for Janet's murder. There was no way she could ever be connected to that homicide, despite Gillian's threat. Freida did what she had to in order to protect her mother, and Ivory kept that secret to protect her daughter.

If my heart's a secret, you're the keeper.

Freida's probably already halfway to the state line, and I'll let her keep going. No one will ever know the truth but me.

Chapter 52

The neighborhood is quieter now. A hush hangs over Doomwood Falls, like the whole town is embarrassed by what it let happen. Or maybe it's just relieved the truth finally bubbled its way to the surface, even if half the people still pretend a woman wasn't murdered in small-town America.

The scent of lemon oil is sharp enough to sting my nose. It's the smell of a normal Saturday, of chores and order while Mamma stands on her tiptoes, a feather duster raised like a scepter. She's humming something low and off-key, attacking the upper shelves of the built-in mahogany bookcase. Dust motes dance in the shaft of afternoon sunlight cutting across the room, oblivious to the darkness resting just inches behind the wood.

"Mamma," I start, keeping my voice level and eyes trained on the bookshelf. "You don't need to do that."

"Oh, hush, Shari." Her gray hair slips out of her loose bun as she dusts. "I like being useful. Your father always said a dusty book is a neglected friend."

She reaches up and her hand hovers over the vintage collection of Nancy Drew mysteries she gifted me when I was ten. The yellow columns are cracked and faded, but they are the only things on that shelf that matter. Her fingers curl around the spine of *The Secret of the Old Clock*.

"Should I do the honors?"

"Mamma, I really wish you wouldn't." But it's too late. She's already pulled the book, tilting it on the hidden hinge.

A heavy, mechanical *thunk* follows, the sound of a deadbolt sliding back, followed by the groan of greased metal. The entire center section of the bookcase shudders and swings open, breaking the illusion of a solid wall. The smell hits us instantly—no longer lemon oil, but something sour. The thick, humid stench of unwashed skin, damp concrete, and excrement. Instead of running away like a normal person, Mamma steps forward.

"Please let me take care of it." I lunge for her arm, but she's already crossing the threshold into the gloom.

"It's fine, honey. You don't need to do this alone," Mamma says.

I follow her into the dark hole, my hand instinctively pulling the thread that clicks on the light. A naked bulb buzzes to life overhead, casting harsh, yellow shadows against the soundproofing foam I stapled to the walls.

The room is small, a converted storage closet that doesn't exist on the house's blueprints. And in the center, huddled against a heavy pipe, is Ramsey Shenk.

He looks like the pathetic piece of garbage that he is. The man who destroyed my life, murdered my husband, framed me for embezzlement, and manipulated my best friend is currently reduced to a shivering heap in a stained undershirt. A heavy iron chain runs from his ankle to a pipe. Next to him sits a plastic bucket that serves as his toilet, radiating a pungent odor. A box of adult diapers was his reward for good behavior, which makes both of our cleanup jobs easier. On the floor, a paper plate is licked clean, nothing left but the red smear of dried marinara sauce, sitting beside a crinkled, empty water bottle.

Ramsey's winter gray eyes—a perfect match to his son Marshall's—blink rapidly while adjusting to the sudden light. He scrambles back until his rear end hits the wall and the chains rattle. His beard has grown in patchy and wild, and he looks hollowed out, like a ghost haunting my walls.

"Please," Ramsey croaks. His voice is wrecked from disuse. He looks from me to my mother, his eyes widening with a desperate, delirious hope. "Please, ma'am. Help me. She's crazy. She's kept me here for—I don't even know how long."

A little over a year I would remind him if I wanted to be cruel. But I'm not cruel, I'm fair. Right after I got out of prison Luca thought he was being a supportive brother by faking Ramsey's death and bringing him to Doomwood Falls for me to deal with as I saw fit. It was a shame such a nice boat was sunk in the process, but hey, some sacrifices had to be made.

Though, I still to this day don't understand how my brother thought delivering Ramsey here in the flesh would bring me comfort, but then again, Luca's concept of justice isn't the same as most people's. He feels personally dealing with a problem the *mafia way* is better than letting the courts handle it. Maybe my brother's right, because the justice system put the wrong person behind bars when I was convicted and Ramsey went free.

I stand rigid, waiting for my mother to scream. I expect her to turn on me, to run for the phone, to look at me with the horror I probably deserve. But no, my mamma Rosetta stands perfectly still staring down at the man, taking in the chains, the bucket, the wretched state of him. Pressing a hand to her chest, her expression remains unreadable.

Slowly, she turns to me with a clinical curiosity. "What now, Shari?"

Ramsey starts to sob. "She's going to let me die here! Please, just let me go!"

Mamma ignores him. She looks at me, and I see the gears turning behind her bifocals. I'm sure she remembers my desperate phone call from jail, Stew's closed casket funeral, the letters I wrote her from behind bars pleading my innocence despite overwhelming evidence. She had bought into Ramsey's lies just like everyone else, and I know her guilt still hurts.

The tension in her shoulders drops. She doesn't scream or recoil, or fling her hands in expressive Italian style. She simply nods, a slow, grim movement of her head toward the daily to-do list of cleaning out Ramsey's makeshift jail cell.

"I'll get the bucket."

She looks back at Ramsey, eyes narrow. To her this man isn't a victim; he's a pest she stumbled on.

"Thanks," I say simply. There isn't much else to say. "Here's your fresh diaper."

I toss Ramsey an adult diaper for his poop, since I discovered it's much easier to clean up after than him pooping in a bucket. He throws his previously used full diaper back at me and misses.

"Though I have to ask something." Mamma smooths the front of her apron and maintains her composure. "What are you going to do with him? In the long run, I mean."

At this point Ramsey has stopped begging, realizing that the sweet old lady isn't going to save him. He shrinks away from her.

"I don't know," I admit.

And I don't. Some days I think about unlocking the cuff and telling him to run, to disappear and never come back. Other days, like today, when the grief is a physical weight pressing on my chest, I think about leaving him down here until the darkness swallows him whole.

"I haven't decided if I'm going to let him go," my voice drops to a whisper, "or if I'm going to finish what I started."

Rosetta reaches out and squeezes my hand. Her grip has remained as strong as it's always been. "This man took your husband from you. Whatever you decide, he earned his place in this room." She turns back toward the bright, lemon-scented living room carrying the sloshing pee bucket and empty paper plate.

My secret room behind the bookshelf stands open for someone else to see for the first time in a year, exposing the real me. I look at my mother, then at the man who ended my life with a single, selfish act. I think of Freida who must live with the memory of what she put Ivory through in order to stop her from destroying both of our lives. And then Fred, whose affair was exposed to the world. Of course there's my brother's hand in Ramsey's disappearance. Plus Gillian and Marshall, and the greed that drove them all the way here to my doorstep and now behind bars. And course I think of myself, and everything I've hidden from those closest to me.

I guess everybody has a secret.

Did you know that reading provides health benefits including better brain connectivity, lowering blood pressure, reducing stress, fighting depression, and increasing longevity? While the victims in my stories clearly did not read enough Pamela Crane books, you don't have to be one of the statistics. Enjoy a long, healthy life by grabbing your next read at www.pamelacrane.com.

Do you want to find out when I'm hosting a giveaway or releasing a new book? Follow me on Facebook, Instagram, or join my mailing list for chances to win free prizes and pre-release offers.

About the Author

To know PAMELA CRANE, you first need to know her husband. He sleeps with one eye open. He checks the knife block to make sure none are missing. It could be because they have four kids and a farm full of mischievous animals. Or it could be because she writes murder mysteries, or about characters who have lost their marbles (not based on her real-life psyche, she swears!). Don't worry—her husband is safe...for now. Her books range from witty whodunnits to psychological suspense and even humorous women's fiction thrown in for good measure. She's a USA TODAY bestselling author of over a dozen novels (who's counting?), but her biggest accomplishment is keeping her zoo of animals alive...and her husband in check. Grab a free book at www.pamelacrane.com.